DATE			

MEG

MEG

MAURICE GEE

ST. MARTIN'S PRESS
NEW YORK

FIC
R00215 06176

Although George and Edith Plumb owe
something to my grandparents, the other
characters in this novel are imaginary. No
reference is intended to any person living or
dead.

M. G.

1 The priest phoned to tell me Sutton was dead. It was all I could do to stop myself crying, "Goody," and clapping my hands. I managed to say, "Oh, well, I'm sorry." There was a singing in me. After our long marking time we were off. When the priest hung up I telegrammed Robert: *Sutton no more. Will collect you tomorrow.* After that I was a little ashamed. Facing facts was all very well, but rejoicing in someone's death going too far. Even Sutton's.

In twenty-five years I had had only snarls from him. Memory of them brought on a stronger attack—an assault by what my father would have called Sutton's "selfhood". A blunt instrument. I retreated before it: and told myself it would not be right to hurry down to his cottage with mop and "Camfosa", and the man's body not yet trollied to the hospital morgue. An hour seemed little enough to offer one whose life had been no life, through a fault not entirely his own. In that hour I fought back fairly strongly: he was interfering between Robert and me! I was giving in to his spiteful demand! My need to get the cottage ready made me jumpy as a cat.

I gathered my things and made them ready on the back verandah: sandsoap, brush, disinfectant, half a dozen cloths, window-cleaner, all in the bucket; mop at attention by the rail, with its fringe of sun-dried white hair on its brow. No—I must avoid these fancies, Raymond says they spoil me as a writer, he calls them coy and clever and tells me I must be plain or fall into self-regard and falsity. I'll leave this one (I rather like it, that's the puzzle) as an example of what I must steer clear of. So—I sat on the verandah with my mop and watched the housewives over the creek pegging out their washing. Their children rode tricycles on the footpaths, screeching down concrete so white it hurt my eyes and braking with their feet on the sun-dried grass. One came close to the old brick bridge but I had no fear for him,

9

it's gated and padlocked on that side and carries the Council's notice warning of danger. The child urinated at the water, but missed reaching it by a good many yards. The clear rainbow of his urine sparkled in the sun. (Raymond would approve of my recording this, but object to "clear rainbow" as inaccurate. He is right. I must be careful. He would not like my seeing the concrete footpath round the turning bay as a noose, nor as my father's "perfect round". He is right again. It's a concrete path and I am not to spill my emotions over it.)

The children played and cried and fought, their mothers scolded and slapped them, cuddled them too (I must be fair), and took them in to biscuits and fizz in their own or each other's houses. Several of the young women noticed me and one or two waved. I'm not disliked, though considered odd. I waved back. I hoped none would invite me over for tea. I have little to say to them, but they miss their mothers or fathers, or their freedom, poor young things, and they pour out their sadnesses to me— and their happiness too, with a desire to fix it, I suspect, before it washes out of the bright new cloth of their married lives. (Raymond would be cross—with reason, I think.) Some of them I like. Some not. They make me feel useful for a short time.

Robert was to make me useful again. His coming down would turn my role to nurse's. I hoped our love would not suffer from it. I believed my skills of subtlety and quiet and wordless doing would prevent his taking fright and running for cover. I wondered how much of gift there was, to me, in his surrender to his illness—for his move into the cottage, into my care, was that: confession, surrender. And gift? Not in a way open to such plain statement. It was part of a natural movement in our affairs. And possibly it was a relief to him.

Dad's old clock in the hall struck the hour of eleven. It has a brassy, gonging, Eastern sound, bringing to mind eunuchs and Turkish harems, echoing marble courts, fountains, palm trees, Moorish warriors in flowing robes, triremes or asps in the bosom—depends on my mood—and its dark English appearance, antique calling-up of a mythical Home, is the least of its qualities. For me. Always that. Others feel differently. A lesson that took me far too long to learn. I mistook my recognitions for an absolute.

Anyway, eleven struck, Sutton was in the morgue, and I could scrub out his cottage.

I walked through a greasy heat filling the driveway. The hedges and shrubs and the trees by the humming creek were rank with a growth that seemed almost tropical. I have never been at home in the Northern summer, with its thick nights and its moody skies, and the biting insects that breed in its tepid swamps. I long for the clean summers of the South. But I love the spring up here, a green bold tender time before all turns to competition; to a seeking, a strangling, a rankness, a pungency—and I love those acres of ground my mother named Peacehaven; the house and gardens. They had seemed, for a time, outside the laws of this place. It was my doing, it was my seeing and blindness, which set them on the outside; and now they are subject to reality. Have been for many years. My vision was false, and I learned to see with a usual eye, and have learned much more that way, and am happier. So, with bucket clanking and mop in hand, I walked down the drive, at home on my piece of the valley, though it's not the magical home I had once made of it.

I do not want to spend my time looking back. Yet I am forced to turn there. Much has to be looked at with a cold eye, there is much to be stripped of its clothing and seen nakedly. This is a duty, and it is a need. If I am to hold myself steady in my shape, which is a sensible one, a shape that makes me useful, I must look at the person I came from. There was a girl, a sister, a wife, sentimental, tender, green, open, painfully open, closed, darkly closed. I was that woman; brought surely, unknowing, to my doom—which was to see. See life, understand circumstance, know death—to get an eyeful, as my sons would say. I have got more than that. And to understand how, must look at that girl, etc. But not yet, not yet a while. Let me set my feet on these days.

I went out the gate, along the footpath a little way, and let myself into the cottage that had been lived in by my brother Willis, by Wendy Philson, by Bluey Considine and Roger Sutton, and by Sutton alone after Bluey's death. Traces of them all remain. The hearth Willis laid about the fireplace forty years ago is there. And the name he carved in the mantelpiece, *Mirth*, can be traced with a finger under the layers of paint slapped over it. Below is a heart pierced with an arrow. Willis never grew up. Mirth was his lady-love, who became his wife, and made him happy, and gave him children, but he never abandoned with her all the paraphernalia of romantic attachment. He clings to them still, flowers and kisses, although she's a crumpled eighty and he sixty-five. It has been a happy marriage.

Wendy's traces are a few scraps of brown paper pasted in corners and behind the doors. Wendy went mad in the cottage, and pasted over the real world in order to bring an unreal one into being, where she could survive. Which she did, at a cost—and came back with many parts missing, and went on with a life of lesser madnesses. My mother scraped her paper off the walls, but missed a scrap here and there. I am moved to see them; for they bring her strongly back, my mother, who was a woman less clever than Wendy Philson but wiser by far.

Bluey. Now Bluey. The place on that morning seemed to reek of him, in spite of Sutton's long residence there. Forgotten racehorses, polished and impossibly refined, posed in dusty frames about the walls. Bluey had money on all of them, and won a bit and lost a bit. That, he used to say, was the story of his life. I took them down, found a cardboard carton and laid them in. But I could not deal with the smell so easily—the mutton-fatty smell that established itself in the cottage in Bluey's time. It will, I think, never go away. It's the smell of Bluey as much as of his food. Other people are not sensitive to it. But I knew him; better even than my father knew him, who was interested only in his mind, and better than Sutton, blinded by his need. I knew him, and loved him grudgingly; and could not abide the man. I set about the impossible task of scrubbing him out of the place.

I forgot my lunch, and would have forgotten afternoon tea if the priest had not come in. I made him a cup and found a damp biscuit for him. He was the man who had helped Bluey back into his church (or is it their belief that one cannot leave it?), who had been with Sutton lately, helping him die. Father Pearce. He had come about Sutton's few belongings, which he had been told he could take for some Catholic charity or other. If I would help him sort them out he would send a van to pick them up. I was pleased to get rid of the rubbish: a broken sea-grass chair, a low-boy with jamming drawers, a tin trunk stuffed with clothes, Sutton's surgical boots—though how Father Pearce expected to get rid of those I don't know. I put out things that had been Bluey's too: the racehorse pictures, a museum of walking-sticks, his old wind-up gramophone and his collection of comic and sentimental Irish songs. We piled them outside the door.

"Did you know Mr Sutton well?" Father Pearce asked.

"Nobody did. He wouldn't let them."

"I believe I was getting to know him. He was—making progress."

I told him I was not interested in Catholic things; but asked him if the Church would bury Sutton, and what the rites would be for one who had only made progress and not reached the goal. He looked at me patiently, and changed the subject.

"Mr Sutton seemed to think you were going to evict him."

"Nonsense," I said. "He was trying to make trouble. It's typical of him."

"He wasn't an easy man."

"He lived in this place rent-free for ten years. And Bluey Considine I don't know how long before that."

"He told me he paid five pounds a week. And had to mow your lawns."

I laughed. A cripple mowing lawns. Sutton had a real gift for malicious invention. "I fed him and spring-cleaned for him. And for Bluey too. And Robert never charged them a penny rent. They had this place from the time my father died. *I* mowed *Mr Sutton's* lawn."

13

"Thank you."

"If you found any good in Sutton I'll be surprised."

"Oh, there was good all right. You had to dig for it."

"I'll bet."

"And Mr Considine was a good man."

"Bluey's a different kettle of fish."

The priest went away. I made myself a new cup of tea and drank it hot. My anger was for Robert. He had never had thanks for anything, only blows and sneers and contempt. That is what goodness gets. He made no complaint. But I complained for him. That black little vulture Sutton—to spread lies about him! I was glad he was dead.

I took a third cup of tea into the sun and sat on Bluey's bench by the front wall. I calmed down there. Sutton had not been all bad. That was a proposition, and I looked for something to stand it on, and found after some searching of memories (and that was a walk through dark and smelly rooms—he lived determinedly in such, with a kind of dogged glee, proving a point substantial enough to him, God knows), found before me, in the real world, his ruined garden, his strangled plantings of the spring. Cabbages on knotted legs, collapsed rows of butter beans, split radishes of turnip size, rattling corn: all awash in a sea of convolvulus. Convolvulus is the curse of this section. Willis, Wendy, Bluey-and-Sutton, fought against it over forty years. And Sutton had only given up on the day they had carted him, snarling, off to the Mater for his "man's operation". The thought of Sutton in starched sheets, catheterized, tended by nuns—hump in pillows, club foot naked of its iron boot—forced a squeak of amusement from me. Or was it pain? I could not tell. I turned my mind firmly on to his garden.

Mother held that gardening was a moral act. It's easy to see what she meant. One puts back what one has taken, hands in soil are the medium of life. So—the man who gardens cannot be all bad. But was Sutton aware, if not with his mind, then his heart? I had thought I was moving nicely to my conclusion but suddenly I was trapped in uncertainties. Capitals reared up and hung like clouds over me. I thought of my brothers and sisters in the Dark Wood: following fairy lights, sinking in swamps, lying down and dying. One had been torn apart by wild beasts. . . . I thought of them on the Black River, floating by; and saw them grey and blind, deaf and tongueless, in the Land of Missing. There is no help for me in this. I have these attacks. They don't come as often as they used to.

I've banished other Capitals altogether: the Plumbs as Chosen Ones, my Father as a Giant Among Men. Drunk on family, I lost all judgement. Well, it's over. I see these happy titles for the false things that they were. I'm grown up now. The Plumbs have a human shape. They're nothing special.

But I've forgotten: the Plumb Zoo. I've taken it over from Felicity, who visits us from Wellington and wanders round the cages, clucking her tongue. I use it from time to time, consciously. Sometimes I simply need to be comfortable. So I fit stylized beings in front of the real ones: a wine-gulping, poker-playing, bookie-ringing Esther; a Willis among his grapefruit, plucking yellow suns from his leafy trees; and Emerson looping the loop in his Gypsy Moth. I can even get Oliver in a cage—wigged and gowned, sitting high above the mass of men; and Felix, flashing with a cold Catholic fire. They are not real. But useful now and then.

So, on that day, I turned aside from the Land of Missing and entered the Plumb Zoo. I strolled there grinning at furry things, coloured things in cages. It's always fun. I don't stay long.

I tipped my lukewarm tea in the roots of Sutton's parsley. No, I don't stay long. Alfred is not there—not since his death. Back in the kitchen, rinsing cups, I took another look at that. I have no rest from it. I carry his death in me as part of my life. I saw him in the flowering onion weed, with his ribs splintered and his jaw broken and his mouth full of blood and urine. I looked at it, in the familiar sickness and the pain. It happened, so I looked. I failed to understand it, but that was neither here nor there, I did not expect to.

Then I dried the cups. I mopped the floor.

2 Two men came in a van and took the furniture and other rubbish away. I threw in several things at the last moment, including Sutton's mattress.

"We don't want this, lady," one of them said. He held his nose.

I asked them to drop it off at the tip for me. They were getting the other stuff free, so it was the least they could do.

When they were gone I saw I would have to bring down a new mattress from the house, and some mats and bedding, and some pictures too. I clanked my way back up the drive; put my cleaning stuff in the wash-house, and went to the kitchen. Fergus was leaning on the bench, with a glass of whisky.

"Pour you one?" he asked.

I told him Sutton was dead and put him to humping the mattress and blankets from the spare room down to the cottage. I got sheets and a pillow case, and the two pictures from Raymond's old room—the Dutch (or are they Flemish?) ones of peasants harvesting wheat and making hay—and carried them down. As I hung the pictures I saw I had made a good choice. Robert would understand them. I put one on each side of the fireplace. Fergus watched and told me when I had them straight. He was anxious to be helpful, but I put off looking at what that might mean. I sent him back to the house for mats, and made the bed while he was gone.

"Where do you want them? No, I'll do it."

He laid one beside Robert's bed—I called it Robert's now, with its fresh linen—and one in front of the hearth.

"Have you heard from him?"

"Not today."

"How do you know he's going to like living here? He hasn't seen it for more than twenty years."

"He'll like it."

"It's pretty run-down."

"Robert's used to run-down places."

"Did you tell him what I said?" He spoke in an off-hand way, thinking perhaps it would make me less angry if he seemed not to care.

"I told him. He wasn't interested. He's not selling this place Fergus, so you can stop thinking about it."

He shrugged. "It would have helped me out. Him too, I guess. He must be pretty broke. But O.K.," he said, seeing me move angrily, "if he doesn't want to sell he doesn't want to sell. Suits me."

That was so plainly not so, and so much in line with his other confusion, that I felt sorry for him. "Fergus," I said, "getting Robert's land wouldn't really help. It would put things off, that's all."

"You don't know."

"What would you have? Another half acre? Another two sections?"

"It would let me put a road in and open up the other four. . . . I'd give him a fair price."

"No, Fergus."

"It's in your interests too."

"The only thing that's in my interests is to get Robert down here so I can look after him."

"If we go broke it doesn't matter?"

"Are we going broke, Fergus?"

"We could." He forgot me. I saw his look go inward, saw him begin to pick again at that giant knot, his entanglement with his brother-in-law, Fred Meggett. I watched him for a while and wished I could help. I had known he was giving away part of himself when he went in with Fred. I had warned him. But he saw the chance of money, real money, and he betrayed himself. He is a loner; alone he knows his shape, he sees what he must do and sets about it. Fergus is a man who believes in duty. But with Fred, as a part of the Meggett empire, he lost his sight of duty, and lost sight of himself. He began to suffer from other temptations than greed.

"Can't you get out, Fergus?"

"I'm trying. It's not as easy as you think."

"I don't think it's easy. Not with Fred." And not, I added to myself, with the woman either. I knew she was on Fergus's mind as much as his other trouble. And I knew he both wanted more and wanted less to be out of his entanglement with her. I was less sure he would manage that escape than manage the other. He had come to believe he owed her something—and I was ready to say, if it would help him, that he owed me nothing, all he had ever owed me he had paid. But I knew it would be no help. He had his delusions, poor man, and one was that I needed him. He was quite wrong. I loved him, but did not need him any longer.

I took a last look round the cottage. It would do. The peasants with their scythes and jars of wine brought it alive. I closed and locked the door and walked with my husband up the drive to Peacehaven. I cooked us a meal and we ate it in the kitchen— tycoon and wife, eating off a wooden table among the pots and pans. It was like our meals of thirty years before, and I supposed it said something for us that we were still at home in the kitchen. Fergus had taken off his jacket and tie and rolled up his sleeves. He has the strong forearms of the young man who was able to hit a cricket ball out of the ground, and the hands of a plumber. He has a weathered face, an outdoors face, and good thick hair, nicely pepper-and-salted. It brings to mind the man behind the desk. So he belongs in two worlds, which increases his attractions one hundred percent. You cannot tell his teeth are not his own. I saw how a young woman might come to believe she loved Fergus and could not live without him.

We did not talk of her over the meal. But when we had taken our coffee out to the verandah, I said, "Have you seen Miss Not Quite today?" That was my name for her. (She's Miss Neeley.) It helped Fergus into the subject of his guilty love. He was able to suppose me fighting back, and he soothed me with accounts of how nothing happened; and soon was deep in the pleasures of talking about her—to his wife, which made it legitimate. He had to go through this, and much else, and I saw my part as something I could do. I said *Miss Not Quite* though with some malice.

"Now, Meg."

"Oh, I'm not jealous. I'm interested, that's all. I like to know how office affairs are managed."

"There's no affair, I've told you."

"Just a few kisses."

He reddened. "That was a mistake. We'd both had a few." They had embraced beside her car after the office party. I had a letter from *A Friend* describing it: *Ha, ha Fergus Sole loves Beth Neeley. I saw them in the carpark, feeling each other up.* It had come in the mail between Christmas and New Year, when we had Rebecca and Tom and their children staying. I saved it till mid-January and showed it to Fergus then. He could not speak for several moments. Fergus took a blow. He's a simple man and he believes in goodness. The letter gave him glimpses of things he would rather not see. It also made him look at what he was doing. Until then he had kept it under the headings, "a bit of fun", "a bit of flirting". Those phrases rattled out when he began to talk, but he was simply getting rid of rubbish. He had to say he liked Beth Neeley much more than he should. And she liked him. But he would tell her nothing could come of it. He would tell her she should look for another job.

"You can't do that."

And of course he agreed. He has a sense of honour. If anyone should go, he should. But how could he, when he was boss of the place?

"I'll finish it, that's what I'll do. We'll just be friends."

"Will that work, Fergus?"

"Of course. Nothing's happened, Meg. It's just an infatuation." That was not his sort of word at all. Not a man's word. He kept it in his mind for a good long time as a weapon he could turn on himself.

Now, in March, he let it go. This was the new thing I had sensed in him.

"Fergus, why don't you take her away? Go away for a week.

Maybe you can work it out of your systems."

Again his face went red: this was dirty talk. He was shocked to hear it from his wife. But I had had enough of evasions, and more than enough of his proprieties; I meant to lay it down for him, make my position clear.

"Take her to a hotel. As man and wife. Then at least you'll know if you want to go on."

"You don't know what you're talking about."

"If you don't you'll just explode one day. And think of the poor girl. She must be dying of frustration."

"Stop it, Meg."

I saw I had made a mistake. I had wanted to show him I would not be hurt. I should have known he would take my flippancy for pain. I kept on for a while, but his face had taken a stubborn set and my thirty years experience of him told me I would not get anywhere. So I lit a cigarette and looked at the houses over the creek, with their lights coming on in the dusk and their front rooms turning blue from TV sets, and I wondered what it was that had happened today. More kisses perhaps, in a corridor, behind a door. That was the sort of behaviour Fergus disapproved of. He was a man for the open, for honesty. A week in a hotel really was the answer. I hoped he would see his way to it soon. It was no fun waiting.

"What happened, Fergus? Did your hands brush or something?"

"Meg, I'm sorry. It's not fair to you."

"But I'm finding it funny. Come on, tell me now."

"We had a talk, that's all."

"What sort of talk?"

"About ourselves. And you."

"Me? How dare you talk about me?"

"She cares, Meg. She cares about you. She doesn't want to hurt you."

"It's a good line for her to take."

"No, Meg. You're wrong about her. She's not the sort of person you think she is."

20

"I've no ideas about her at all. She's just a face. A body."

"She's not. She's more than that."

"It's the first thing you see though, isn't it?"

Simply in talking to her Fergus had found himself involved in sex. It unbalanced him, poor man. He had had his diet of me for thirty-five years and I'm thin gruel. Beth Neeley was apples, peaches, she was roast beef and red wine. Fergus had never been at a feast before. Or, I should say, been so near a feast—so far he had not had a bite—well, no more than a nibble. And thinking thus, elaborating a fancy, I wanted that food for him. I wanted him to have it. I almost found my own mouth watering.

"Oh Fergus, for heaven's sake stop all the talk. Take her away. Be a man for once."

I struck him sharply with that. He sees himself above all as a man—tough, decisive, a person who gets things done. He stammered in his anger, but got nothing out. The trouble is that though he is a "man"—no doubt about that—he has pockets in his mind where corrupting influences work. (1) He has a sense of honour—for that *I* admire him. (2) He has a sense of things unclean. It cripples him.

He could not admit he just wanted Beth Neeley in bed.

3 I listened to him ramble about her sentimentally. He was not himself. He believed this sort of talk was realistic, especially as it took place with his wife. It was "bringing things out in the open". I felt like telling him he was indulging in a solitary vice.

We were rescued by the arrival of Bill McBride, Fergus's accountant. Bill and Fergus and Jack Short, his lawyer, had been having meetings at our house all week. They were trying to save some of Fergus's money—my money, too. Meggett Enterprises was collapsing on itself, sucking all its parts in with a convoluted roar. And they were searching for ways of keeping

Fergus out of court. Fred was definitely going. There had been no charges laid, the police were still investigating M.E. (*Truth* had played great games with that acronym.) These things move with a dreadful slow inevitability. But we were close now to the day of arrests. Dippers-in-the-till would have bolted long ago. Not Fred. Fred was a big-time swindler, no petty thief. A police team had taken away his books, the affairs of M.E. had ground to a halt, its glossy prospectuses had been carted off in van loads to the tip, and its staff laid off, except the construction staff (Fergus's side). Fred was ruined. Shortly he would occupy a cell. But it made no difference to the way he lived. His laugh still racketed through the members' bar at Ellerslie. He led a winner back to scale now and then, and was clapped for it. People touched the cloth of his coat, hoping even now to carry some of his greatness away with them.

It was different with Fergus. Fergus was cast as the fool. He had had no idea what Fred and his smart managers were up to. That did not mean he was safe, Jack Short explained. He was head of the M.E. house construction side, and as a director was, at least nominally, a party to the consortium's money-raising activities. The thing Jack Short must demonstrate, he said, was that Fergus in practice was a field man. It would help too that he had been trying to get away from M.E. for years. The police might decide to grab just the inside boys: Fred Meggett and John Gundry, Graham Tarleton and George Sloane.

I hoped that would be the case. I did not want to see Fergus in prison. That sounds cool—but my concern for him was that he should retain his idea of himself as an honest man. He could keep it in the face of a legal judgement, and keep it in prison. But if he judged himself a thief he was lost.

Jack Short drove up and parked in the yard. He sidled by me with an embarrassed nod.

"Don't keep him too late, Jack. He needs a good night's sleep."

"Right, Meg. Right, Mrs Sole." He cannot work out whether or not he knows me socially.

"See if you can persuade him to take a holiday."

"He can't do that. There's too much going on."

"What he needs is a few days away with a chorus girl. Or a secretary or something."

"Ha, ha." Not a convincing laugh. In his eyes I'm another burden Fergus carries.

Well, I thought, I try. "I'll bring you a cup of tea later on."

When he had gone I turned the verandah light off and sat in darkness on my sea-grass chair, watching the goings-on in the little tongue of suburbia over the creek. (The orchard had been there. Robert had grazed his sheep under the pear trees.) When I say goings-on I mean the occasional switching off or switching on of a light, or the passing of a figure in front of a window. I mean the blue flicker of TV sets. Once though a man went out, slamming the door behind him. He drove away with a sound of tyres like a screech of pain. A few moments later his wife ran out of the house, carrying her children wrapped in blankets, one on each arm. She went two doors up the street and someone drew her in. Her house was left empty, blazing its lights over the shaven lawn and the ornamental shrubs. I knew her. She had told me only the day before how good her husband was and how the children had drawn them closer together. Perhaps it's true.

On the rise beyond the turning bay the Butters house stood on its acre of ground. A blue porch-light gleamed on the backs of half a dozen cars. Merle was holding a séance. She is the *grande dame* of Auckland spiritualist circles. Messages from the Beyond enter our world through Merle and her favourite medium, Mrs Peet. Naturally some are for me. We played a game of hide and seek. I would see her floating out from her house. She speared a finger in my direction as she bossed the driver. (A taxi for that quarter-mile trip!) It gave me time to lock my doors and curl deep in a chair. She wrote messages on a little pad and pushed them through the windows. I saw them flutter in. *Your father came through last night, Meg dear. He and Alfred are the best of friends now. He says beware of electric stoves and bottles without labels.* At first

23

I tore them up, but later I thought it would do no harm to put them with Dad's papers. (Wendy Philson goes pale when she finds them there.) After all, I owed something to Merle. She had made no complaint about losing a large sum of money in the M.E. collapse. I hoped though that the messages she was receiving tonight would not include any from my father. It disturbed my calm to have his voice, even though spurious, come fluttering like a bird through my living-room window.

At nine o'clock Wendy Philson's car turned in at our gate.

"Bother," I said. I had forgotten she was calling. She clumped up the steps on her swollen legs and sat down in the other sea-grass chair. Fergus put his head out of the study to see who it was, and went in again. He and Wendy make each other nervous. His maleness is a force she cannot ignore. There is in Wendy a deeply buried ember of sexuality and Fergus sets it glowing now and then. She hates it. She is filled with contempt for herself and puts on the hair shirt of her lost ambition—to find the Way and write wise books about it. When she speaks of things like that Fergus finds a reason to leave the room. He is no fool. He has intimations of a world beyond his own. Wendy makes him glimpse it. He does not like that. Questions and discomforts would never stop, and there's more than enough in the world he understands to keep him busy. He gets out. And he knocks Wendy down in his mind by saying that what she had really needed was a husband to look after and some kids.

Wendy, dropsical, diabetic, sighed at the pleasure of sitting down after her struggle with the verandah steps. She took out a bag of nuts and offered me one.

"No thanks." I rolled a cigarette.

"Those things are bad for you, Meg. Your father never smoked."

"It's my only vice. Are you sure you're warm enough? Are the mosquitoes biting you?"—and I went to the bathroom for some insect repellent. Wendy and I do not care for each other and we disguise it by handing small courtesies back and forth.

She rubbed the stuff on her arms and legs and dabbed some

on her face. Then we sat in the luminous night, conversing politely. She noticed the cars gleaming in Merle's driveway.

"What? It looks like another table-rapping night at Madame Merle's." She gave the name the full French treatment, but somehow made herself, not Merle, seem foolish. "Who goes to those things? What sort of people are taken in by it?"

"Bankers," I said, "schoolteachers, bricklayers, housewives, old maids, hospital matrons—"

"Yes, yes, you've made your point."

"Have you seen her latest book?"

"That rubbish! It's full of bad grammar. She speaks of Perfection in one sentence and misrelates a participle in the next."

"It all comes from a Japanese man."

Merle's books—there are three so far, all published by herself—are the versified thoughts of a thirteenth-century Japanese court official. He dictates them to her. I have not liked to ask how he comes to know English. Or why he leans so heavily on Kahlil Gibran. Or where he could possibly have seen pohutukawa trees in bloom. Wendy would ask, if she and Merle ever met. She would point out the bad grammar and proofreading errors. And explain Merle's motives to her.

"She's been writing bad verse all her life. She knows it's bad. And now she's found a way of putting it in print without being held responsible."

"It makes her happy."

"That's not a good enough reason."

I think it is, but I did not argue. I asked Wendy how she was getting on with her own work.

"Ah, well," she dug in her bag and brought out half a dozen of Dad's notebooks and a packet of letters. "I've brought these back. I'm ready for the next lot."

"Was there anything useful?"

"Those were his political years. Pretty much a waste of time. It's the twenties and thirties that really interest me. When it was all coming clear for him."

I smiled at that. She was getting ready to write my father's life. It was not to be the usual sort of thing. "A spiritual biography, Meg." Mundane things would have no place: politics, orthodox religion, domestic life. She had warned me several times I would not figure there. I did not mind. It sounded like a piece of fiction to me.

But Wendy was a methodical worker. Dad had left mountains of notebooks and letters. I sorted them into chronological order after his death, and fought off Oliver and Felicity, who wanted to carry parts of them away. If people—and that included family—wanted to look at Dad's papers they could do it in his study. That was my rule. I had relaxed it for Wendy. She would not want to burn or tear or annotate or hide things away for fifty years in cupboards. Her concern was for evidence; for marking in my father's steps on the Way to Illumination, to that moment of permission received to step off the Wheel and proceed to Nirvana. (I may have mixed her terminology up, I'm not all that interested.) But Wendy was methodical, as I've said. She had started at the beginning and was working through to the end. Now and then she congratulated me on the way I had put Dad's papers in order. She regarded it as proper that one of the great man's children should have become custodian of his relics.

I took the notebooks and letters and went along to the study. The three men were in a cloud of tobacco smoke, busy with their papers on Dad's huge desk. They looked up like conspirators when I came in. I apologized for disturbing them and told Fergus I had come to get some notebooks for Wendy. I went at it quickly: some inhibition prevented them from working while I was there. The notebooks were in a glass-doored shelf. My reflection grimaced at me as I approached. I do not like Dad's notebooks. Filling them was a habit he had, like chewing gum. They're fat little books, easy to handle. There are seventy-one. Dad had bought them in dozen lots. And I had done my duty when he died—numbered them, strengthened their spines with tape. Today I handle them without care. I banged in Wendy's six and pulled six out. She was up to twenty-four. I took a

26

blue-ribboned packet of letters from a hidden drawer in the back of the desk. "Love letters, Jack."

"Ha ha." What a nervous little man.

"Come on, Meg. We're busy," Fergus said.

"Right. I'll bring some tea in soon," and I left them in their tobacco smoke, smiled on by Dad's brass Buddha, who had been a smoker himself (thin sticks of incense). I gave Wendy the notebooks and letters.

"Ah, thank you." She took them with an air of reverence. "This looks more like it. 'He who knows God will need no priest.' That's Emerson."

"Is it?" I took little notice of her as she dipped here and there and read out quotations and gems of Plumbian wisdom. I was tired of all that. Wendy salivated like a cow. I wondered if I should mention again that Dad had written his own life. I had offered her the manuscript more than once, and seen her fingers creep on it greedily, like caterpillars. But no; she stroked and patted it but would not turn a page. He had "composed" it last, she would come to it last. It was the fabulous peak she climbed towards.

"Wendy," I said, "it's not like that. There's nothing spiritual."

She smiled at my ignorance. *She* would take the real meaning from it.

I made tea and brought her a cup and took some to the men. I was glad not to be partner in either quest.

Wendy sweetened her tea and drank it hot. She kissed my brow in a manner I thought Eastern, and drove away, treasures deep in her bag. I hoped the George Plumb she was so busy creating would be one who would keep her satisfied. If he failed her it would be the failure of the main prop of her world. But I had little fear for her. She had great cunning as well as strength of mind.

Jack Short and Bill McBride came out of the study at half past ten. They made toothy goodbyes and purred discreetly off in their fat cars. Fergus sat with me for two or three minutes. He smoked half a cigarette and stubbed it out.

"Did you get anything settled, Fergus?"

"It's a bloody mess. I can't understand how it happened."

"It'll sort itself out."

He sighed. "I suppose so. I'm off to bed. I'm bushed."

"I won't be long."

Merle's séance guests came out of her house and drove away. I watched that dark-clad lady on her porch. She seemed to be peering at me. I wondered if perhaps she had some message to bring over. But after a moment she went inside, the blue light went out, and soon her house was in darkness.

I fetched the men's cups from the study, emptied the ashtrays, opened the windows to clear the room of smoke. Then I went back and sat on the verandah for another hour. I knew I should go to bed. Tomorrow I was driving north for Robert. Getting there and bringing him back and settling him in the cottage would take the whole day. But I was not ready for sleep. The present: I was determined to live in it. But the past was demanding admittance, my deep past. Robert had been with me all through the day; and Robert was *there*. He had a dimension everyone lacked. Wendy and Merle, even poor Fergus too, were like cut-out figures from a book. Robert on that murmuring night was flesh of my flesh, bone of my bone: I sat there living over our childhood together.

Sometime, midnight said my watch, the angry husband from the house over the creek came home in his car. He searched his house, then stood on the front lawn bawling for his wife. Lights went on. Up the street a door opened and the woman came out. She went to him, bravely I thought, and coaxed him inside. The children, it seemed, would stay at the neighbour's that night. Then the lights went out again, one by one. The suburb was quiet. Only the car lights burned outside the garage. I wondered if I should ring the man and tell him. By morning his battery would be flat. But he would not thank me. And I was pleased to see this evidence of disorder, passion, of the primitive thing, burning in the darkened suburb.

I went to bed and listened to Fergus breathing heavily on his side of the room. Tomorrow morning I would go for Robert. I lay in the dark smiling about that.

4 Robert saved me from the sackman. He rode away in the sackman's cart to a dungeon where he would be kept in a cage and fattened up for breakfast. The sackman was old, the sackman was filthy. He wore a coat with the lining poking out. He had whiskers on his chin, grey and white and yellow. He made noises in his throat and spat fat gobs of phlegm into the gutters. His cart was full of lumpy sacks with captured children in them, and his horse had one white eye. His horse never ran, it walked, clump, clump, slow as an elephant, and sometimes it stopped and rested with its head hanging down and the sackman talked to himself while he waited for it to go on.

It was best to hide in a ditch when the sackman came by. The ditches on the long road home were deep and running with slime. But my brother Alfred had told me the sackman liked girls best, they tasted sweeter. If he caught one as fat as me he would eat me on the spot and spit out the bones. So I hid. I hid deep in the ditches. I crouched with my bare feet in the slime, with the hem of my dress bunched in my hand, and watched the hairy feet of the horse go by, and heard the sackman talking to himself and heard him spit and heard him make rude noises from his bottom. Then I ran home crying, and mother gave me bread and jam and told me I was a funny little thing.

One day in autumn I was close to home when I heard the slow sound of hooves and saw the sackman's cart come round the corner. I thought if I ran I would beat him to our gate, and then I knew I could not, my legs would stop moving and he would lift me into his cart and tie me in a sack with the other children. I hid in the ditch. His cart creaked up, clump went the horse and blew shudderingly, and the iron rims on the wheels cracked stones and sent bits of them flying into the grass. I put my forehead on the mud wall of the ditch and closed my eyes. Under my breath I prayed, "Please God, save me." Over and over I prayed—until the sounds stopped. I felt my back go cold, and all the hair moved on my head like ants. Then the horse blew again, right over me, and I opened my eyes and saw his milky eye so close I could have touched it. Through the long grass I saw flies on his skin; and I saw flies sitting on the sackman's coat and on his beard. I saw a piece of meat stuck in his beard. He was right above me, up against the sky. There was the tall wheel, with spokes like a ladder, and the broken boards of the cart, painted green, and the black flies, warm and happy on his coat, and his face, bigger than a moon in the sky, hanging down like his horse's face—but not at me. That stopped me from screaming. Spiders and frogs in the ditch—I did not care. "Oh God save me," I prayed. The sackman laughed. He made noises in his throat, round and round, like scraping a pot, and he spat, and I heard something wet smack on the fence post behind me. "I'll skin 'im alive when I catch 'im," the sackman said. "Aarg," he said, "bustid, I'll skin 'im alive."

He was quiet. His horse swished its tail. I knew they would stay till he saw me. His head would come round like a door. He would bend down from his cart and put his arm in the ditch and lift me out and drop me in a sack and tie it up. (I did not believe he would eat me straight away.) Then he would spit and the horse would clump away. "Oh God, please save me. Oh Mummy, Mummy, please." But it was Robert who came. He came with a sound on the road—feet padding in the dust and clicking stones together like glass marbles. He looked at me in the gutter.

"She's a right 'un, ain't she?" the sackman said.

Robert touched the horse. "She only wants some grass, Meg." He tore a handful from the ditch and fed it past the horse's rubber lips and yellow teeth.

"Climb aboard, young 'un. Up you come."

Robert stepped on the wheel like a ladder. He went up in

three steps, sat down with the sackman. The horse leaned forward and they clopped away.

I scrambled out of the ditch. I left my books and slate. I ran home crying, into the kitchen, into Mother's skirts.

"The sackman's got him," I wept.

She wiped my face, she warmed my feet in the oven, she gave me bread and jam, and said I was a strange little girl and Robert was all right. Then Robert came in. He grinned at me.

"Went as far as the corner."

"How did you escape?"

"I go with him lots of times. He lets me hold the reins."

"Don't you go bothering him," Mother said.

"He taught me to say whoa."

I believed none of this. I had no need of it. I had need of the sackman, and his lumpy sacks, and of the children he ate. Robert had saved me. How he had done it was not something I wondered about. Mother sent me back to the ditch for my books. Robert came with me, throwing stones at fence posts all the way. He jumped into the ditch, tossed up my things, and stood there a while, letting long-legged spiders run up his arms.

I was six. He was nearly five. He saved me from the sackman in the year the Great War started.

5   On Belinda Beach we saw a troop of soldiers singing war songs. One of them was my brother Oliver. He looked as if he was only moving his mouth and not saying words, but that was because he hated people looking at him. He believed in war. My father said so. He believed in slaughtering his fellow man.

Oliver was in a khaki uniform and a hat with the top squeezed in. He had come home in those clothes the day before and Father had ordered him to leave our house, and Mother pulled him away to change in the boys' bedroom. But Oliver shouted he was proud to wear his country's uniform and proud to fight her enemies. Father was a traitor, he said, and the sooner he was locked up the better. Father rushed to his study for his cane but Oliver climbed out the bedroom window and ran away. He did not come back. Mother cried, and she and Felicity talked to Father a long time in his study. Father caned Emerson that night for saying "bum" (which was not the worst word he could say, that would have been Hun or bayonet or Attention, stand up straight). "Look," Emerson said, pulling his pants down in our bedroom, "I've got a mark on my bum." Esther told on him, and Father caned him again. Then he came into the sitting-room and took down Oliver's photograph from the mantelpiece and put it on the fire like a piece of wood.

On Belinda Beach we waved to Oliver. He did not wave back. Soon he went away to camp and before long Mother told us he had gone to the war. He was a Lieutenant. That was a French word, Mother said. It meant a man who fills a place for somebody else. It would have been a good word if the military men had not got hold of it.

Oliver started fighting straight away. He was in the Dardanelles. Felicity showed us where that was on the globe. It was round the other side of the world. She told us secretly; Father would not have the war talked about in our house, unless he did it himself with his friends Mr Jepson and Mr Cryer. But I dreamed about the war, day and night. My Turks were storybook Turks. They wore turbans and baggy blue pants and black moustaches and carried swords like sickles curved the wrong way. I saw one of them hit my brother Oliver and Oliver's head jumped from his shoulders and rolled along the ground.

My Germans, though, were real. There were no Germans in the books I read, but pictures of them in the magazines. In an *Illustrated London News* Mr Jepson brought to our house I found a picture of a man with a nose like a snout and fat cheeks and a bristly chin and ugly eyes. He had an iron hat on his head. Underneath it said: *The Physiognomy of the Hun*. I asked Mother what that meant. She told me physiognomy meant the way a person's face was made: it showed what he was really like. She would not say the other word. But I said it to myself when I was alone, and felt myself grow hot to be using it. It made me frightened and I knew Hun was a real word whatever Father said.

The other word that frightened me was *missing*. The paper had lists of men who were missing. There were killed and wounded too, but I knew where they were, in hospital or in heaven. I wondered and wondered where the missing had gone, and what sort of world was Missing. I thought it would be grey and if you went to it you would not be able to taste anything or hear anything or see any colours, you just walked about waiting for someone to come and let you out, but nobody came.

I had a dream that Robert and I were in the vegetable garden and we heard the Germans coming. We hid under the trellis with the scarlet runner beans on it and we saw the German boots go marching by and then one German stopped and lifted up the runner beans. It was the Hun from the magazine, the one with the physiognomy. He reached down with his hands and if he caught us we would go to Missing. But I screamed and woke up and found myself sleeping on the floor in our empty house. Robert was beside me, sucking his thumb. His head was on the boards. I lifted it up with two hands like a ball and put it on the pillow. It was warm, and heavier than I had expected. I began to feel safe. I knew where all my family were. Father and Mother and Felicity were in the kitchen drinking tea and talking about tomorrow when we were leaving on the train for California. Esther and Rebecca and Alfred were over the room from me, sleeping on cushions. I saw the moonlight shine on Alfred's hair. Emerson was in the shed out the back, where he had made a bed for himself in an old seaman's hammock. Edith and Florence were staying with friends on the other side of town—in proper beds, for they were almost grown up and it would not have been right for them to sleep on the floor. Agnes was outside under the trees, saying goodbye to her sweetheart. She had been crying all day, but Felicity had told me not to be sorry for her because

33

Agnes was enjoying every minute of it. I did not see how that could be, but I always believed Felicity. And when Agnes came climbing in the window soon afterwards she was smiling. She saw me watching her. "Still awake, Goody two-shoes?" "Did you kiss him, Agnes?" "What do you know about kissing, little dope?" She took off her dress and put on her nightie and wriggled into her blankets. Soon she was fast asleep. So Felicity had been right. I felt very happy about it. We were all safe. I did not even mind going to California. Once or twice I had thought it might be like Missing, but if we were all together, the Plumbs, nothing bad could happen. Our father could preach peace there without being put in prison.

I began to go to sleep. My face was on a wet patch on the pillow where Robert had dribbled but I did not even mind that. I remembered I had left my blue tea-set in the hedge. I hoped somebody nice would find it. I hoped my best friend Madge would find it. I would write her a letter from California telling her where to look. I went to sleep thinking of Madge and the tea-set and kissing and how warm Robert's head had been and Emerson in his hammock, bent like a banana, and trains and boats, and the Plumbs all up on the sunny deck where the sharks could not get them.

When I woke up we all went to the station—"Keep together or you'll get left behind," Felicity cried—and we went to California. We were safe on the deck. The sharks never got us.

6 But I had been wrong about California. California was the Land of Missing. Nothing there looked right. When I talk to people about it now they say I must be making it up. Children are like weeds, they say, they grow anywhere. But in California I did not grow. Mother said I was a tree that would not transplant. Perhaps I make up a physical wasting-away— my cheeks all hollow and my bones sticking out. My skin could not have been as white as I see it—not in the California sunshine. But inside, there is no doubt, I wasted away. I longed for Thorpe with a longing like that for food. There I was in a land all brightly coloured, a land that became for my brothers and sisters a kind of Arcadia, I saw the leafy suburbs, I saw the golden Fall, my friends at school—for I made friends—put grapes into my mouth. I swam on the warm beaches, swam in the millionaire pools. And all the time I saw Thorpe—saw grey ditches full of frogs, and saw the black pine row where goblin toadstools forced their way through needles, and saw cold willows over narrow streams. I talk of these things in an adult way. They were not cold for me then. They were not uncoloured.

There were other things too. I wrote about them passionately in my language book at school. There was the traction engine, chugging across the paddock, pulling the cookhouse behind it. Its loose belt flapped and thundered and flew round fast enough to tear our arms off. The ground shook, we felt it up to our knees. Chaff filled the air and wheat began to pour into the sacks like yellow water. We sat in the cookhouse talking to the cook. He gave us scones to eat. We asked if we could sleep in the bunk-house with him. But Felicity called us from the far-away fence. The men finished work and stopped the engine and the sun went down behind the pinerow. Our bare feet hurt as we walked home over the stubble. They stung in the tub—Robert and I back to back so we could not see each other—and stung in bed as we went to sleep. But tomorrow the engine would start chugging again and chaff would fill the air like golden rain, and the cook had said he would bake us something nobody had ever tasted before.

I wrote about the traction engine. The teacher called me out to read my story to the class. But I could not. I read a few words and I began to cry. She thought it was shyness. It was not that—it was longing, it was hunger: for the engine and the cookhouse and the cook and the stubble fields, and Felicity waving us home from the far-away fence.

I did not live in this state for the whole of our two-year stay in

35

California. That would not have been possible. I would not have survived. But I ached from time to time with the kind of ache one feels in a missing limb. Anything could set it off: a leaf, a footfall on a stair, the taste of a vegetable, a colour in the sky, a word in a book, a word spoken in another room that was, suddenly, not a room in Thorpe. I think I remember truly when I say I always felt myself in danger. I felt us all in danger, but Robert especially, for Robert was dearest to me, and Robert was, I knew, the one who would meet my danger and try to save me.

I have a small notebook in which I wrote at that time. I find in it a poem called *A Mother's Love*. It is dated 1917.

> Silently it made it's way upon that little bed,
> Silently it went to sleep just near that curly head,
> A fierce-eyed poisness dreaded snake.
> O mercy if that child should wake,
> Or if that little arm should bend
> It certainly would bring the end,
> For a sleeping snake is a dangerous thing
> And if wakened makes ready to use its sting.
>
> And so it was a mother came to kiss her little son.
> And so it was she crept upstairs to get that awful gun.
> Some minutes passed, a rifle shot, a baby's startled cry.
> That loving woman's work was done,
> Yes saved was her precious son.

The danger is more convincing than the rescue. I was, I think, pleading with our parents to take us home. Robert had stopped me that day on our walk from school. He had made me stand absolutely silent on the sidewalk, listening for something—he would not tell me what. In a moment he handed me his books. I heard a rustle in the dry leaves in the gutter. It moved along and Robert followed it.

"Is it a lizard?" I whispered. There had been lizards in Thorpe.

"Shh," he said. At last he made a dive. He threw handfuls of

36

leaves on the pavement and scattered them with his shoe. I saw a wriggling thing six inches long, earthy brown, with patches of pink on it, like sores. Robert dived after it as it squirmed away, and held it triumphantly in the air. It was a snake. He held it by the tail and it wrapped itself like rubber round his hand and opened its sharp mouth. Robert held it out for me to see. I was making little screaming noises but he told me not to be a sap. This was not a poisonous snake—and he showed me the inside of its mouth, clean as a baby's. But I screamed. I could not help myself. Snakes were from the dark, the dangerous place, they were poisonous, they killed—and I wet my pants. Robert put the snake down in the gutter. He took his books and mine and made me run home with him through the back streets so people would not see my legs were wet. He took me into the garden and made me hold my dress up while he turned the hose on me. What a sap I was, he said. He told me he knew where there were tarantula spiders, but he wouldn't show me in case I did something worse than wet my pants.

I wrote my poem that night, sitting cross-legged on my bed. The child is Robert and me both, and perhaps Alfred too, with his curly hair, but I did not show it to them, for they liked California. I showed it to Mother and she was pleased with it. She took it though as an exercise not a plea, and told me I had spelled poisonous wrong. When she showed it to Dad he wrote *Good girl, Meg* in the margin and corrected poisonous. Neither of them understood. They had their own troubles. The greatest of them was that they too were unhappy in California—but I did not know that. I did not know they were searching for ways of getting back to New Zealand.

7 I had another dream. I dreamed it often. And when I woke crying or calling out one of the others would come into my bed, Esther or Rebecca, and with them lying against me I would drift back to sleep; or Mother or Felicity would hear and come from the kitchen and sit with me, stroking my face or holding my hand and I would tell them I had had my dream, but it faded so fast I could never describe it, I would say just that it was about floating, and sinking in water, and they would stroke me kindly and say, "There Meg, there little one, it's gone now, go back to sleep," and with them sitting on the edge of my bed it was easy, that is what I would do.

Mother thought I dreamed because I was displaced, because I was the tree that would not transplant. "It's a California dream. When we go back to New Zealand it will stop." I believed her. For a wonderful thing had happened. Felicity had been charged with the message and she came to me first, sitting in the shade out in the garden reading my book. I had been sick again and was wrapped in blankets and had on my new red slippers with the blue pom-poms. I loved them so much I was certain they came from Thorpe. "Meg," she said, closing the pages, taking my hands, "what would you wish for most?" I read her as clearly as I had the print on the page, and I laughed and said, "Thorpe. We're going back."

"Not quite, little goose. But very close. We're going to Christchurch. To New Zealand."

"When?"

"Soon. As soon as Father and Mother get the money."

"Will Father be able to preach there?"

"Yes."

"Will he go to prison?"

"Probably. But you mustn't worry about that. Now, shall we tell the others?"

38

"Can I tell Robert?"

I found him and Alfred in their tree hut and I told them. I yelled it to them and their heads poked out and they looked at each other, not knowing whether to be pleased or cross, until Robert said, "Hey, we'll go on the ship again," and they yelled and thumped each other.

Felicity told my sisters and they cried. "I'll be able to go to Thorpe and get my tea-set," I said to Agnes. "Oh shut up, Goody two-shoes." She was leaving another sweetheart in the garden.

So the Plumbs got on their ship and sailed to Christchurch, and I stopped having my dream of standing on the banks of a dark river, while my dead family floated by, Mother first, and then my brothers and sisters, one by one—I reaching out my hands to catch them until I found myself in the water too and sinking down. I had it once on the ship but Mother said that was because the boys had been talking too much about U-boats. She said it would not come back any more, and it never came back.

I was happy in Christchurch. It had not been Thorpe I needed, but something in the air and in the ground. I could list a hundred particulars, I could tell of deep and instant recognitions, of things seen and touched and heard, of faces on which a nose, a mouth, sat rightly—I do not joke—of voices making just the sounds they should. But there's no way of taking the clumsiness off such declarations, so I will leave it. It was delicate and hidden, never clumsy. Mother said I started to grow again. I grew in more ways than one.

Our house in Shirley was larger than the one we had left in Thorpe, almost as large as our California house. I do not know who paid the rent, but think it was our father's friend Mr Jepson, who owned a soft-drink factory, and perhaps some others of Dad's followers, and perhaps even Grandfather Willis. We had an orchard and a rose garden and a creek with willows growing on its banks. The boys swung out on the branches over the water, and I made playhouses under them, sometimes with my nearest sister Rebecca, although she was too old for that sort of thing and joined me out of kindness. For a while I watched for the yellow water snakes that had lived in the California swimming pools and watched for tarantula spiders under the rocks, but I soon got out of that. There was nothing poisonous in New Zealand. I did not feel threatened. I did not even feel threatened when Dad went to prison and people started throwing stones on our roof. They crossed to the other side of the street when they saw us coming. I did not mind. It was part of being a Plumb, and Plumbs were special.

The headmaster at school knew they were special. The day after Dad was sent to prison I saw him watching Robert and Alfred in the playground and I heard him say to the teacher next to him, "We'll have to see the others don't pick on them." When the other teacher, a returned soldier, who coughed a lot and had pains in his chest, muttered that he didn't care too much, the headmaster said, "You'll do what I say, Mr Gibbons. I'll not have any sins visited on the children here."

It was soon after that I stopped saluting the flag. The drum and fife band played, dressed in their belts and Glengarries, and the classes marched into school one by one, saluting the flag as they went. I had made up my mind to stop. It was something I could do for my father in prison, and for Mother. I had found her that morning in his study, hunched up on the footstool like a child. She was crying in her hands. So I went by the flag without saluting. Mr Gibbons's little slug moustache jumped up and down. It looked as if it was trying to get up his nose. He took me by the ear, and caught some of my hair too and gave it a painful tug. He marched me off to the headmaster's office. I waited there like Mother in the study, all alone. I was frightened when I heard the headmaster coming. He sat behind his desk and looked at me. I waited for him to get his strap from the cupboard.

"Tell me why you didn't salute the flag, Margaret."

"I don't know." That was the truth. The reason had gone away from me. I looked at this man with his big head and big nose and yellow stains on his teeth and knew that I would have to do what he said.

"Did Mr Gibbons hurt you?"

"He twisted my ear," and I began to cry.

The headmaster filled his pipe. "We have to make allowances for Mr Gibbons. He was badly gassed. He's very sick. But I don't want you to tell anyone that."

"All right." I didn't see how being gassed gave him the right to twist my ear and pull my hair.

"The flag means a lot to him."

"Yes."

"Is it because your father's a pacifist that you didn't salute it?"

"He doesn't believe in flags and war and I want to be on his side."

"Yes, I suppose you do. . . . Will you salute it tomorrow?"

"I still don't want to."

He lit his pipe and puffed a while. The room filled with smoke, like the gas that had got Mr Gibbons. It made me cough.

"Well Margaret, we'll make a bargain. When the first bell rings in the morning you go into your room and start your work. That way you'll miss assembly and you won't have to salute the flag. But you must be very quiet and you must do some work."

"Won't Mr Gibbons be cross?"

"Oh, he'll be cross all right. But you leave him to me." He smiled at me as if we had a secret. And nothing, not even Mr Gibbons, not children punching me and tipping water down my dress and knocking my lunch bag out of my hand and calling "Passifisst" at me as I walked home, could frighten me at that school any more.

Oliver came home from the war a Captain. He came to see us once then stayed away. He had a medal, which he showed us, and a wound in his leg which he would not. He said Father deserved to be where he was, and Mother told him he was in Father's house and he would please have the courtesy not to talk in that way.

41

"You understand he's ruined my career," Oliver shouted, but Mother said only Oliver could do that.

His visit made me unhappy. But I was inventive enough not to remain in that state. My reading showed me a way Oliver might be expelled from our family. I worked up a story in my mind: Oliver was the child of our father's enemy—one of the "wicked men" who, according to Mother, had been against him from the start of his time as a "crusader". The child was left an orphan, and our parents adopted him and brought him up a Plumb and tried to make him good—but it did not work, Oliver's bad blood was too strong and he became Father's enemy too, and worked against him. It remained for me to declare him no longer a Plumb, which I did, secretly, in my playhouse by the creek, kneeling in an Islamic pose, tinkling a little hand-bell three times and intoning words of banishment: "Out into the Darkness Oliver Plumb, we banish thee from Light." It was done, and I shivered for him, but felt very warm myself, and immensely powerful. I felt strong enough to put the world to rights with a word and make our father king. He and I would see that people were happy, for evermore. Meanwhile Oliver was gone, and although in the months that followed I saw him from time to time, in the streets of the town, even in our house, I knew that was just the wraith of him come to see what mischief it could do, for his real self had gone to the grey land of Missing and could trouble us no more. Alfred told me he had seen the wound in Oliver's leg. It was sucked-in like a mouth without any teeth. But that could not frighten me. Oliver was no more, I had seen to it. Even today Oliver does not seem quite real to me.

So our times went by. Nothing could touch us. Sometimes I was sad, but it was a pleasant sadness, for animals, for birds, like the blackbirds Robert killed and plucked and baked into a pie—which I had a small taste of. I could not swallow it. The birds had looked so sick with their feathers off. And sometimes I wept for no reason at all. It did not bother me, I felt it was special, and the tears were so warm and friendly running down my cheeks. The doctor came to look at me and said I was shooting up too fast, and he and Mother spoke privately about some other thing—I was only mildly curious. After that I had to drink water that had a few drops of iodine put in. Mother kept it in a big jug on the bench, and although I hated the taste I drank it willingly for I made of it a magical brew that only princesses drank.

I knew the 'flu would not touch us. I knew it would touch none of our family. Mother said it was the fault of the war (the dead soldiers, I heard someone say, had not been buried in time and the germs came from there), and as we had been against that it seemed to me we must be immune. Besides, I had tinkled my bell again and driven the germs away. So I watched with a kindly interest as the epidemic worked its way through our town. Two people died in our street. Every day we saw funerals and we stood silently as they went by, and the boys took off their caps, and sometimes I wept and felt the relatives must be pleased to see me weeping for them. Although we were immune we too had to walk through the tram drawn up by the shops and open our mouths for the spray the nurses squirted down your throat. It made our noses tickle and our eyes water. When we came out we pretended to be crying. We kept our S.O.S. stickers in a drawer. Robert pasted one on the lavatory door. We counted stickers in windows, but Robert always counted most because he went furthest from home. Mother could not keep him from wandering. He said he was hunting burglars.

There were a lot of burglaries, especially in the houses of rich people who had gone to stay in the country. Agnes said it wasn't fair that we weren't rich as well. She said our father was a bad man for making us suffer so much. If he really loved us he would not have gone to prison and made people talk, he would have earned us some money so we could go away and be safe from the 'flu; and she rushed away crying to her room and lay sobbing on her bed for a long time. I listened to Mother comforting her. The worst thing, it seemed, was that the girls in the embroidery shop where she worked would not sit with her in the lunch hour. Although I felt sorry for Agnes I began to wonder if she had been

43

adopted like Oliver, and I hoped I would not have to send her off to the Land of Missing. But that very night Grandpa Willis called and told us he had rented a cottage for us at New Brighton beach. We were to go next morning and could stay until the 'flu epidemic was over. We all shouted with delight, and Agnes looked so pleased I knew she was one of us, so she was saved.

We sat in the parlour talking to Grandpa Willis and while we were there the widow lady from next door ran in and said her boy had jumped out the window and run away to the creek. He had gone down with 'flu that day and was too hot in his bed and wanted to get cool. We all ran out. And there the boy was, Tommy Bracewell, lying in the creek under the willow branches, naked and sick as Robert's plucked blackbirds, splashing up and down with his arms and looking like Tom in *The Water Babies*. Alfred and Grandpa Willis pulled him out. Robert helped too. They pulled him all the way back to Mrs Bracewell's house. Tommy bit Robert's finger. He didn't mean to, Mother explained, putting iodine on it in the kitchen. He did it because he had fever and didn't know what he was doing. But it seemed unfair to me, and suddenly we weren't as safe as we had been, the 'flu had closed in. Grandpa Willis felt it too. It was just as well we were off tomorrow, he said.

So we went to the country, like rich people. (Felicity stayed behind to look after things. Oliver would come to be with her, so there would be a man about the house. Esther winked at me when Felix said that. It wasn't Oliver who would come, Esther said, but Dan Peabody, our father's friend and a married man. Felicity was sweet on him, and he would take the chance with all of us gone to make her do with him the dirty things that married people did. At least, I thought they were dirty, and thought them made up as well, but Esther said they were fun or why would people do them all the time. I did not listen. Felicity was a Plumb, and not like that.) We packed our summer clothes in suitcases and put them on the porch for Grandpa Willis to pick up. Then we went along the street and caught the tram to New Brighton. Seven Plumbs together: Mother and me, Agnes and

Esther and Rebecca, Alfred and Robert. The same number, I thought, as the seven little Australians from the book that had made me cry so much when I read it the week before. In the end the big sister, Judy, was crushed under a falling tree, saving the little ones. I had thought her sacrifice beautiful, and the saddest and noblest thing I had ever heard of. I shed a few tears on the tram, thinking about it, but cheered up when New Brighton came into view.

It was lovely there. There was hardly any work to do in the house, and we were able to run on the beach and the sandhills all day long. Grandpa Willis brought our groceries out to us in his trap and sometimes his son John, whom we called uncle, brought them in his motor car and took us for rides on the roads at the back of the sandhills. Grandpa was always cheerful, although he was ill and was still mourning his wife, our grandmother, but John was a gloomy man and did not talk much. I thought perhaps he had been in love and been jilted. He drove our mother out to Paparua prison on visiting days. Sometimes they took Alfred or Esther or Rebecca or picked Felicity up from town. They thought I was too young, and that suited me. I did not want to visit Paparua prison. I knew it would be—I will not say too real, but just *ordinary*. It would not be the prison I had built in my mind, with stone walls and towers and iron doors and dripping passages, and the deep cell where our father languished, chained against the wall, waiting for the day when he would come out and put the world to rights. I stayed at home with Agnes. I modelled castles and dragons in plasticine.

So my waking dream went on. I sat alone in the sandhills with my book, or I followed the shapeless marks of giant feet until they became lost in marram grass. I was lost in there too. Each hill was like the next, and it was easy to think you were in a desert, or that the little bowl you rested in was the whole of the world and outside was nothing but blue with you floating in it. Lying on my back, I watched the sky move. There was no sound, unless you counted the sea rustling away, thumping away, telling the direction home.

I found a grave in there. I thought it was a grave, but I did not dare dig it up to make sure. It was shaped in a mound and had a jam jar with red geraniums at each end. It wasn't long enough to be a grown-up's grave. I sat down by it and felt very sad and queer. Someone's child had died of 'flu, I thought, and there hadn't been enough proper people to bury her, and so her family had carried her quietly into the sandhills at night and buried her there. I was sure she was a girl like me and I wondered what it was like to be dead. I got very frightened. I listened for the sea and ran down to it and ran all the way home. I told my brothers about the grave, but when I tried to take them to it next day I couldn't find the place. Alfred said I was dreaming it because I was a dope and so romantic. He went home. But Robert and I made a new grave. We decorated it with shells and pieces of wood. "Now all you need is someone to put in it," Alfred said, when we told him.

The next day was our last at New Brighton beach. A wind from the plains lifted the sea into sharp little waves that slapped our cheeks and blinded us. We swam all morning, shrieking in the tide that lifted itself up the dry sand like a live thing to swallow the world. It swelled and grew, and frightened me and drew me in, and I saw no reason why it should stop at the sandhills or the houses, or at the city beyond, and the cathedral and the park, or stop at the hills. I would not go as far out as the others. I saw them diving like porpoises in the waves. Alfred spouted water from his mouth. "It tastes like old Meg's iodine," he yelled. I ran in to the beach and wrapped my towel round me and sheltered from the wind in the little group of Mother and Grandpa Willis and Uncle John.

"This child's cold," Mother said. "It's time we all went in." She called my brothers and sisters, and we went single file through the sandhills, like Indians, and dried ourselves in our rooms with our coloured towels, and gathered for lunch. Then I looked round and I saw one of us was missing. The world went grey, like tin. Colour went from the sky outside the window and the flowers on the table in their vase, and the food and the faces, and death came in for the Plumbs. I knew who the grave in the sandhills was for. Agnes took me by the shoulders and pushed me to the table. "Come on, dreamy," she said.

Then Mother knew what I had known. She turned from the bench where she had been cutting bread. "Where's Rebecca?" Her face was like a face in an old broken book.

We ran down to the beach. Uncle John found her in the waves. He ran in up to his waist in his Sunday clothes and carried her out and ran through the sandhills with her to the cottage and we stood and looked at her—Rebecca dead. They laid her on her face on a towel on the floor and turned her head side on and pulled her tongue out. Water ran out of her mouth. Robert gave her artificial respiration. He was the only one who knew how to do it. He knelt beside her and pressed with his thin hands on the ribs of her back, and lifted his hands away, counting one, two, three, one, two, three. More water came from her mouth. But even Robert, I knew, would not bring her back. Robert would not save the Plumbs. Presently a man came in from the cottage next door, and lifted him aside and took over from him.

I walked out of the house into the sandhills. I sat down. I did not look for the grave. I knew it was there. I did not cry. My dream had been a true one, my California dream. It had been sent to show the way things were. The Plumbs were floating by on the Black River. One by one they were sinking. Rebecca was first.

8 We had shared many things. Her dresses and dolls were handed down to me. I came to the books she had read, crossed her neat *Rebecca* from their pages and wrote *Margaret Plumb*. She told me the ones I would like. *Seven Little Australians* had been hers. She had come to me in my bed when I had bad dreams. She saw things I was able to see. Like me she drew wizards and witches, magical doors and sleeping princesses. I

loved her next to Robert. When she died I came to love Robert with a kind of desperation. I knew we were doomed.

That was long ago. Now Robert's turn was coming. I drove north for him on a summer's day. Rebecca had died, and Mother and Father had died, and Alfred had had the life kicked out of him. Agnes was dead in San Francisco, from a stroke that had come at a bridge party, just when she was on the point of slamming, her husband wrote. And now Robert, who once I had thought might save us, was entering the last few months of his life. He was fifty-four.

I hummed a tune as I drove along. I was not unhappy. Robert had taught me this. I drove through vineyards and orchards, and pine forests where the trees were of Christmas-tree size. I drove past sawmills and yellow heaps of sawdust falling into the mud of mangrove creeks. Men in black singlets stood upon the logs. I drove by the muddy harbour and through a little town, and went along a dusty road beyond the furthest houses, and there I came to Robert's iron shack. It stood in the fenced-off corner of a field where cattle grazed in the shade of manuka trees. Its corrugated walls were green and its roof tarred black. Robert's garden came up to the door. Corn stood at shoulder height. Pumpkins and marrows lay on beds of straw. The fields around were baked to a grey colour by the hard summer, but coolness seemed to rise up from the ground on Robert's section. This was no magic. I do not claim any special relationship for him with "the soil". He worked at it, that's all, and knew what it needed; so he could keep it healthy, even when sick himself. He had rain-water tanks and an artesian bore and compost bins. He collected animal manure. He left trees about his property for shade. Looking at all this, I was guilty to be taking him away.

I walked up the path and looked in at his door. "Robert." I went to his bedroom, treading softly in case he was asleep. The bed was neatly made. Folded on it was a patchwork quilt Mother had sewn thirty years before. There were squares in it from the frock I had worn at Esther's twenty-first birthday party—forget-me-nots, blue on blue—and squares of midnight serge

48

from my Epsom Grammar gym frocks. I had given Robert the quilt to bring him back into our family. It made me smile—not convincingly: I am still prone to symbolic acts. The quilt at least kept him warm at nights. But I put aside any meaning from that, and went back to his kitchen—living-room too. I looked about in a sharp housewifely way. Although no larger than our bathroom at home, it did not seem cramped. Nothing was out of its place. On the table was a cloth embroidered with birds. (Mother's work too. Dad liked to see her making pretty things. She put useful tasks aside when he sat with her.) An easy chair stood by the range and a box of kindling wood on the hearth. Clean dishes from Robert's breakfast sparkled in a drying rack on the bench. There were books in a shelf, a calendar over the mantelpiece, with tide times pencilled on it, and on the wall by the door a hand-drawn map of the south side of the harbour, showing the creeks and mangrove swamps and shoals. Fishing grounds were cross-hatched in red pencil. It had been a good many months since he had been well enough to take his boat out fishing.

I went through the lean-to on the back of the house, past his iron bath and copper and tubs, and walked down through the garden to the orchard. Black Orpingtons scratched among the trees. They had blood-red crowns and crazy eyes: Renaissance kings. A beehive hummed, with guards darting at the door. I kept well clear of it; and startled a wild black cat, which ran away to a blackberry patch in a field. A path led to the river. I went along it through ripening fruit that banged me on the arms. He had planted sensibly: apples, peaches, plums. But here was a row of guavas, and there a persimmon tree.

When I came out by the creek I saw him sitting on his jetty. That was of his making too. It had his mark. For me jetties mean rotting piles and sun-warped planks—the romantic view. Robert's was tarred and creosoted. Its thick legs grew out of the mud like trees. A dinghy was tied at the foot of iron steps. It lay tilted on its side, lapped under half its length by rising water. Robert had named it *Susan*. No woman of that name was in his life. It was simply to Robert the sort of name one gave a boat. In the old days at Peacehaven his cow had always been Daisy and his goat Nan.

He turned when he heard my feet on the jetty deck. "Don't get up, Robert." I put my hand on his shoulder. He made a place for me and we sat with our feet dangling towards the mud.

"Good drive?" he asked.

"Not bad. What time's the tide?"

"It's half-way in. Dick'll be bringing his boat up in an hour."

"Is that the man you're letting have this place?"

"That's him. He's a good bloke."

I knew that was all I would get about Dick. It was strange with Robert, he reversed so many things. What would have come as meanness from other people emerged from him as a sign of his fullness.

"I've tidied your place up," I said. "I hope it will be all right."

"Sutton died? I got your telegram."

"Yesterday morning."

He nodded. I watched the warm salt water advance on the mud. Air bubbled out of crab holes and mud-crabs darted here and there with the sun glistening on their backs. The flanks of the river gleamed, the mangrove trees lay yellow-green, croco-dile-still. As a rule I did not care for this scenery. Today I thought it beautiful. And Sutton's death seemed right, as Robert's death would be, and mine.

He had lived twelve years on this piece of land. I had been visiting him for ten. Silence was as good as conversation to us. I pulled my cardigan off and enjoyed the sun. Robert took out his handkerchief and knotted it at the corners for a hat. He was bald, as all the Plumb men were. He had the round Plumb face that even in the worldly and selfish ones appears innocent. Suffering had not taken that away. If anything his disease had made him seem stronger. It had given him a barrel chest and thickened him round the shoulders. But I had spoken its name to my doctor in Loomis and he had told me what Robert kept to

50

himself or perhaps did not know. I knew of the broken lung tissues and air rattling in the pleural sac, and of his heart swollen by the pressure and strained to the point where soon it would collapse. On the mudflats I heard a continuous crackle, a salty sound, as the tide advanced; and from Robert's chest a noise like gravel shaken in a sieve.

"Does your doctor say it's all right for you to come?"

"He thinks it's a good idea. He's written me a letter. . . . Who is it down there now? Still Doctor Walker?"

"He died. It's a man called Webley-Brown."

"An Englishman? Is he O.K.?"

"He's not English. I suppose he can't help his name." I was moved by the way he had spoken of Doctor Walker. When Robert became an objector in the war, Walker, a fierce old gun-boat Britisher, had steamed round to Peacehaven with abuse—"worse than a rapist", "shooting would be too good", etc. Yet Robert would have gone to him now. His innocence, his acceptance, made me want to cry.

"If I put the kettle on, Robert, will you come in for some tea?" I wanted to get away by myself for a moment. But he struggled to his feet.

"It's getting hot."

We went slowly along the jetty. The dinghy *Susan* was afloat, rubbing on the piles. The water, pushing a rim of scum, eased into the roots of the mangrove trees. We walked through the orchard, Robert first, no taller than me in the bent-forward stance his illness forced on him. He picked a few late plums and offered them to me.

"Burbanks. They weren't very good this year."

"Can you really leave this, Robert?"

"Dick'll look after it. He's been helping already."

"You'll miss your grapes being ripe."

He shrugged. It meant, I think, they would ripen without him. Again I accepted it; and the guilt that had had me argue for a moment against his leaving lifted from me. The trees that had taken twelve years to grow, the grape vines over the shed and

51

along the trellis, the fowls in their seventh or eighth generation, the sheds, the tanks, the jetty and the boat *Susan*; and the bach—he was leaving these for Sutton's smelly rooms and dusty garden (he knew, I had described them); and he shrugged at it and took it as his next step—so it became acceptable to me.

I put the kettle on and we had tea. Robert drank his in his easy chair. "I'll kill a chook for you before we go."

"Oh no, Robert."

He grinned at me. "You don't have to watch. You'd like a chook for your dinner, wouldn't you?"

I had to admit that was true, but the thought of Robert's hatchet falling on one of those beautiful red-combed birds I had seen in the orchard disturbed me terribly. So did the dreadful accident of selection. Which would it be?—its death already approaching as it scratched happily under some plum or peach tree. The others, I supposed, would squawk a bit, and then carry on with their feeding.

"There's a couple that aren't laying too well. I'll take one of those."

I looked at him sitting there, with his round face and bald head and badly-shaven chin and crooked teeth, and looked at his body, new-shapen by his disease; and told myself what I had known since my girlhood—that he had no intelligence to speak of, and little imagination, but that he was good. I had seen goodness in him, plain as blue eyes and rounded chin. (Raymond snorts at this, and uses words like quietism, passivism. "Was he driven to goodness, did it come from an inner compulsion? Seems to me it might have been the line of least resistance." He claims Alfred was the better man. "Alfred tried to help people, he didn't just take off for the bush like a hermit." He finds the very idea of Robert tiresome. When I took him with me on a visit he enjoyed the fishing, but found his uncle's simpleness a bore. *Robert*, he believes, is my creation. That's not so, but I do not argue. I look for less contentious ground, and say that what was just as impressive about Robert as his goodness was that he had known himself. But Raymond won't allow this any importance. "Oh we all get acquainted. Just by staying alive. It's the self you find that matters. Wouldn't have taken much effort for old Robert to know himself." I get angry—and grow silent. I'll do that now; and not swell Robert up with meaning. He would strut through my story like a pouter pigeon, and that is not him at all. Someone said, "I know what Time is, but I cannot tell you." That is how I am with Robert's goodness.)

Now all of this does not mean I was ready to see him cut the heads off chickens. I told him I was happy to go without. "Don't spoil your last day here by killing things, Robert."

He laughed. "All right. But Dick'll soon have them in the pot."

"Have you sold him everything?"

"I've given my boat to one of the boys down the road. He helps with the garden."

"Have you got the house sale sorted out?"

"We'll stop and see the lawyer on our way through town. Dick's got it arranged."

"What about packing?"

"I haven't got much."

"Whatever it is, we'd better get it together."

So we went about the rooms, he told me things he wanted to take, and I packed them up: his clothes in a suitcase, and mother's patchwork quilt and embroidered cloth in a cardboard box. I made him take blankets and pillows, sheets and towels— but other things (cutlery and plates and pots and pans and his hearth shovel and brush, and tools from his shed) he told me he had promised Dick. It was all in the price. I did not believe him. The real reason was that Robert placed no value on things—no, that is wrong. He felt that things belonged to places, belonged where their use had been. He had, I think, an instinct not to possess. I did not keep on at him. He was in distress from his emphysema and leaned over the table for a few moments to ease his pain. He allowed me to pack his books. That was no pleasure. Wiping the dust from them, placing them neatly in an apple box, I was a prey to emotions as different as sentimental love and bitter hatred. I had thought myself past both, long past, on a sensible ground, but here I had tears on my cheeks and the hardness of rage on my mouth. The books had been Dad's. His own were there: *The Growing Point of Truth*, *New Reasons For the Future Life*, *The World's Disease*. He was good at titles. And each had its tag of Latin, boldly pencilled at poor Robert: *Post tenebras lux* and *Tempori parendum*. They confused me too. I wanted to cry, "Onward!"; yet was saying, "Enough of this stuff, Dad, enough!" I closed the books roughly, packed them in.

"Do you ever read these, Robert?"

"I'm not much of a reader." He pushed himself up painfully from the table. "I never really knew what he was getting at."

"You became a conscientious objector."

"That was for me, not him. I'm glad it made him happy though."

"Was he happy? To see you in that place?"

"Yes. He never thought things were easy."

"Do you?"

He had himself almost straight by now. "I've never worried about it."

I opened another book. A silverfish flashed into the spine. " 'To Robert. Yours to right the wrong and wrong nothing that is right.' "

"I wasn't doing that. . . . I don't know whether I want to take them, Meg."

"I'll have them then. I'm collecting his old stuff. Did I tell you Wendy Philson is writing his life?"

He shook his head.

"And Merle Butters is getting messages from him. From the Great Beyond."

"What does he say?"

"Oh, weed the carrots. And, love makes the world go round. It's him all right." But my bitterness was passing, and my love, and I began to be ashamed of myself. It was a long time since I had suffered an attack of that sort. I came back to normal. What

I had for my father these days was an easy love, a calm respect, an eye that made no distortions.

We carried Robert's belongings out to my car, packed them in the boot and the back seat. Then we walked to the jetty. The mudflats had gone. Green water stretched to the creek mouth. I saw small schools of sprats darting through the piles. Robert sat down, taking the slightly forward-leaning position that eased his chest. It gave him a dejected look, but I knew he was not dejected. I took my place beside him and we sat without speaking, letting the warmth touch our bones—pleasant for a few moments, but soon I had to put on my hat and Robert covered his head with his handkerchief. I heard his breath rattling, endlessly turning.

"What does the doctor say about you, Robert?"

"Just take my pills."

"Do you?"

"Yes. No trouble. I think from the way it's going I'll die about the middle of the year."

"What makes you think that?"

"Just the way it's going. It kind of grows. It's got times—and new stages. . . . And it feels as if it'll all finish in winter."

"So," I said, "you'll have your last few months back at Peacehaven."

He nodded. "Not at the house, Meg. I want to be at the cottage."

"You'll come up for your tea? I thought we agreed."

"Yes, that's all right. But I won't be able to get there. Not always. It's getting worse pretty fast."

"Then I'll come and cook it down at your place."

We left it at that. Presently Robert said, "Here's Dick," and I saw a launch come round the farthest mangroves and head towards us.

"Who is he, Robert?"

"A retired fisherman. He lives in a little shack on the edge of town."

"I hope you're getting a good price from him."

I had my answer when Dick climbed on the jetty. There was something furtive in the way he looked at me. He was like a man who has won a lottery and is afraid it might all be a mistake. He climbed back into his launch—the most down-at-heel boat I had ever seen—and threw a fish on the jetty.

"There you are, Bob. There you are, Mrs Sole. Beauty, ain't she? Caught her out at your spot this morning, Bob."

It was a schnapper, all rosy-coloured and plump and beautiful. It must have weighed ten pounds.

"Scaled her and gutted her. Don't find them that big much more." He was trying to make Robert some return. The fish was all he could manage, and it did not seem inadequate. It made me hungry just to look at it. Robert was pleased too.

"We'll have it tonight. You can bake it, Meg."

"Stuff it with a few onions," Dick said. "She'll feed your whole family." He climbed back on the jetty, picked up the schnapper, and we walked to the house.

"You'll have a good crop off those tree tomatoes, Dick," Robert said.

"Looks like it, looks like it," Dick answered, looking uneasy.

We wrapped the fish in newspaper and stowed it in the car. Then I made lunch. I felt sorry for Dick, and was impatient with him. His smiles and silences were a poor thing for a man who, from the look of him, was used to speaking out. I was glad when the meal was over. I cleared the dishes away and started to wash them. Robert went to his chair and sat there, looking exhausted.

"Are you sure you're up to travelling today?"

"I'll be all right. I'll help you with the dishes in a minute."

"No you won't."

"I've got the thing for you," Dick said. From the window I saw him heading down to his launch. Presently he came back with a bottle of beer. He poured Robert a glass.

"Mrs Sole?"

"No thank you." But I was pleased with Dick. Robert sipped the beer and seemed to grow easy.

"How about some plums?" Dick said. He picked a bag and

56

put them on the table. He was getting lively. "Not finished yet." He winked at Robert and made another sortie down the orchard. I could not see what he was doing. I had the dishes away and was ready to leave by the time he came back. He slapped something on the table with a heavy sound. "There," he said, "a pot-roaster. Feel how heavy she is," and he dug his thumb in. It was a fowl; beheaded, gutted, plucked. "Run like a rabbit, she did. But I got her. She'll make a good couple of meals, eh Bob?"

Robert laughed: a wheezy lurching sound. "I guess his number was up, Meg."

I was furious. "Mr Webster, until Robert signs the papers this place is his. And the livestock. And the fruit. I think you could have the courtesy to ask before you touch things."

"Now, Meg. Now, Meg," Robert said. "She doesn't like killing things, Dick. She thought she'd saved old chooky here."

"I'm sorry," Dick began, but I cut him off.

"Come on, Robert. It's time we were leaving."

"We'll take the chook. Can't waste that. Thanks, Dick. I hope you didn't get one of the layers."

"She was the one you showed me. With the torn comb."

"I won't cook it, Robert."

"Yes you will, Meg. See how fat she is." He had come to the table and, like Dick, he dug his thumb in the fowl. "Get us some paper, Dick, and we'll wrap her up."

So we took it. We put it on the back seat of the car, along with the bag of plums and the hump-backed schnapper. Then Dick went off to his launch and chugged away. He would meet us in half an hour in the lawyer's office in town.

Robert got in the car. I was disturbed at his easy behaviour. I would have wandered round touching things. I started the car and drove away. At the corner he looked back—a painful turning of his misshapen torso. "She wasn't a bad little place."

I was satisfied. I am still satisfied. I have these attacks of sentimentality, and am glad to have them. It would be un-natural, I would be some sort of monster, if I had entirely put off the habit of mind that dominated my life for thirty years. I take

57

these things as a sign of my health.

We drove along the dusty road and through the town to the wharf. Robert got out and sat on a fishing crate in a band of shade tight under a wall. I sat beside him and looked over the harbour at the hills. The water was green, a salty colour, and striped with yellow where the mudbanks lay. Soon Dick's launch came round the nearest headland and turned towards us.

"Dick's not a bad bloke," Robert said.

I did not want to talk about him. With the wide view ahead of me, the sun on the boards, the sound of gulls, I felt very peaceful. I felt my mind expand to take in the past. I thought of the years Robert had vanished from us to a community—I shall have to call it Christian—run by a crazy man called Parminter. Robert was no Christian, no believer in whatever variation Parminter taught. But he was happy on Parminter's farm. Dad had a letter from him, and went to visit him there, and said he was happy. He seemed to believe Robert's mind was healed of the wounds it had taken in his four years in the camps. So I was pleased, moderately pleased, to think of him there, living out his life. But then a letter I wrote him came back to me. Someone had written on it in a neat hand: *Gone to join his Master in the Pit.* I wrote to Parminter, asking what had happened, but had no reply. So Robert was lost again.

Now, on the wharf, I said, "You never told me why you left the farm. Parminter's place."

He shrugged. "Long time ago, Meg."

"What sort of man was Parminter?"

"He was mad."

"Dad said you liked it there."

"It was all right."

"And you had a wife?"

"I just lived with her, that's all."

We had had this conversation before, and got no further. I believed I was going to get no further that day. I sighed, but was not too discouraged. Then Robert surprised me by saying, "They stopped talking to me. Even Betty stopped. They made

58

her move out. So I packed up and got out of there."

"Betty was your wife?"

He nodded.

"Why did they stop talking to you?"

"Money."

I did not understand.

"It was when Dad died. He left me the cottage. When I told Tom Parminter, he wanted me to sell it and put the money in the farm. Everything belonged to us all, he said. But I had a letter from Bluey Considine asking if he could stay on there. I told him he could have it without any rent. And that's what I told Tom." Robert grinned. "He said I was the Anti-Christ."

"So you left?"

"After they stopped talking. More than two weeks Meg, and not one of them said a word to me. I tried to get to Betty to see if she'd come but they locked her up. And then Tom started saying he could see my cloven hoof. So I left that night. It was too crazy for me."

"And you came up here?"

"Wandered around a bit. Then I found this place."

That was his life, these were the places of his life: Peacehaven, then the camps, Parminter's farm, his bach by the creek (Dick's place now), and Peacehaven again, or at least its fringes. Until he died. I had no doubt that would come in the winter. I looked calmly at it all. I did not see that his life should be called a failure, as Oliver and Felicity call it.

On the other hand I did not see why I should be happy with all he did. In the solicitor's office I could not keep quiet. I saw the price he was asking Dick for his property.

"Are you crazy, Robert? It must be worth three times that much."

"It's the price I paid. I told Dick he could have it for what I paid."

"But what about your improvements? You told me yourself it was falling down when you bought it."

"I don't want any profits."

"It's not a question of profits, it's a question of what it's worth. Property values have gone up three or four times. You ask Fergus, he'll tell you."

"Meg—"

"I'm not going to stand here and see you cheated."

The solicitor made an angry sound. Dick said, "Nobody's cheating him, Mrs Sole. I've told him all of this a dozen times."

"I wonder."

He looked miserable, and I understood a future he had dreamed of was slipping away. And suddenly I had had enough of my anger and talk of money. Robert would be dead in the winter. What he was getting would keep him very comfortably till then.

"I'm sorry. I didn't mean that."

"Yes, Meg, you keep out of it. We've got an agreement and that's what I'm going to sign. Now," he said to the lawyer, "where do I do it?" He put his name on the paper and that was that. He grinned at me. He knew I was ashamed of myself.

We said goodbye. Dick got into his launch, and Robert and I in the car. I drove south, through the forests and farms, and came to Peacehaven.

The journey exhausted Robert. I made him lie down while I unpacked. Then I went up to the house and baked the schnapper. Robert was not well enough to come up. I took some to him in a covered dish.

The next day he felt better. He was able to come up.

I roasted the fowl.

9 Robert looked at the garden and shook his head. There was little he could do with it. He dug a small patch out the back and put some seeds in. I tried to burn the convolvulus he had weeded out but it made a thick white smoke that set us coughing. I had to walk him up the road to get away from it.

The doctor called and spent half an hour with him. Afterwards we talked out by his car.

"He'll need a lot of care. He'd be better staying with you."

"He won't do that."

"It's got to the point where he's in a lot of discomfort. He's finding it difficult to breathe."

"Can't you give him something?"

"I've given him what I can. It's not much help. I'd be happier if someone was in the house."

"I'll shift down."

"Yes. Soon, I think. I suppose we can't talk him into going to hospital?"

"No."

"That's what I thought." He drove away and I went in to see Robert. He was resting on the sofa.

"Seems to know what he's doing," Robert said.

"Did he leave a prescription?"

"Here. I wonder why he calls himself Webley-Brown." He was as near to being offended as I had ever seen him.

Later in the day we walked in the grounds of Peacehaven. We went by the ruins of the summer-house and round the edge of the lawn till we came to the bridge.

"It's not safe, Robert."

"Looks sound enough to me." He went on to it and looked at the water. "I wonder if there are still any eels."

"I think the boys from the houses have caught them all. Sutton used to fish for eels. It's a long time since I saw him catch any though."

"What did he do with them?"

"Bluey used to say he ate them. But I think he just caught them for fun."

Robert walked to the other side of the bridge. He looked past the danger notice at the houses stretching up the line of the creek.

"Nothing left."

"There's an old pear tree in one of the back yards up there."

"Merle's garden looks O.K."

"She pays a man. She's not short of money."

"How is she?"

"Since Graydon died? I thought she'd fold up. They were more like Siamese twins than husband and wife. But of course all she did was get in touch with his spirit. She'd managed that before he was even buried. Now it's mostly Dad she's getting through to. And her Japanese man. Graydon hasn't got much to say any more."

"You sound as if you don't like her."

"She's all right. But I've had her for forty years."

"I'd like to go and see her."

"You won't have to. She's coming to see you."

Merle was floating down through her garden, through the roses, through the hydrangea walks, like the Queen of the Fairies. She had a marvellous air of commanding nature. But when she had opened the gate at the garden bottom and come on to the concrete suburban paths she looked ridiculous. She had always affected a flowing style of dress, taking it from Graydon's mother, Ella Satterthwaite, who had claimed to be a poet—or, as she put it, poetess. But Ella preferred blue or mauve. Merle chose darker colours. Today she was in black, with purple at the cuffs and at her throat. It was easy to see why the children in the houses called her a witch.

She crossed the turning bay and came across the broken ground to the fence. She moved with amazing lightness for a woman of her age. Robert met her. They kissed by the pad-locked gate.

"Robert, my dear, my boy. I knew you had come home. Your father told me. You've no idea how pleased he is."

I had told her too, on the telephone, but she did not mention that. She caressed his cheek. "Robert, it's so good you've come. How could you not come? All your dear ones from the Other Side have been making the path, and now at last you've travelled along it. And dear Meg fetched you in her car. What a good girl she is." She is like that, she makes such easy passage between her

62

worlds that she disarms me. She held Robert's hand. She smiled at him. It was an unlikely conjunction: the stately and beautiful—Merle had always been beautiful—eighty-year-old witch-woman, in her black and purple clothes, in her rings and bangles and scarf and cameo brooch, with cheeks of silk, with English voice; and Robert, my slow brother, misshapen Robert, in sleeves rolled up tight under his arms, in waistcoat from somebody's suit, and thick trousers, and thick boots—his ugly clothes of thirty years ago. They held hands. Something was passing between them. Perhaps it was just affection. I was not jealous. Not at all. I was mystified, and envious; and thrown into confusion by something not complicated enough for me to understand.

"And so," Merle said, "you're starting on your passage. What an exciting journey. You are fortunate."

"For heaven's sake, Merle," I cried.

She smiled at me. "Meg doesn't understand. We understand, don't we Robert? Your dear ones are waiting for you. There'll be a great celebration when you arrive."

"You'd better remind them Robert doesn't drink."

For a moment I thought I had managed to offend her. But she smiled at last and said, "Meg dear, death isn't what you think. You mustn't allow it to frighten you. It doesn't frighten Robert."

"I'm not dead yet," he said.

"We never die. There is no such thing as death. The body may decay but our spirit will go on and on until it reaches God."

"In the meantime," I said, "weed the carrots."

"Oh Meg, oh Meg, you don't give yourself a chance."

"What else did Dad say the other night? Did he have a message for me?"

"He said you must be brave. Grief is a part of it all. Now my dears, I must go. Mr Fujikawa always speaks at two twenty-seven. He gets very cross if I keep him waiting. He pinches me, do you know that? I really don't know how he manages it, but I have the bruises on my arms for weeks afterwards. Robert dear, you must come and visit me. You can walk that far? Don't bring Meg. Her aura has a jagged edge and it hurts my friends."

"I can come," Robert said.

"Not between half past two and three. Mr Fujikawa can't bear interruptions. Goodbye, dear." She kissed him again. "It's a pity your illness has made you look so ugly. But never mind. Your spirit is beautiful, isn't it? That's what counts."

She went away up the slope, but stopped on the turning bay and called, "Oh, Meg dear, I almost forgot. Your tomatoes have got borer. You need some arsenate of lead. I can let you have some." And she went on, up the concrete path into her garden, through the hydrangea walks and the roses, into her house—and to the dark drawing-room with the inlaid table, where she entertained her Japanese gentleman.

"She doesn't change," Robert said.

"She changes all the time."

He shrugged. "All that spirit stuff is new, but that's not important."

"Don't let her hear you say so." I had spoken to no one about Robert's death. That meant Merle had seen it for herself. I supposed it was plain. It was plain to me—but I did not want others to see it; and if they saw, did not think it right for them to say so. Not even Merle. I was sure she looked on her own body as more than a parcel of flesh, a sack of bones. She dressed it up as though it had great importance.

Robert said, "We had a spiritualist in Shannon camp. He was the happiest bloke there. He reckoned his spirit used to leave his body every night and spend the time at home."

We strolled along the path by the stream. Fergus kept the section in reasonable trim, and I did my bit. He mowed the lawns, pruned the fruit trees and dug and mulched around them. He planted the heavy crops—potatoes and kumara. I looked after the rest. I did not grow many flowers. After Dad's death I had Mother's rose garden rooted out. There was too much snipping and pruning. And the budding of those fragrant lovely flowers from a stem so arthritic, so dangerously barbed,

64

struck me as a falsification.

Robert noticed they were gone and said it was a pity. "They were too much work," I said. "Mother only played games with them anyhow." I meant that in moving in hat and gloves among her roses, cutting here and there a perfect bloom, she had been playing the lady she might have been. It was her only pretence. I understood her need of it. But roses did not work that way for me. I made a bonfire of them by the creek.

Robert said, "You kept the fruit trees though." He walked round trees he had planted thirty years before, but was not moved by any great emotion. He was simply happy. We made our tour, he admired my tomatoes (Merle was right, they had borer) and ate half a dozen gooseberries, stripping their paper clothes with his rough hands; and up by the bend in the creek, where pine roots make a ladder down to the pools, he watched three boys building a dam and called advice to them. (They thought he was crackers.) By then he had had enough, his breathing was painful, and I took him inside. He rested for an hour on the sofa. I brought him a cup of tea and played popular tunes on Mother's piano. This was as I had imagined it. I too was simply happy. I thought later if caring for Robert was my pretence there was no reason why I should not have it. I did not believe, though, it was all pretence.

Robert came up to the house for tea that night. I had asked if he would mind meeting Esther and Fred. "Whatever you like, Meg." So I asked them over: not for the meal though. Robert's breathing made an invasion of the dining table. We ate, Fergus and Robert and I, and Fergus was good with Robert. That gravelly rattle did not trouble him. He remains an accepting and a natural man. I saw his worries come swimming to the surface of his eyes—swift and flicking and irritable for M.E., and for Beth Neeley slower, somehow eel-like, with a trace of red. Poor Fergus, I thought, I really must try to help him. He smiled and talked with Robert about fishing and about gardening, and about Bluey Considine and Sutton. He had gone to Sutton's funeral. There had been only the priest and one or two others.

Fergus had been moved by the words of burial. He could not find masculine terms to admit it in, so he did no more than say it made you think.

He came with us after the meal when I showed Robert Dad's study, and I could not resent his air of proprietorship. He worked there nightly. His study was one thing, Dad's another. The desk was his place of activity, and Dad's books, floor to ceiling on every wall, were as distant from him as a ring of mountains. When he saw them at all he took them for scenery.

Robert had no entry to that world either. But he had come to the study as a child and taken his turn on the stool while Dad scratched away above him at essay or lecture or commentary or letter to some fellow-crusader in Sydney, London, Bombay, Thorpe, or Kumara. We had all gone through it. I will not say it had no value. I will not even say there was no pleasure in it. I made many discoveries on that footstool, and Dad's hand on my head was a natural blessing. He was kinder with me than with most of the others. But even I was nervous. We never knew when a question would fall—come rolling down like thunder out of the sky. We learned not to say we had liked a poem or we would have to say why. Our reasons were never good enough. We crept out with the knowledge of having failed him. At least, I had thought it so until that night. But Robert grinned when I spoke of it.

"I told him I didn't like reading. He let me play with his ear trumpet."

I could not believe it. Nobody touched his trumpet. *I* had never laid a hand on it.

"I used to carve heads on his walking sticks. This is one I did," and he took a stick from the stand in the corner and looked at it and grinned. "Pretty good for a kid." It was an ugly goat's head, roughly done. I had often wondered about it. "Later on I used to polish the Buddha." That was on a stand in a corner and he went to it and slapped it softly on its shining head. "We used to grin at each other. Have you got any incense?"

"No," I said.

"He let me light the incense. We always had some when I came in here."

I was thinking, a little bitterly, that it would have been better to be dull. Dull Robert. Slow Robert. Dad had never let me light the incense. He had burned a stick for me when I brought home my school report with every subject marked *Excellent*—but in his canny way had stubbed it out. "We'll save a bit for next time." He had not offered a next time. I was jealous. But I looked at Robert grinning there, patting the Buddha on its head, and the feeling went away.

Later I asked Esther, "Did Dad ever light any incense for you?"

"Never, the old skinflint. He said it cost too much."

"George was one of the good guys," Fred Meggett said. Since his first big success with U.S. Army surplus after the war, Fred had been full of Americanisms. They marked his moments of sincerity. He had always admired my father. They used to spar with each other, play a game: Fred felt the qualities he admired in himself thrown into relief by Dad's semi-comical judgements, while Dad relaxed with him, suspended judgement, and treated Fred like a naughty boy. It was easier for us all than open war.

Esther said, "We're all good guys as long as we help you make a buck." Her Americanisms mock her husband.

Fergus poured Fred a whisky, and Esther helped herself from her jar of port wine. (She carried it in a brown-paper bag everywhere she went.) My sister had grown into what her husband called "a big soft pudding". It was a description full of inaccuracies. She was hard rather than soft, even her fatty swellings (and these, I suppose, are what Fred was talking about) were firm to touch; and as for sweetness, there was not the slightest bit of that in her. Once she'd been able to love, in her noisy way. Not any longer. Love had been treated to doses of what she called "life", and it did not survive. Fred called her Fatso, Guzzleguts, Pisshead, and worse names. That was his response to "life".

I looked at her with affection. I had no other way of seeing her. She wore expensive clothes, and wore them badly. She rolled up the sleeves of her blouses like a man. Her buttons came undone and her seams went crooked. She did not care. Her dresses rucked at her waist (though she had no waist) and rode up her thighs when she sat in a chair. That was a pain to us—her legs were a pain. She would not wear a suspender belt, but secured her stockings with tight garters, just above her knees. Over the years a trench had been cut there. Her thighs were white and lumpy as scone dough. Esther knew she had grown ugly. But she laughed at me when I tried to make her take better care of herself. She saw her ugliness as what she deserved. But greedily she hunted after comforts. She guzzled her sugary wine by the tumblerful, she gobbled cakes, ate mountains of fried food—chips and chicken and sausages done in batter—she smoked without a pause, lighting her new cigarette from the butt of her old. Her talk was all of racehorses and poker schools. But her winnings gave her happiness only briefly. She soon looked on them as a dirty trick—and lost soon enough.

So Esther lived a life turning from her girlhood to this end. She had chased after pleasure ceaselessly, and it left her disappointed, wanting more. Fred had meant parties, kissing, drinking beer—so she married him. Love was not part of it. They never had a special private place.

I cannot go on. Although I have opened my eyes and see things clearly, and accept what had to be and cannot be changed, Esther makes me want to weep. There is nothing for me but to offer her love. But she had wanted love only from Alfred. They were close, as Robert and I were close. A special private place? She had it with Alfred. He kept her human in her Meggett shape. To her children she gave an impatient care, love of a kind, but for Alfred she kept an open door into a self she could not find unless he took her hand and led her there. I am being sentimental. Am I? My son Raymond would certainly say yes. But am I? Is this not the way it happened—charged like this, charged to its brim, with feelings all confused? With Alfred she entered herself. Then Alfred died. And she believed she had killed him.

Enough. I will come to it in its place. On this night in the sitting-room at Peacehaven she grinned at her brother Robert without love. She tried to get him smoking cigarettes and drinking port. He smiled at her, but her loudness knocks one about. He was soon exhausted.

"Leave him alone, Esther. He can't smoke, you can see that. Or drink that stuff of yours."

"What a pair of wet blankets. I thought we came here for a party."

"Nobody mentioned a party. You came to see Robert."

"Well, I've seen him. What happens next?"

"We can talk. Like civilized people."

"You sound like our dear old dad. I'm not civilized. I want a bit of fun."

"Shut up and drink your plonk," Fred Meggett said.

They make me angry. And they make Fergus angry. He wants to take Esther into a corner and give her a good talking to. And he wants to punch Fred on the jaw for speaking to a woman in that way. Fred knows it. He looks at my husband with a contempt that I find even harder to bear than his treatment of Esther.

I said, "I'm going to take Robert home. I think he's had enough of you two."

"Hold on, we came to see him. Let's have a look. You haven't got any prettier looking, Bobby. What's that noise you make?"

"For heaven's sake, it's his lungs. Now behave yourself."

"She can't, can you, Fatso?" Fred said. "But you can shut up while I talk to Robert. I've got a business proposition for him." And he came right out with it in the way that had earned him his reputation for "bull-headedness". He offered Robert three thousand pounds for the cottage.

Robert struggled out of his chair. He shook his head at Fred; and with my help he went behind the chair and bent forward over it, letting the back take his weight. He rested there a moment, then managed to say, through a dry bubbling in his chest, "No, Fred, thanks. I've had an offer from Fergus so he'd have first option. But I'm not selling it. I'm leaving it to Meg. Maybe when I'm dead she'll sell it to you."

Fred's eyes drooped; his sign of displeasure. "Pretty quick off the mark, eh son?" he said to Fergus.

"He's not selling, Fred, so we can both forget it."

"What do you need property for? You've got M.E. looking after you."

"M.E.'s going bust and you know it."

"Everybody have a drink," Esther cried.

"Who said it's going bust? Things don't go bust when I'm running them."

"Come on, Fred. When are you going to admit it?"

"Christ, what a party. Everybody bitching," Esther said.

"I'm taking Robert home now, so you'd better say good-night."

"Goodnight, brother. Take something for that throat. You sound like a blocked plughole."

Robert took my arm and we left. We walked down the drive of Peacehaven and along the footpath to the cottage.

"Is she always like that?"

"More or less."

"And Fred?"

"Him too. He was fairly mild tonight. . . . I don't know what to do for Esther."

He shook his head. His breathing was horrible.

"I don't think you need to see them again, Robert."

"I suppose not. I've always brought out something funny in Esther."

I took him into the cottage and helped him to bed. I gave him his drugs and sat with him until his breathing settled down. Then I went back to Peacehaven.

Fergus and Fred and Esther were playing poker. They dealt me a hand and I played a while. I even drank a glass of my sister's wine. "To help me sleep."

"Little Goody two-shoes."

At half past ten I went to bed. The wine did help me drift off into sleep. Esther's cries from the sitting-room became a sound from my childhood. I dreamed of her as a happy ten-year-old.

In the morning, Fergus told me they had played poker till one o'clock. Fred won more than fifteen pounds from his wife.

10 My first sight of Fred Meggett was memorable. When I feel at a disadvantage with him I have only to bring it to mind. I have seen his face naked and greedy, I have seen it charged to the vein-ends with gobbling hunger. Today's false-hearty man-breaking tycoon cannot scare me. I have only to think of it and I want to laugh.

We had travelled north from Christchurch to settle in Loomis. A year had turned about. Peacehaven, the house and grounds, were tight around me. I was twelve. I had heard of this sweetheart of Esther's. He was a butcher. My revulsion was aesthetic more than snobbish. But I wanted to see him; I had a curiosity turning about the flesh—ugly, ambiguous, attractive—and my sister's meeting with it in this man. She brought him home one Saturday afternoon. I was reading in the orchard and did not know of his visit until I came down. Mother came from her cooking and looked at my eyes. She was worried I was straining them and she laid her hands on the lids to cool them down.

"What are you reading, dear?"

I showed her. She was disappointed. "You'd better not let your father see. One shock for him a day is enough."

"What's he shocked about?"

She would not say. She never spoke against people. But when I went to my bedroom I saw Esther disappearing down the bank by the creek in company with a young man, and I knew my father's shock had been his meeting with the butcher.

I did not want to meet him. But I was determined to *see* him. I used my rights of ownership as an excuse. The bank above the creek where she had taken him was my place, Robert's place. Our tracks were over it; and my reading places, soft and warm and peopled from my dreams, were flattened into the grass from the edge of the eely creek up to the rhododendron by the lawn. Esther had no right there, especially with Fred Meggett, a butcher's boy. I worked up my indignation. I combed and plaited my hair, and composed my face. Then I set off to come on them and with my presence drive them from my ground. I saw it more as poetry than drama. Of course, before they went, I would take a good look at Fred. He would have clothes with stains on them (it made me shiver), and meaty hands and a red hot face. Yet with all this, he would have a power—a dark magnetism, turning my sister Esther into his slave. I was familiar with this sort of thing from my reading. It was likely Fred Meggett had it. How else would he get Esther? She was a Plumb. I thought my purity would be a match for him.

I approached, though, with a shrinking confidence. I sensed the closeness of some mystery, and a danger of revelation. I stepped into the dreaming ground of my childhood, but advanced on another level into a place where adult things might happen. Shadows fell across the summer bank. Heavy insects flew up from the grass and went ahead of me with whirring wings. I walked light-footed, straight, imperious; with a frightened crying at the heart of me.

What I came upon was an idyllic scene: lovers resting on a grassy bank. But standing out from it was Fred Meggett's face. It had a colour, a greed, a vulgarity, that drained the life from everything around it—from Esther, who was no more than a black and white figure from a photograph, from the sky and the clouds and the trees and the bank. The sunlight faded. I was dry, with the white dryness of dust. I was a vacuum, I was null. I will not exaggerate the moment—the moment I caught sight of an enemy and was slain by him. It lasted only the space of a heartbeat or two. I came back to life. I came back with a thumping in my heart. Esther saw me. Her face rose up like a shape from under water. It burst into the air, took colour from the light. I saw her grinning at me, winking at me.

Today I am impressed by the comicalness of the scene, and a certain rightness it has. There was my sister Esther, lying on the bank in her blue summer dress, holding Fred Meggett in one arm like a giant baby. She had a look of interest on her face. Fred had his blind face at me. His mouth was open. His nose appeared to be swollen. I could see his tongue. Esther's hand was down in his trousers, through his opened fly, at some work. She stopped it when she saw me. "Don't stop," he whimpered. So she went on. Interest on her face. Yes. And a little boredom. A little contempt. I am probably imagining it. What I do not imagine is the spurt of enjoyment she felt on seeing me there. She grinned at me. She winked at me. Her hand got busy again. Easily she took me into the play and got more from it. Fred began to gasp.

I laugh at it now. On that day I turned and ran. My plaits urged me on with heavy bangs upon my back. I scrambled up the bank and through the branches of the rhododendron tree, and ran past the rockery and through the garden, and burst at last with a hot face into Mother's kitchen, where she stood peeling potatoes at the bench.

"Easy child, easy." She looked at me more closely. "Go and wash your face in cold water and you will feel better." My world jolted back into something like its shape. I ran to her and pressed myself against her. She wiped her hands and took my face in her palms. "What is it, little Meg?"

"Nothing. Nothing."

"Go and wash, there's a dear. Then you can help me put the dates in my pudding."

I did as I was told. We made date-roll, which was my favourite pudding. I helped Mother tidy up the bench, and together we set the dining-room table for dinner. Laying out the serviettes in their rings, making a box with knife and fork and spoon, I gained a balance. I was able to giggle at what I had seen, and feel pleased at my daring. I was worried though about what

Esther would do. She was seventeen. She was big and strong. I kept within a step of Mother, chattering all the time, until she raised her eyes in mock annoyance.

"Stop getting under my feet, child."

"Shall I take Dad a cup of tea?" I would be even safer in the study. But Mother said no. "You might spoil his line of thought."

Esther came in. She was unhurried, she looked cool, and she sat at the kitchen table and gave a wide yawn.

"Put your hand over your mouth," Mother said.

"Too tired."

"A lady covers her mouth when she yawns. A gentleman too. In fact it's better to yawn in your room if you must."

"Ho hum," Esther said. She grinned at me. "You live and learn, dopey."

"Has Mr Meggett gone?" Mother asked.

"Yep. I had enough of him."

"He seems a nice young man," Mother lied.

"I guess he'll do."

"Really Esther, you shouldn't talk like that. You should speak of him with respect if you really like him."

Esther yawned again. She grinned half-way through and covered her mouth. With horror I realized she was using the hand that had been in Fred Meggett's trousers. She had not even washed it.

"What are you looking so goofy for?"

"Nothing," I squeaked.

"You're going cross-eyed. That's the second time today."

"Leave her alone," Mother said. "She's got a nice face. She's got a very kind face."

"Yes, like a cow. Moo-oo. Watch out the bull doesn't catch you."

"Go to your room if you can't speak like a lady."

"I'm going. I hope tea's early. I've got to go to a party."

"Well," Mother said sharply, "I hope you're not putting any of that lipstick on your face."

74

"Of course I am. That's half the fun."

"You're prettier without it. And you'll meet nicer young men."

"I knew you didn't like him," Esther said happily. "Never mind, Meg likes him, don't you dope?" She winked at me. "You can meet him if you like when he calls tonight."

"I don't want to meet him."

"Of course you do. I've told him all about you."

"You keep your young men away from Meg. She's not ready yet."

"I'm beginning to wonder if she ever will be."

Esther went to our room and laid out her dress. She had a bath. Alfred and Robert hurried in with buckets of hot water from the copper until it was full enough to please her. She put in bath salts and soaked for half an hour, then called me in to scrub her back. I did it with eyes turned away. I could not look at her woman's body. Later she called me to the bedroom to button her dress at the back. I found then I could look at her. In fact, I could not take my eyes off her. She glittered like the bad queen, I could imagine her mirror telling her that she was most beautiful of all. She had eyes like Pola Negri—"dark lagoons wherein men drown"—but had the trick of widening them and darting them about. She laughed with them, she used them. Light seemed to sparkle out, and life sparkle too. Her features were not pretty. She had a mouth too large and a flaring nose. But that was not something you noticed about her, unless to notice that her mouth smiled happily, and her nose seemed to drink up life. I exaggerate. I have worked my way to that, hunted it out. Her young men heard her laughter, saw her beautiful eyes and painted mouth, and asked no more than that. Asked though, perhaps, favours of her hand. Fred was not the only one. But I do not believe she obliged with more than hand. Not at that time.

She let me watch while she put her lipstick on. She dabbed some of her perfume behind my ears. Never once did she mention my spying on her, she did not hint at it. That was past, she was looking ahead to the next thing. I had the beginnings of knowledge that she had gone too far, too carelessly, she was out of her depth; and, like Rebecca, she would drown.

Fred called for her in his father's car. She brought him into the living-room to say hallo. Alfred looked up from his book and gave a nod so small I don't think Fred saw it. The rest of us were polite. But I could not look at him, I could not meet his eye. He shook hands with me, and I pulled my fingers quickly out of his grip—it was a jerking-away I could not help, as though from something unclean. Esther's had been the hand, but I was not in any reasonable state. I had seen his tongue, and the whites of his eyes, and his nose swollen like—I shall not say. I could not stand chatting with him in our father's house and Mother's house, in my clean world.

Dad said, "You have Esther home by half past ten, young man."

"Half past ten?" Esther screeched. But Dad had spoken. He lowered his ear trumpet and took no more part in the argument—which determined that Esther should be home by half past twelve.

Mother said, "I mean it, Esther. You're only seventeen. And don't you smoke. Mr Meggett, you must not offer her cigarettes."

"I can't stop her smoking, Mrs Plumb. She doesn't listen to me."

"You must treat your bodies with respect," Mother said.

"We will, we promise," they choroused. Their hands behind their backs were highly amused; began, in a clump of three, secret ticklings, a dirty game. I felt sick. I wanted to scream at my sister, and beat Fred Meggett out of our house with my fists. Instead, I left the room, I ran to my bed, and there I dived for safety into my book. I bathed in it like a spring of water.

Mother was right, *Bab of the Backwoods* would have shocked Dad. But on that summer night, as the warm air brought a dampness on my skin and the dark made noises, as Esther's laugh by the car and the butcher's red guffaw and the sound of a palm smacking rump, and words like damn and bugger came

76

through the trees, it gave me Monte Baron to set against Fred. Monte. His name still brings a faster beat to my heart. And her name: Bab. It was so like Meg. For the rest of that year I secretly called myself Bab, and even more secretly her other name, Running Water. The only flaw in the book was that it was set in California. California made me cold, it fell like an icy hand on me; and still does that. But the magic world Monte and Bab made for themselves, their world of love, was safe inside and cut off from the California that threatened me so, just as my new world of Peacehaven was safe inside the north. I had no Monte yet, but I waited for him. Fred I saw as Conroy. "Conroy, a gross man, licked his lips." I found the sentence in my mind whenever I thought of Fred. I made him helpless in those words, he was no threat to me. I waited for Monte Baron to come and take me by the hand. I waited for his kiss. I ran my fingers softly over my lips and felt them tingle. "She lifted her eyes to his; her lips were lifted, slightly parted, inviting. . . ." I practised that. Physical realities throbbed below the surface in that book. But other realities had not the smallest place there.

Fred followed me into the orchard one day. By this time I was fourteen. I had grown breasts, of which I was suspicious. He tried to put his hands on them. He told me how much he liked me. I was not the least bit frightened, but felt very sure of myself and powerful. Fred was lusting after me, in his Conroy way. I said, "I could never be interested in a man who handles raw meat all day." He went the red of steak. He grabbed me and tried to kiss me but I jerked away from him, in a dignified way, still not frightened, and his mouth came down by my ear. "I'll give you something you won't forget." I began to worry then. I could not break out of his arms. Down against my hip he butted at me with a part I had never thought of as so leathery and long. I could not scream. The best I could manage was to say, "You smell of meat."

I must have excited him terribly. He pulled me hard against him, as if his body wanted to take in mine. His face nuzzled and ground into my neck and his loins rolled on the hip bone I still managed to present to him. He groaned and drew in long shuddery breaths. I stood stiff, my face turned up and away from him. I was not part of it. When he had finished I stepped away and began in a bored way to walk into the trees. He followed me, panting, almost crying. "That was your fault," he managed to get out, "so don't blame me." "Go away." I began to be pleased. Whatever he had done, it was inside him and had nothing to do with me. I saw it as a kind of animal tribute, the pathetic groping out of a lower nature. I laughed at it.

He said, "If you tell anyone about this I'll run you over in my car."

He meant that, or thought he did. I said, "Go away, Fred. I'm waiting for somebody." I was waiting for Monte. One day he would come and say, "You precious girl! . . . Kiss me!" "Yes," I would say, "yes." And he would say, "I want you for mine, for all time. For this life and the next and all through eternity. . . ."

Fred was real all right (had left a damp patch on my dress to prove it), but I had weapons against him. He did not scare me.

11 Mother was my life-line. She was always there to bring me back into the world. Most of my memories of her are kitchen memories. It seems to me she passed her life in the kitchen. I came in warm from my bed, came in to the sound of bubbling porridge, the cat's miaow by the meat-safe, Mother's slippered feet as she moved in the triangle, table, stove, bench—endlessly: table, stove, bench—sometimes humming a tune, always with a smile and a word of greeting. She served us all (she served the cat), and the help we were able to give her with washing-up, and cooking, and laying the table, made only a small reduction in her work. At night when I came to kiss her, there she was at the bench, setting our father's tray with teacup and biscuits, and pouring tea to carry to his study—not too hot, not too strong, always perfect tea. She would not let me take in his night-time cup. That was her job. She guarded it jealously. (Sometimes though, when he tinkled his spoon on his saucer, she let me fetch the tray for his second cup.)

It may seem contradictory to say that Mother always had time. But she was always ready to sit down and talk. The dishwater was left to go cold in the sink, the fire in the range die down, if I had a trouble. She sat me down at the table and made me tell it. It was the same for the others. I came in to find Alfred with his eyes full of tears and his voice grown shrill (soon she would calm it); or Robert there, grumbling softly, with a grin; or grown-up Agnes, hoping for California; or Emerson with a dream that receded from him—new motor bike, or Model T, or flight into the clouds. Mother heard us all and calmed us down, and taught us what it was we might properly hope for. (Esther came there too, sometimes, but Mother never taught her.) Mother told me I must not hope my brown eyes would turn blue or my teeth grow straight. "Crooked teeth are no great tragedy. Now a crooked soul, Meg dear, that would be something to worry about." I took it from her because she spoke of souls, and hearts, and God, and love, and truth, as easily as if they were carrots and potatoes. And Mother was never high and mighty or censorious. She could be stern. Wrong was as much a part of her talk as right. But everything came out of a ground of love. She put a serenity in me, under my troubles. I look for it and find it there today.

So I came out of Monte's world into the kitchen. I forgot my name, Running Water. I was Meg Plumb. This was my home. Mother was mixing a dough-boy for the stew. Dad was in his study, smiting away at the war-lords with his pen. No more was needed for my happiness. I must not forget what a happy girl I was.

I was happy on the night of Esther's twenty-first birthday party. I had helped Mother all through the day with her baking. I had tidied the house and polished the furniture. Esther did not help. "Why should I? It's my birthday." Her contribution was to throw open the double doors between the dining-room and the sitting-room. Her eyes shone at the expanse for dancing. Emerson and Alfred had pushed the furniture to the walls and rolled up the mats. She caught Emerson, who was nearest her, and waltzed into the centre of the room, trailing one arm in an extravagant way (one could almost see the gauze scarf floating from it), throwing her head back languorously. Alfred went to the piano and fitted a tune to their rhythms. Robert and I watched, grinning a little with embarrassment, and Mother came from the kitchen with a mixing bowl in her arm and stood in the doorway, turning with her wooden spoon and smiling approval of the stately dance.

She was less happy when Alfred played a Charleston and Esther flung herself into double-jointed motions. Emerson could not keep up with her. She gave us a solo performance. "Like a rag doll having fits," Alfred said later. "Remember how Jehovah looked on his mountain?" That was Dad. He had come from a stroll in the orchard. We did not see him in the doorway until Esther was done. She fell into a posture of exhaustion: loose at the knees, arms hanging loose, and her tongue poking out. Mother said, "Esther, that's vulgar." At the same time we heard Dad's voice: "A Hottentot," he said, "a Hottentot." He had the look of a man who has come upon something not just outside his experience but beyond imagination.

"It's the new dance, Dad. It's all the rage," Esther said.

He was without his trumpet. "A Hottentot." I don't think that word expressed it for him at all. He put his hand on his forehead in a way that meant he must find the peace of his study or go mad. It was a stagy gesture, but usually it made us feel guilty or contrite. On that day, when he had gone, we spluttered with laughter. Even Mother gave a smile.

"I hope you won't be doing that tonight, Esther."

"Of course we will. None of them can do it as fast as me."

"I'll have to keep your father well away."

She handed me the mixing bowl and went to the study to calm him. Alfred, clever Alfred, played their conversation on

80

the piano, thundering with the bass notes for "Jehovah", and soothing, soothing, overcoming his thunder, smoothing his brow, in the treble for Mum. We laughed until we cried. Those fading rolls of thunder, those tinkles at once so gentle and so strong! For me it was wildly funny; and it was sad. My tears fell into the mixing bowl. Emerson had to take it away from me.

"Sorrow cakes," Alfred said. "Or happy cakes. Is it sorrow from the left eye Meg and happy from the right or vice versa?"

"I'm not eating them," Esther cried. "What a sap you are."

That night we had a special tea, just for the family. We had it in the kitchen because the dining-room table was set for the party. It was a crush. Dad sat alone at the head with plenty of room for his arms, and Mother had the other end to herself. The rest of us had our arms pressed in to our sides. We girls were in our party frocks and one or other of us was always rushing off to the bathroom to sponge out some gravy spot or custard spot. Dad frowned at this. We had given up saying grace long ago, but he started the meal with a prayer.

"Lord, in your mystery, in your immanence, suffer our voices to find a path to Thee. We ask for Thy blessing on one who has come to adulthood. May she put off the childish ways that cling to her—" Esther bridled. "—and grow into wisdom and maturity, and exercise her mind and discover her heart and come out of selfish strivings—" "Do I really have to listen to this?" "Hush," Mother said. "—and learn modesty and a womanly restraint. And may she find Thee Lord, and know happiness, for at present she is lost on a darkened way." "Really!" "And we ask that our children, our brother and sister, Agnes and Emerson, know Thy comfort on their travels in the world. They have chosen to leave us. We pray that they may grow in wisdom, and that the love that surrounds them now may go out with them into those places where they will pass their lives. . . ." Agnes and Emerson looked uncomfortable. Dad had not meant his disapproval to come so strongly through. But California, where Agnes was booked to go, had always been for him a land where frivolities reigned and vices thrived. (I take the words from his essay on the place.) And Emerson's plan to get to England and somehow learn to fly was one he had no sympathy with.

Willis and Mirth arrived at the end of the meal. "Ah," Willis cried, "just in time for some pudding,"—(which sums up his life). Mother gave them bowls, and the Auckland part of our family was complete, eating peaches and cream. Mirth was in the last months of her pregnancy—her second with her second family. I confined myself to looking at her face. I could not bear to look at her swollen body. (No more could Dad. He insisted on the beauty of women expecting, but when faced with them he turned away.) It made me feel choked and gave me the feeling some great slippery thing was on the point of sliding out of my mouth. When Dad had gone she invited us girls to feel the baby kicking, but Mother reminded her sharply the boys were in the room. She believed in a *purdah* for women in their last months. Mirth apologized, and Willis took out his mouth organ and knelt in front of his wife and played the unborn baby a lullaby, which had us all laughing; even Mother.

When I had helped with the dishes I went to the bedroom to rub some of Esther's cold cream on my hands. She gave it to me grudgingly—a waste on my fat paws. My hands were thin and beautiful, one of the things I was sure of. I smiled at her and scooped out a large fingerful. "Take it easy," she cried.

Alfred grinned at me. He was sitting on my bed, watching Esther put the finishing touches to her hair. He liked to watch this sort of thing and pass comment on it, and usually we listened with respect. He had a flair. As a last touch Esther tucked a red hibiscus in the dark waves of her hair and fastened it with a diamante clasp. I thought it made her even more beautiful, it made her look dramatic, but Alfred said, "That's all wrong."

"Why?"

"You girls always overdo things. You want one or the other, not both."

"Which then?" She turned her head this way and that.

"The flower," I said.

82

"No one asked you."

"The clasp," Alfred said.

"I could have the flower on one side and the clasp on the other."

"You could not. Not unless you want to look like a *fille de joie*."

I was thrilled by the term, which I understood instantly. But Esther said, "Talk English. Tell me what to do."

"Take out the flower."

She tried but the stem tangled in her hair. "Why didn't you tell me before I pinned it?"

"How did I know it would make you look cheap?" I thought he probably had known. He sometimes played with Esther like a doll.

She redid her hair and repainted her lips.

"Wipe all that off and put on half as much." He was watching with a deep interest, and an emotion that made him irritable. I thought it strange.

"Is mine all right, Alfred?" I had barely touched my lips.

He glanced at me. "Yours is good. You've got taste."

"Angel face," Esther sneered.

"She knows when to stop."

"Her? She doesn't even know when to start."

He watched her coolly. "You've got on too much. It makes you look like a tart."

"What would you know about tarts?"

"As much as I need to. Come on Esther, wipe it off and start again."

"No."

"It'll be over half the men in town by morning."

"You," she cried, "you pig!"

"Who are you laying the net for? I thought you had old Pickled Pork all wrapped up."

She threw the lipstick at him. It struck him on the forehead and fell on the bed. He picked it up and put it in his pocket. "I'll keep it for that."

"Give that back to me."

"It's wasted on you."

"Damn you," she said. "Damn you."

"Language," Alfred said.

"Get out. Get out of my room."

"I'm going." He stood up. His eyes were watering from the blow and a red mark was coming up on his brow. But I saw he was happy; and in a way she was too. I could not understand it.

She rounded on me. "You clear out as well."

"It's my room as much as yours."

"Just for once, on my birthday, can I have it to myself?"

"Come on, Sis," Alfred said. He took me by the hand and pulled me out. Esther slammed the door.

"A real fire-eater, ain't she?" Alfred said. He took the lipstick out of his pocket and tossed it in the air. "Tell you what, you could do with just a touch of this. Come here." He stood me up against the door and painted my lips. "There you are, young Meg. You look like a *femme fatale*." He was doing it for Esther, on the other side of the door. I knew she was listening. I felt as if I had stepped, not into the adult world—that was serious—but into a world where make-believe was on the point of being real. I liked the strange excited feeling it gave me, but did not like the danger I felt I was in.

That night I had a heightened sense of things. I look on it as the last night of my girlhood. Nothing dramatic happened. But I was in my family, deep in my family, in a blissful, accepting, elegiac way. Everything that happened on that night was confusing yet absolutely right. I was happy, I was taking it all deep into myself, yet I was weeping at the loss of it all. Today I would probably put it down to hormonal imbalance—being a modern woman. I am glad I was not modern on that night. I was outside the party. I understood that perfectly. Esther's guests were glittering apes and birds. Only the Plumbs were human. From time to time I danced with some Alan or Morrie or Murray, with some Tiny or Knuckles or Squidge. They had brought along a gramophone and a stack of records. I even tried the Charleston,

84

and didn't do it badly. Noise and colour tumbled in the room. The dizzy music turned us upside down. But through it all there strolled significant beings: Alfred and Emerson, Agnes and Esther and Robert, Willis, Mother and Dad. Yes, Dad put in an appearance. He made a speech and presented Esther with a key cut out of box-wood and pasted over with silver paper. He talked for too long, too heavily—of youth, and duty, and the tasks of life and its rewards. The Dust of Conflict and the Palm of Victory. People sneaked on to the verandah and came back when it was over. Dad watched Esther blow the candles out with a mystified air. He had not come across that tradition before. He ate a piece of cake. Then he put his hand on his forehead, and went to his study. I loved him for it.

The food quietened everybody down. Willis snored away on his mouth organ, then sang sentimental songs while Mirth played the piano. His voice was naturally tearful. After *Danny Boy* and *Kathleen Mavourneen*, which dampened his eye, he grabbed two spoons from the table and played a tune on his wooden leg. Then he asked some of the girls to carve their initials on it. I shivered at their cutting, I felt sharp pains in my leg; and then came worse, I felt that tearing-off at the knee he had suffered in Copenhagen. I limped outside, and sank down on the lawn and was nearly sick.

"Come here, goof," a voice said from the dark. I saw a cigarette glowing by the peach tree.

"Is that you, Agnes?"

"Of course it's me."

"What are you doing out here?" I hobbled over.

"Sit down and talk to me. What have you done to your leg?"

"It's nothing. It's gone away now."

"How can you stand it in there?"

"Willis singing, do you mean? He's all right."

"What a family. Thank God for California."

That was all right too. That was acceptable—it was, I under-stood, her role in the family to say this thing and run away from us.

"I love you, Agnes," I said.

"I love you, too. Do you think I don't?" She rubbed her cheek and I knew she had rubbed away a tear. I felt the same one tickling on my cheek.

"What will you do over there?"

"I'll find a man and get married. There's plenty of men. But I won't let him treat me the way *he* treats Mum."

"They're all right, Agnes." I knew they were all right, though I could not explain it.

"They're not. She's just his slave. I'll never be like that for any man." She smoked, and puffed out furiously, and suddenly she began to cry. I put my arm round her and she bored in close to me and soaked the whole of my bodice with her tears.

"Agnes," I screamed, "your dress is on fire." She had dropped her cigarette on a fold of it. We beat the smouldering cloth out with our hands.

Agnes laughed. "It was an ugly dress anyway. I was going to give it to you." She lit another cigarette. "Here, have a puff."

"No, Agnes."

"It'll do you good."

"No, I don't want to."

"Come on, no one's watching. You can't be a goody-goody all your life."

The smoke burned me deep in my chest. I coughed and sagged on the grass and Agnes, laughing, banged me on my back. When I was better she showed me how to smoke. She took the smoke into her mouth and let it trickle out her nostrils. Every time she drew on the cigarette her wet cheeks gleamed.

"Willis and his leg," she said. "Oh, God. And his awful wife. And Esther and that butcher. She's a tramp. And Alfred."

"Alfred's all right."

"He's not all right. Can't you see?" Just for a flash I did. I could not hold it.

"Alfred's going to be a poet."

"Thank God I'm going." She brooded. "And *him*, and *her*. How could he make that awful speech? Telling us to go out and do those things? We can never do them. People on the porch were laughing at him." She puffed. "And you mooning like a cow. What a family."

"Please don't cry again, Agnes."

"I won't cry. Not me.—Tell me Meg, do you know how babies come?"

"I think I do."

"You think? But you're not sure?"

"I can't understand some things."

"I've got a book. I'll give it to you. It will be my going away present. That and a dress with a hole burnt in it."

"Will you come back, Agnes?"

"No. Not ever. It's California for me."

"I didn't like it there."

"You wouldn't. But I'll like it."

Emerson came over the lawn to us. "Which one of you's first for a joyride?"

"On your bike? No fear. You'll break our necks," Agnes said.

"Come on. They all want one—" he waved towards a group of girls coming down the verandah steps, "—but I said I was going to take my sisters first."

"I'll come, Emerson," I said. I had never been on his bike, it terrified me, but tonight I felt I must meet everything my brothers and sisters offered, they were revealing themselves and I would see things I would never see again, and perhaps I would help them; certainly I would take a grip on them that would never be broken. Emerson wheeled his bike out of the shed. With admiring girls about him he kicked it once, twice, three times. It roared like a mountain lion, then sank to a gargle. One of the girls tried to climb on the back but Emerson held her off with a straightened arm. "Come on, Meg."

"Goodbye," I said to Agnes.

"What do you mean? I've got two more weeks here yet."

I meant goodbye. I went across the lawn to Emerson, the girls parted unwillingly to let me through—I was a nobody to them—and I sat on the pillion seat of the Indian and wrapped my arms about my brother's waist.

"Gangway," Emerson yelled. He wriggled the bike through them and suddenly we were free, thundering with an impossible noise, yet sliding as though on oil, down the drive between the bank and Mother's rose garden. The gate was open. We broadsided out. The road leaned up to meet me and fell away, and off we raced through the white dust and spitting metal, chasing the rigid beam of light that shone out of Emerson's face. I was not frightened. I held him with arms tight locked, one on the other, knowing he was all that kept me alive in the tiny dangerous world he created on this pitch-bright road. I knew at last where he lived. I laid my cheek hard against his spine and screamed with joy. And he, poor wordless fellow, yelled back at me, "Fun, eh Meg?" He did not need words. We went to the end of Millbrook Road and crossed the thundering wooden bridge. The wind blew water from my eyes in trickles back into my hair. We raced through the main street of Loomis, where people were coming out of the picture theatre. A boy I had once had a Monte crush on, Fergus Sole, was there, holding his girl by the hand, and as their faces flickered like movie-faces I laughed at them. We roared up the concrete Great North Road past the vineyards until we came to View Road. Skidding and scrambling, we came down, down to the wooden bridge and Millbrook Road, and zoomed back past the giant pines— "Doing fifty," Emerson yelled—leaning over this way, that, my dress hem brushing in the dust, until we came again to Peacehaven's gate; and there Emerson puttered up and stopped us safely on the lawn.

"Thank you Emerson," I whispered into his back.

"O.K. Meg?" He unlocked my hands. I climbed off the bike and ran away into the dark, past those cold girl-faces staring at me. Emerson had showed me where he lived.

"My turn, my turn," cried the girls.

"Esther. I want Esther," Emerson yelled.

Off they rode; and when they came back he went to Agnes, smoking in the dark, and picked her up and put her on the seat—so she went too. Then, though the girls screeched at him and slapped him on his arms and swore at him, he pushed his bike into the shed. "That's enough for one night." He closed and padlocked the door. He had never meant to take more than Agnes and Esther and me. I laughed from my place by the creek. We were a family.

After that I wanted no more of the party. I do not mean I wanted it to be over. I was content to swim on the edges of it—no, I shall change that. I wanted to stroll through the party like a zoo, and feel the pity one feels for caged animals. I wanted no more dancing with Murray and Morrie and no more plates of food delivered by Squidge. I wanted to see how Murray and Morrie and Squidge, and Betty and Rae, behaved in their little cages, and see whether any realization came to them that they were not Plumbs, not strolling free. After a while I found Alfred at what I took to be the same occupation. He was coming down the steps from the top lawn. I waited for him on the path.

"Hello, Moony Meg."

"I'm not mooning, Alfred. I'm watching people."

"A great sport, isn't it? A great sport for those who can't join in."

"Do you want to join in, Alfred?"

"With that lot of Woolworth girls?"

"And butchers and bakers."

"And joystick makers. Sorry Meg, you wouldn't understand."

"Where are you going, Alfred?"

"I thought I might climb a tree. But I'll walk with you instead."

We went across the lower lawn to the summer-house. A glow of cigarettes turned as away.

"I don't think that was Esther."

"Do you envy them?"

"No."

"You mustn't always be alone, Meg. Don't you want a boyfriend sometimes?"

"Now and then I think it would be nice. Not just any boy though."

"Sir Percival, the perfect knight. Me too, but where on earth do we find him?"

"Do they have lady knights?"

"Ah Meg, 'you do me good."

"Why are you laughing?"

"It's that sort of night. You laugh or cry."

We came to the rhododendron trees. Beyond them on the slope voices murmured, bottles clinked. "The Carcase Cutter and his friends," Alfred said. "They've got little stores of beer all over the section."

"That's Esther's voice."

"She's there. She's where the fun is. Good old Esther."

We went along by the trees, following the curve of the creek. The cottage windows turned into our view, making a framed picture in the dark. Wendy Philson sat at her table, writing. From time to time she raised her head and listened to the cries in the grounds of Peacehaven.

"That's what I should be like," Alfred said. "Cut off from the monkey house. Writing poetry. She's probably copying recipes though."

"She's marking school books, I think."

"Well, she's busy, that's the thing. She's got a meaning."

"You'll write poetry, Alfred."

"Oh, I do, I do. Sentimental odes. Dirty limericks."

"You'll write something good."

"I've got to, Meg. I've got to write something better than good. Or else I've got no meaning. Meg, love is no good for me. Love is out. It's got to be work. Forget Sir Percival. That's a dream. That's for kids. I've got to find the Grail myself. Alone."

"You will, Alfred."

"Will I?" He laughed. "Will I? Perhaps I will. Thank you, Sister." He was quiet for a moment. "Meanwhile, listen to the denizens of the zoo." Beyond the rhododendrons a bottle smashed. Esther's voice rose scolding, Fred guffawed. In the cottage Wendy Philson stopped her writing, sat up straight. After a while she put her pen down. She stretched her arms and yawned. She scratched beneath her breasts.

Alfred said, "That's what happens to the ideal. Suddenly it gets fleas."

"Oh Alfred, that wasn't fleas."

"If we watch long enough we'll see her pick her nose."

"Come with me. It isn't right to watch."

"Most things that are any fun aren't right."

He let me pull him away. We walked back past the summer-house and climbed the steps to the top lawn. A few people were dancing in the sitting-room. We watched through the open French doors. Moths turned into the room and the music flowed out. Mirth was sitting in an easy chair, watching with patient adoration while Willis danced energetically with a lopsided fat girl in a purple frock.

"How does he manage, with his leg?"

"Worth more to him than a thousand golden words. Look at that girl, she's in love with it."

"Mirth doesn't seem to care."

"That's how she keeps him. Shall I tell you something, you won't be shocked?"

"No," I said, believing I probably would be.

"He told me the other day he's had ninety-six women in his life. Do you know what I mean?"

"I know."

"Course some of them he paid for. But ninety-six!"

"Fancy counting."

"He takes it seriously. This girl looks as if she'll be ninety-seven."

"When he gets to a hundred we'll bake him a cake."

Alfred laughed. "Good girl, Meg. You're coming on." We were quiet for a while. Then Alfred said, "There's no such thing as love, you know."

"Yes there is. There's got to be."

"I agree with the second part."

"There is love. Look at Mum and Dad."

He stared at me. "I really think you mean that."

"I do. They love each other. Why can't anybody else see how happy she is? And Dad."

"Oh, *he's* happy all right. But I don't know why you think it's love. It's not much better than Willie in there, cutting another notch in his belt."

"You don't believe that. I know you don't believe it."

"I do, Meg. But I've got a feeling—you might be the one who gets it. Love, I mean." He made a sudden violent cut with his arm. "God, the bilge I talk."

"Why aren't you happy, Alfred?"

"I'm not, that's all."

"You'll find someone."

"Will I? Will I?"

"I know you will."

"Unless I do, unless I find that person Meg, I'll never find out who I am. I—can't—find—out."

"Alfred, you'll find her soon. I know you will."

"Ha!" he cried, "find her! I do like that. What a chump you are, Meg. Well—well—there is some love you know, because I love you. And crazy old Esther down there in the bushes. Here—" he took something out of his pocket, "—give this to her. She needs it more than me." He put her lipstick in my hand.

"Alfred, you've put some on." I saw his face clearly in the light.

He grinned. "I like to try things out. It tastes like cherries."

"Where are you going?"

"I think I'll climb that tree now."

He went down the steps and ran away into the dark. Even that did not make me unhappy. His talk of there being no love, for him, for anyone, of Mum and Dad not being in love—these did not, on that night, make me unhappy. I was drinking my family down. My family made me drunk. I was at that stage of intoxication when even pain is good. Sitting on the stone wall in the garden, I saw Mother come into the sitting-room. She looked startled to find only Willis there. She asked him a question but he shrugged and went on dancing. She came towards the door, with a look on her face I knew well—that look she got when she meant to round up her children. But half-way there she stopped, she gave it up. She said something to Mirth, sprawled in her chair. Mirth smiled and sat up straight and closed her legs. Mother went out of the room. I understood it all, in detail, perfectly. I lived the moment with her. Then I walked down the steps and down to the creek. Agnes was gone from under the peach tree. But on the brick bridge I met Robert. I had not seen him since early in the night.

"Where have you been?"

"Over at the Butterses'. You know what Meg, they believe plants have souls and they're trying to talk to us. Merle was kissing a begonia."

"Oh, Robert." I laughed until I was gasping.

"Yeah, it's a lot of hooey. I'm hot. I'm going for a swim." He began to take off his clothes.

"Robert."

"I'll keep my underpants on."

"You can't swim there. It's dark."

"I know where the rocks are."

"What about the eels?"

"They don't hurt you."

I looked down into the water—into the dark, for no gleam showed. It might have been a pit dropping forever. The blackness seemed to suck all the blood from my body and flesh from my bones. It seemed to suck the whole world into it. On the edge of terror, on the edge of Missing, I knew that Robert would turn it into water, make it our creek. He lined himself up carefully.

"If you dive out towards that tree you miss the rocks. It's just deep enough."

"Go on, Robert." Others would fall down the hole into Missing, but Robert, Robert would do it like walking down a wide street. I saw the white blur of his body as he dived, and heard his splash, and another sound. It was flat and deadly, it met nothing in me that understood, and my heart stood for a moment utterly still, I believe I died. For one missed beat of my heart Robert vanished from the world. Then he splashed up and yelled at me, "What was that?"

I could not answer. The swelling beat of my heart left me no room. Robert splashed about down there, a blur, and soon he said, "It's a bottle. Someone must have bished a beer bottle in."

"Are you all right?"

"I hit it with my elbow."

"Come out, Robert."

He swam to the side of the pool and put the bottle on the rocks. It made a musical sound.

I said, "It was probably Fred. He's been drinking."

"Probably was. He's got no sense." He swam across the pool. "This is good. Come on in. Hey, that was an eel. He's swimming up my back. Eee, it's like a snake."

"He might bite you."

"It's just a little one. Hey, that one was big. He's nibbling my toes. Come on, they don't hurt."

If I had gone into that dark water with the eels I might not have been afraid of anything again, for the rest of my life. Robert was down there swimming in the stream, conquering it. Yes, I have worked it up, it is no longer pure, but once it was below my consciousness and it was pure. It would have given me life if I had been able to go down there. I stood on the bridge and did not go, and presently Robert came out and dried himself with his shirt and pulled his trousers on.

"That was great. I wonder if I can tame those eels. We could go in a circus."

We walked up to the house. Music still splashed into the night. Couples sat on the lawn, smoking and kissing. On the verandah steps Emerson sat with a group of young men, talking about motorbikes. He was already a hero. Robert said goodnight. He meant to sleep in the garden shed to get away from the noise. When I had left him I walked along the gravel path by the bedrooms. I put my head in Agnes's window. Her dark head moved on the pillow.

"Agnes?"

"Meg. What do you want?"

"Goodnight."

"Goodnight, Meg."

I went to the sitting-room and found Mirth there, listening to the music dreamily.

"Where's Willis?"

"Outside with some girl. He won't be long."

I blushed.

"He'll give her a few kisses Meg, that's all."

"Don't you mind?"

"No. I don't think anyone's ever kissed her before. Willie's a very kind man."

"Won't he enjoy it too, Mirth?"

"You're a sly little thing. Do you know what men and women do yet?"

"Agnes is going to tell me." I wondered why they made such a fuss about it. It was interesting, no doubt, and disturbing, but there were more interesting things, and much more disturbing. Things, I mean, that men and women did. I knew that already.

I went down the hall to my bedroom, but on the way noticed Dad's study door slightly ajar. I stood there a moment wondering if I should go in. We had set times for visiting. Then I heard Mother cough. I pushed the door a little and put my head in. They were having one of their "paper chats". She handed him a sheet of paper; he read; wrote something and handed it back. Then he saw me and cried, "Ho, it's Meg. Come into my parlour."

Mother did not look pleased. I had interrupted one of her times with him. I said to her, "I'm sorry. I was on my way to bed and I thought I'd say goodnight."

"Goodnight, Meg."

"Sit down, my dear," cried Dad, who had heard none of this. "Pull up a chair and join our paper chat."

Mother put the paper sharply away. "What are they all doing?"

"Oh, talking," I said, "wandering round."

"It's time they all went home. Where's Alfred?"

"Up a tree."

"What's that?" Dad said, "what's that?"

"Alfred's up a tree."

"Is he now? Writing poetry?" That excused all sorts of odd behaviour; and I wondered if it would have excused Robert in the creek with eels and Esther with her butcher down the bank—even Willis off in the orchard with a woman not his wife. I hoped Mother was not going to ask me where they all were. I should have to lie.

"Well," Dad said, "we'll light some incense. It isn't often I get a visit from my wife and my daughter at once."

Mother softened to me. She had to work at hardness, it was not in her. She gave me a chair to sit on, and we stayed there, paper-chatting while midnight passed and the spice-and-sugar of incense filled the room. Buddha smiled on us.

It's been a lovely party, I wrote. *The night's so beautiful.*

Have you all been happy? Mother wrote.

It is a beauteous evening, calm and free, Dad wrote.

"Did you all get enough to eat?"

"We had happy cakes."

The holy time is quiet as a nun, breathless with adoration, Dad went on.

Screams came from the night, and Mother smiled. "It's time we sent them home," she said to me.

I stood up. "Going already?" Dad cried.

"It's half-past twelve." I pointed at his clock.

"Well bless my soul!"

I kissed them. Dad looked at me. "Stand still, Meg." Then he said to Mother, "She's grown up, Edie. When did she do that?" And to me: "You've grown up behind our backs."

96

"She's still a child and she should be in bed. Off you go, Meg."

I went, and closed the door, and washed, and brushed my teeth, and climbed in my summer nightie into my bed. I sighed with happiness. I heard Mum and Dad calling everyone in, sending them home, and heard Mum clattering dishes, tidying up. Esther slammed into the room and pulled off her dress and threw it on the floor. She got into bed in her underthings.

"Goodnight, Esther."

"Shut up."

I smiled and went happily to sleep. Later I woke and saw her dressing. I kept still but she said, "You can stop pretending."

"Where are you going?"

"It's none of your business.—No one's sending me to bed any more." She went to the window and raised it. "If you tell anyone this I'll murder you."

"I won't tell."

"I'm twenty-one. I can do what I like."

"Why don't you go out the door then?"

"The window's more fun." She grinned at me, and climbed out, and was gone.

After a while I went back to sleep, happily still; and it seems to me now I slept through the rest of that year, through winter, and Esther's wedding in the spring, and woke up only in late spring, in December. That was the time when uncle John Willis stayed with us. John Willis: I thought of him as having a physiognomy—but the physiognomy of what? As I watched him mooning about, it seemed almost of darkness and of death. I did not like him. He was a closed-up man, he seemed to carry about him odours of deception and odours of private delight. I was the only one to see that somehow, secretly, he made Alfred happy. It was not a happiness I liked. Watching them together, I felt myself cramped up, with all my limbs forced tight into my body, as though I had been stuffed into a sack. I waited in a kind of breathlessness for John to go.

His last week came. One Saturday morning Dad found Alfred

and John Willis in the orchard. Doing something unspeakable? Making love? Both are true. Dad cursed Alfred and drove him out from Peacehaven.

Then I had my dream again: a black river, with the Plumbs all sinking. I did not sleep, but lay wide-eyed in bed, watching it happen.

12 On racedays Fred Meggett was away in the pubs taking bets. With Mother I walked across Loomis to visit Esther. Sometimes Alfred called in. He came alone. Mother did not want to see John Willis. Alfred was hurt by that, he told me so. "She thinks he's my bad habit, like gambling or drinking—but a good deal worse." It gave her love for him a desperate edge.

As for me, I did not understand him. "He's a marvellous person, Meg. He's so good to me." I did not understand. "Yes," I said. By this time they were living together. I wondered if they had a double bed.

"Do you remember I told you I couldn't find out who I was? Well now I know."

"That's good," I said. (Who are you?)

"He's introduced me to some marvellous people."

"That's nice."

He had given up his university studies.

"Are you writing poetry, Alfred?"

"Not yet. But I will soon. I'm getting ready."

I did not think he would ever start. The knowledge came to me intuitively. His happiness might give him weight, but rage and pain made him light, unstable. He would never settle down to work.

"You should have seen Jehovah when he found us. His eyes went red. Literally. He nearly fell over. And his hat fell off—"

"Alfred—"

"He ran away like this, like a chimpanzee."

"I don't want to hear. Please."

"And then when he met us on the bridge with his handful of money. It was straight out of the Old Testament. 'I curse you, Alfred. You are no longer a Plumb. Here's money to change your name.' Half of it went in the water. You'd better tell Robert to fish it out. Sovereigns, after all."

"Alfred, please don't hate him."

"I don't hate him, Meg. I laugh at him. My God though, when I think of his face in that orchard. He was like Moses coming down with his tablets and finding us worshipping the golden calf." He laughed. "That's what John calls me. It's his name for me. The Golden Calf. He's marvellous with words."

"Alfred—"

"Heee, when his hat fell off."

"He loves you, Alfred."

"You're joking. He loves himself."

"We all love you."

"And I love John. No need to look like that. I do."

"You told me there was no love."

"I was wrong."

"You can't love him. Not the way people love."

"Meg, Meg—how can I explain it? You'll understand one day."

I wanted to ask him why he didn't see a doctor. I thought he had a disease. But I did not dare. Instead I asked if he was really going to change his name.

"Yes. As soon as I'm twenty-one. I'm going to be Alfred Hamer. It's got a good sound, don't you think?"

"Have you told Mum?"

"It's best not to tell her anything, Meg. Just let her keep boxing on."

Mother and Esther came in from the kitchen with cups of tea and a plate of the pikelets mother had brought. (Esther did no baking.)

"Mm, I've been missing these," Alfred said.

"Which one of you does the cooking?" Esther said.

"We take it in turns."

"I've had a letter from Agnes," Mother said.

"Whose turn is it tonight?"

"Oh, I do Saturdays. We've got some people coming in. I'm a better cook than John."

"She says she's met a nice young man called Jerry. I suppose that's Gerald. He's an engineer."

"He even burns the toast, John does."

"I hope she doesn't rush into things too fast."

Oh help her, Alfred, I wanted to cry out. Mother sat very pale.

"Mirth is expecting again."

"He's a phenomenon, that man." This time he meant Willie.

"Children are a blessing," Mother said. "Life is nothing without children," she said. I could no longer tell whom she was talking to. When she and Esther took the tea things out I hissed at him, "You said it was best not to tell her anything. And you spend all your time talking about John."

"That's a fact, Meg. John's a fact. You've all got to get used to that."

"Can't you help her?"

"I've got to live my life. If people can't fit in they've got to stay out."

"Mother isn't people."

"I suppose she's not. But what can I do? I can't pretend to be something I'm not."

"Pretend to her. Forget the rest of us."

He tried, but it did not work. Her ear was impossibly refined.

"I planted some spring onions this morning." With John.

"Can I take some of these pikelets home?" For John.

"It's getting late. I suppose I'd better be going." Home to John.

So it went on, through those Saturday afternoons. Alfred turned twenty-one. He changed his name to Hamer, Mother's name. I do not know what she thought of that. Esther became busier. She was always running out of the room to answer the door. Fred was a land agent now, but his more profitable line was bookmaking. People slunk up to the back door with bets, and Esther came back scribbling in a notebook. "What a lot of callers you have," Mother said. She never discovered the source of their new wealth.

"I'll have ten bob each way on Prester John," Alfred said. Prester John? Mother looked at him with agonized love. He saw the love, he was used to it, lapped it up. Only I saw the pain.

At home Dad had locked himself away. He was like a man in sickness, half-way recovered, and one did not know whether he would slip back, and die perhaps, or whether he would slowly, day by day, get well and be his old self. He was in that condition for the rest of his life. I tried very hard to make him well; and coming from an hour spent in his study (holding his hand, and he there scratching a sentence or two in his notebook) I likened myself to Abishag, the Shunammite maiden, sent to warm King David in his old age. But I could not warm Dad. Something had gone cold at his centre, far beyond my touch. There was a little damp closed room in there. I caught a musty smell. He smelt it himself, and for a while he tried to wash it away—bathing and soaping—but then gave up and lived with it. Bodily cleanliness had always been one of his moral aims. After banishing Alfred he gave up cleanliness.

He came out of his study in the end. He and Mother were very kind to each other. After several years they resumed their paper chats. I watched them study each other, puzzling at the way to happiness. They had taken it so easily before. Now they had to think out every step. She would take his arm on Sundays and they would do their round of the garden—but they kept clear of the orchard. They strolled about the lawns, through the rose garden and the flower beds, and they spent a long time in the vegetable garden, admiring Robert's work and praising him for it. They strolled along Millbrook Road arm in arm, she showed him secret places—perhaps in one a bird had made its nest and was hatching eggs, perhaps weeds flowered in one, beautifully as roses in a garden—and he spoke of some political matter, some new cause, some injustice, or in his orator's voice boomed out a poem. It was unreal. I sat at my books in the evenings and heard their laughter coming from the study. It was unreal. It was our new reality.

"I hope we can be like that," Fergus Sole said.

Fergus Sole? Yes, I had him. In that unhappy time I found my husband. He became my lifeline, replacing Mother.

"For God's sake Meg, get yourself a boy," Esther had said. She was kinder to me now that she was married.

"How?" I said, "how?" I wanted a boy, I wanted Monte— Monte/Fergus, Monte/Simon, Monte/David, Monte/Doug.

"Let them kiss you. Let them get their hand up your dress. That's all they want."

"No."

"You're not bad looking. Even Fred says so. You know about precautions, don't you?"

I let them kiss me. But Simon did it in a way I did not like, and David picked his ears and rolled the wax in little balls, which he smeared under his chair, and Doug used bad language to make me think he was a man of the world.

I had gone off Fergus too. He was two years older than me. When I began taking the train from Loomis station on my way to the Girls' Grammar School, Fergus was in the fourth form at Seddon Tech. He wore the green and yellow Seddon cap, which I thought more attractive than the Mt Albert Grammar one— though the Grammar boys were the ones I should be interested in. (Agnes had told me, but I did not need telling. They would be doctors and lawyers, some of them, while the Seddon boys would only be butchers and bricklayers.) I thought none of the Grammar boys would ever be interested in me. It did not make me sad, for they were a rowdy lot, cheeking the guard, smoking cigarettes, throwing water-bombs at our carriage windows when we came into Mt Albert station. One or two made verbal lunges at me, but found me "stuck-up". So they mimicked my vowel sounds and my way of saying, "Oh dear," and they named me Plumb Jam because of my straw cady with the broken top that opened like the lid of a can. They lifted it as they went by and put apple cores in. I thought very few of them would be doctors and lawyers. The world was a complicated place. The most gentlemanly boy on the train was Fergus Sole, from Seddon Tech. He stood back at the train steps to let the girls down. "Watch it," he said, "there's girls here," when his friends said bugger or damn. Once he lifted my bag down from the rack when its handle was caught in the netting. "Thank you," I said, blushing. But then he was gone from the train, apprenticed to a plumber, and I forgot him. For three years I never gave him a thought.

I left the Epsom Grammar School—the gym frocks and ties and starched collars and cady I had sewn up a hundred times—and began to train as a teacher. Simon and David and Doug were fellow students. I found their shortcomings out. I clung to impossible Monte—against the evidence I clung to him. "You precious girl! . . . kiss me!" Simon tried to put his tongue in my mouth, and David had more than one bad habit. Doug used words that seemed to me to give him a bad smell. I think I should have gone on believing in Monte and drifting further and further out of the world, if one Saturday afternoon my walk had not taken me past the Loomis cricket ground. I had no interest in sport. But I saw men in white clothes strolling on the grass beyond the trees, and I heard the crack of bat on ball, and on that afternoon, filled as all my afternoons were with Alfred and Mother and Dad, it seemed beautifully simple and cool and pure. It was part of our mythology that Mother and Dad had met at a cricket match. It crossed my mind, obscurely, that I might find their primal place for them, and bring them to it, and start them on their proper way again.

I went under the trees and walked along the whitewashed circle that marked the boundary of the field. I came towards a small grandstand holding a dozen people. On the grass in front of it players were lounging, waiting their turn at bat. I did not go close. I chose an empty bench in front of a paling fence and sat there in the sun, watching the leisurely game. I circled in a lazy contented way a mystery that would not be penetrated. The rules of the game were strange to me; and the white-clad figures, flicking into time, and out of it, had a meaning I could not understand. It did not matter. Soon it did not matter. The sun warmed my skin and made me want to sprawl and open my limbs and catch it in my mouth and throat, and to my puzzlement and shame, further down. I mean, it made me sexy. That was not a word I knew. But I felt I was damaging my vision of the game—formal and pure—and made it my business to sit up straight and keep my knees together and keep my hands tight folded in my lap.

I heard a smack as the bat struck the ball, and saw the red orb fly into the air and make an arc and fall with a papery sound into a bamboo clump at the far end of the ground. Sparrows flew out in droves. In the stand people clapped. "Sixer. Good old Fergie," someone yelled.

So I knew Fergus Sole. I saw him again. I had been half an hour at the ground, sunning and dreaming in my ladylike pose, watching, half-watching, a man with a bat hitting a ball with it, before I suddenly saw Fergus Sole. He invaded me then, he filled my mind, and somehow seemed to fill my body too. I took into myself his shining hair (that was Vaseline putting light on it) and his widow's peak that made his face so stern, and his eyes of blue (blue of water and sky), and his arms and bony wrists and plumber's hands. He struck the ball and it sped like a weasel at me, deadly, true. It struck the palings and bounced back to my feet and lay there throbbing. A fieldsman picked it up and lobbed it back. But Fergus had sent me a message. On the paling fence was a red bruise. There was a bruise in me—in my heart, on my mind—somewhere in there. I had fallen in love. That is how I saw it. I don't see why I should choose other ways of describing it now. He swung his bat again. The ball clacked on the palings further along. People cheered, and Fergus raised his bat in a small salute. "Century!" Such a cut-and-dried word to take on magic for me. His bat was a sword. I thought of Alfred's

104

Percival, and Monte Baron of the West, and they faded away and Fergus Sole stood there. Or someone like Fergus, a Fergus-shape filled with their virtues.

He struck. The ball sped away. High in the air it curved, and down by the bamboo clump a man got under it and juggled it once or twice and fell down on his knees, and Fergus was out. It did not matter. He had made his century. I was only cross that the man on the fence had made such a clumsy catch. A perfect catch was the end for Fergus. He came back to the stand. His bat was under his arm. He walked by me. He saw me. I knew he did. He made no sign.

And made no sign on the next Saturday. I came there again, I sat in the sun, I watched Fergus Sole fielding, watched him bowl. When he walked out with his bat I could not help it: I felt pure and soulful and sexy. Being there was my declaration. The whole of Loomis saw it. Fergus saw it, though he made no sign. The ball bruised the fence again. It came between my feet, increasing the bruise in me. But Fergus was quickly out. His stumps crashed over—perfect end for him. He walked back grinning ruefully, and wiped his hand on his brow so our eyes should not meet. I smiled at that.

Through the summer, whenever the Loomis side played at the park, I was there. I seldom went with Mother to see Alfred. I became expert in the rules of cricket. Other players sat on the seat by the palings and talked with me. I was a puzzle to them. Once Fergus Sole came with three others and sat by my feet and rubbed oil on his bat and looked at me. "Are you at the Training College?" he asked gruffly. "Yes," I said. It worried him. He snapped dry stalks of grass with his plumber's hands. The time was coming, I knew, when I would say, "I love your hands."

I went with my friend Lorna to a party. Lorna was a girl I had been at school with. She worked in the baker's shop in Loomis, selling cakes by the dozen and loaves of bread. She was an unhappy girl. She could not stop eating and at eighteen her flesh was swelling out on her thighs and arms. She wailed at it, and wept at it, and went on eating Lamingtons and cream buns and chocolate eclairs. Her boyfriend at this time was Jimmy Jessop, a member of the Loomis cricket team. The party was at his place. I went along. I painted myself very lightly and put some perfume on my wrists and throat and put my best dress on (a simple thing Alfred had once passed as "not too bad") and I went along for my meeting with Fergus Sole.

I did not stay long. Jimmy Jessop pestered me. Fergus stood in a corner and pretended not to see. Lorna watched from the supper table, gobbling cakes. This could not be the place. "Leave me alone, Jimmy Jessop. I don't like you." I made sure Fergus heard. I went out into the night and walked down the path and sought the concealing shade of a big macrocarpa tree by the gate. There in the cool dark, with aromatic branches about my head, I waited for Fergus Sole to come and find me. But it was Jimmy Jessop who came in the moonlight, and called my name and sensed me breathing there. He lifted the branches and came inside.

"Meg? Let me kiss you, Meg."

"Please don't, Jimmy. I don't like you like that."

"What's wrong with me? Lorna thinks I'm O.K." He was a stupid boy. He told me Lorna thought he was good at kissing. He was like a weak Fred Meggett, a weak Conroy.

"Don't touch me, Jimmy. I'll kick your shins."

He tried to grab me. I struck him with my fist high on his chest.

"Ow! That hurt."

"Go away. I'm waiting for someone."

"Who? Old Fergie Sole? You've got a crush on him, but he doesn't like you."

"That's all you know."

He grabbed me then and pushed his mouth at me. It was like being licked by a dog.

"Let me go. I hate being kissed like that."

"Hallo," a voice said from outside the tree. Fergus lifted the branches and came along, and stood up straight by Jimmy, half a head taller. Jimmy let me go.

106

"Who asked you in, Fergie?"

"Asked myself."

"I got here first."

"You can leave first then."

"Yeah?"

Fergus jerked his thumb. "Clear out, Jimmy."

"You going to make me?"

"Yep." It was almost as if Fergus too had read about Monte and Bab. "I'll count to three. One, two—"

Jimmy cleared out. "You're welcome to her. She doesn't even know what it's for." From further up the path he yelled, "And don't come back to my party."

"I'm sorry if he upset you," Fergus said.

"I'm all right now." I took out my handkerchief and rubbed my cheek where Jimmy had licked me.

"I'll walk you home."

"My shawl's up there," I said.

"I'll get it. I saw where you put it."

I waited in the aromatic dark. It was perfect. Our meeting was as romantic as I had hoped it would be. Even Jimmy Jessop added to it. Fergus came back with my shawl and wrapped it round my shoulders. We walked through Loomis and along Millbrook Road. The creek shone in the moonlight.

"I used to fish for eels in there," Fergus said.

"My brother swims with them."

"Bob? He's a funny kid, Bob." He took my hand. "Your father's a parson, isn't he?"

"Not any more. He gave it up. He doesn't believe in churches." I was confident that would not worry Fergus, although I had no idea what he believed. Nothing could go wrong, this was our meeting.

"Do you believe in them?" he asked.

"No. I think there's a God somewhere though."

"I don't know what I think."

"My father says God is in our minds."

"I don't know whether it's important."

"You're a funny plumber's apprentice," I said.

He was quiet at that, his hand went still.

"I love your hands," I said. "All the boys at Training College have got soft hands."

"Never done any work." He was unsure still.

"I love it when you hit sixers. I saw you hit one into the bamboo."

"We lost the ball. . . . Do you like it at Training College?"

"No. I don't want to be a teacher."

"Why do you go there, then?"

"There's nothing else to do. I don't want to work in a cake shop either." I want to be your wife, I almost said. "How long does your apprenticeship last?"

"Two more years."

"You'll be a plumber then?"

"Yes. There's nothing wrong with plumbers, Meg."

"I know. I know. They're better than schoolteachers."

"Teachers don't scare me."

He put his arms around me at the gate. He did not say, "You precious girl! . . . Kiss me!" I said it for him, in my mind. I held up my mouth as I had practised, in a way perfectly natural. We kissed softly.

"I'd like to see you again," he said.

"Yes."

"When?"

"Tomorrow?"

"I'd like you to meet my parents."

He did not realize what he had said, or that when I answered, "Yes," I was saying I would marry him.

Mother was waiting up for me in the kitchen. She looked at my flushed cheeks and said, "You'd better splash some cold water on your face."

"I've met the most wonderful boy."

"Cold water's the thing for wonderful boys."

"He wants me to meet his parents."

That worried her. "Who is he, Meg? What does he do?"

"His name is Fergus Sole. He's a plumber's apprentice. You're not to say a word, Mum. Plumbers are all right."

"Yes, Meg."

"He's much better than a plumber."

"But plumbers are all right."

"He's better than Simon and Doug."

"Of course. Whoever they are."

"Don't laugh at me, Mum."

"I'm not laughing. Go and wash your face and I'll make some tea."

I told her all about Fergus. She became very worried. She had not realized how far I had moved away from the real world.

"Don't make him something he's not, Meg dear."

"You did. Remember the cricket match."

"I always saw your father very clearly." But did not know, I saw her add, that he would ever turn out one of his sons. Seeing her pain, I came as close to seeing a real Fergus as I was to come for several years.

The next day he called for me in a small car and drove me into a street of railway houses. They had numbers stencilled high under their eaves. Fergus lived in A27. His father was a big slow heavy man, with grime in his scalp and hair sprouting from his ears. He was a railway blacksmith. He never spoke more than half a dozen words to me on a visit—no more than a hundred or so in his life. Mrs Sole made up for him: a skinny woman, with her skull all plain to see, and scaly clothes-peg hands, and her joints standing out of her skin. She had sinews in her arms, thin as wire, terribly strong, and sinews in her throat; and in her tongue. She was a worker. She told me so. All her life she had worked, she had known nothing else. To make sense of it, she placed all virtue there. I was a soft and useless thing to her. "Look at those hands. Never seen a scrubbing board, they haven't. You'll have to learn to scrub if you're going to have my boy." I was not good enough, she made no bones about it.

They appalled me. I felt a little sick. But they changed my view of Fergus only for the better. I described him in a poem I

109

wrote: "growing to perfection in the mud".

On our second Sunday he took me on the train to Redwood Park. At Swanson station he held up his arms to help me from the carriage, and I, absurdly overdressed, and trying for "a gay insouciance", jumped instead of stepping down, and caught him unready. I had no lightness. The heel of my shoe caught in his fly and all the buttons sprang off and ping-ed on the carriage wheels. We should have laughed. If I had been Esther I suppose I would have gone into the bushes with him and made love. But it ruined our day. We took the next train back to Loomis. He was not even able to walk me home from the station. He ran off in the other direction, waving one-handed, pink in his face as a baby (that pink had been coming and going all of our silent ride home); and told his mother some tale, and she sewed his buttons on.

We recovered. After some months we made love. I will not go into that. It was not much fun, but was a business highly charged with feeling for both of us. We were in love. And as we went on with what I termed, rather oddly, "having a good time", I came to like it fairly well. I mean the physical doings and responses. I always loved the emotional side of it (always in those days), especially the sacrificial part, and I loved his pleasure, and loved to watch while he lost himself, taking that for his finding of me. He said my name.

Well, enough of that. We became engaged. Mother liked him, up to a point. She would have wished him cleverer, and less of the physical man. But she recognized his honesty and goodness. Dad had a much sterner disapproval. And his absurdities led him into a sensible judgement. He was full of ambitions for Man, and full of plans for Eugenic Betterment (that nonsense that became so dangerous). Even his Socialism required an élite, though he never found a way of saying so. What it boiled down to was that Fergus was not good enough. That was not the sensible part of his judgement. Fergus and I were not suited— that was it. I would have loved to hear him talking about it with Mrs Sole.

But I saw Fergus slowly break him down. He did it by laughing, nervously at first, at Dad's innocent jokes and his foolish remarks about women. "Trout, like women, Fergus, are taken by a bit of coloured feather or rag. They jump, my boy, they jump readily." Fergus laughed—a nervous laugh, that one. And Dad told him about the Irish woman coming through customs. "'What's in the bottle?' the customs man said. 'Lourdes water.' 'It smells like gin to me.' 'I knew a blessed miracle would happen before I got home.'" (Bluey Considine had told it to him.) Fergus laughed again, more happily. And before very long Dad began to tell him tales about me as a child. "I came across her once drawing a picture—it was a sort of cloudy presence. 'What's that?' I said. 'God,' said Meg. 'But nobody knows what God looks like.' 'Well, they will when I'm finished.'"

Fergus fixed the spouting on our house and put new washers in our dripping taps. Robert was annoyed about that, but he liked Fergus too. The two of them spent four summer Sundays digging out and re-laying the Peacehaven drains. Dad offered Fergus a pound, which he would not take. So he gave him a book of Emerson's essays instead.

"I can't read it, Meg."

"Never mind, never mind, tell him you haven't got time."

"What does *Mens agitat molem* mean? He wrote it in the front. Is it something to do with teeth?"

We sneaked into Dad's study and looked it up in Webster. "I found out what *Mens agitat molem* means, Mr Plumb," Fergus shouted that afternoon into Dad's trumpet. "Mind moves matter."

"Ah, you're coming on. You're learning, Fergus." He still thought ours a bad match; but he liked Fergus. They went off together to cricket matches.

It made me happy to see them. I thought of myself as possessing (and wrote it too) a gently welling cup of happiness. The books I read, and the language they taught me! *A gently welling cup of happiness*. But Alfred was still banished; and that darkness lay between Mother and Dad. So I wrote that my cup "was held in the Dark Hand of Life". But there was hope. I wept over *Precious Bane*, and rejoiced in its ending, indeed I almost cried out with belief. Kester Woodseaves kissed Prue Sarn on her hare-shotten lip. That for me was realism. A hare-shotten lip came from the Dark Hand of Life. And Kester Woodseaves lowered his mouth and kissed her. I lived in hope. And I had Fergus Sole.

I taught school for a year. He finished his apprenticeship. We married then, and settled down to be happy.

13

To be happy? Our expectations were not impossibly high. But . . . my mother-in-law. The depression. And childbirth. Moony Meg. I cannot blame our fall on one of these; or all of them. There was something else. We tumbled down. But I shall say a word or two first on how for a time we found our rosy future almost coming true.

There was, to begin with, his coming home. How my day lit up. We had rented a house too expensive for us in one of the better streets of Loomis not far from Esther's place. I could not believe it was mine (and was just coming to believe when the depression put us into a three-roomed shack down by the creek—but that comes later). I played in the kitchen nervously. I made the double bed in something between disbelief and guilt. Was it true I had grown up? As the day went on I came to believe it. And Fergus, coming home, stamped on me the mark of womanhood. I do not mean he took me off to bed, though once or twice he did, and we found that "love" did not *have* to be done at night. I mean he kissed me, told me of his day; took off his boots, washed his feet in the bath; I served his meal, and we sat through the evening as man and wife. That lit me up with what I shall have to call *meaning*.

I walked out with my shopping kit and filled it with meat

from Porky Meggett's butcher shop. I gossiped in the baker's with Lorna Tilley—Ten-ton Lorna they called her—and she slipped an extra fruit square in with my dozen. ("Fly cemeteries," Lorna giggled, shocking me.) At the grocer's I bought cheese and butter and flour and a new scrubbing brush. And at Doctor Walker's I learned I was expecting. I went to the draper's and bought some wool to start knitting. Meaning! I wore it like a crown upon my head.

"Who have you told?" Fergus asked.

"Just Mum. I went round this afternoon."

"Did you tell my mum?"

"Not yet."

That was a small shadow. We celebrated with an extra chop and a glass of beer.

Childbirth that first time was not easy, nor too hard. The pain came in waves, and sank away. I could hear it rustling with a shingly sound, leaving a beautiful calm, all light and peace; and feel it building, building to a new wave that might wash me out of life—but always it stopped, just at the point when I knew I should have to cry out and give way and start screaming. It wasn't too bad. They wheeled me into the delivery room and Robert was born. *Meaning* went away and left me holding my baby, feeling him suck. I felt very peaceful, happy down into my bones, and grown up at last.

Fergus brought me flowers and fruit and chocolates. The spring scent of stock filled the room. He knew my favourites. His happiness was different from mine. There was a crowing in him, and a masculine increase, a pushing out. I said, "You won't go chasing anyone while I'm in here?"

"Hey, you're crackers Meg, it's you I love."

"You won't get in any fights?"

He came along the ward the next night with his eyes burning and hurt and his face white as paper. He held his handkerchief to his mouth. "I can't kiss you, Meg."

"Fergus," I cried, "you've been fighting."

"No. I've had my teeth out."

I made a sound like fingernails on silk. Fergus, bending close to me, an anxious giant, suddenly shrank to a goblin size. For me his nature changed. He was Fergus no longer—and he has never grown back, though he grew into other shapes I could admire. But in that moment, as he withered and shrank beside my bed, I felt his loss as deeply as Rebecca's drowning and Alfred's banishment, and I felt a bitter dislike of this strange man bending dumbly over me, bleeding into his crumpled handkerchief. His mouth would grow like the sucked-in wound on my brother Oliver's leg.

"Why? Why did you do that?"

"I thought it would be a good idea. Mum thought so."

"Your mother?"

"I won't have to go to the dentist, Meg. No trouble with fillings and things."

"She's a stupid bitch." I had never spoken that word before.

"Meg!"

"Did you have gas?"

"No."

"Just like you. Proving you're a man."

"You can't blame Mum."

"Who can I blame? No, don't talk if it hurts. Go home, Fergus. I want to sleep." I turned to the wall. After a while he went away.

I lay in my bed wanting nothing except to be back home at Peacehaven with Mother. Home, that was my knowledge. Peacehaven was home. Out in the world was danger and ugliness and pain; and what seemed worse, stupidity. To pull out teeth that were not too bad just so that he need not worry about fillings any more! I made the screeching noise again, and a passing nurse stopped to ask if I had a pain. "Yes, yes," I said, but would not tell her where. I told her I wanted to go home.

"Oh, it's too soon yet. And here comes your mother-in-law."

The woman sat in the straight chair by my bed and held her hard purse on her scrawny knees. I let her have it. She grinned with pleasure in fighting, and answered back, better than I could give. Mr Sole, grimy old blacksmith Sole, winked at me sadly from his post at her back, trying to let me see he cared for me. "Let there be harmony." There would never be that between Mrs Sole and me. We screamed at each other. The sister came running and joined in the shouting too. Mrs Sole stood up, she mounted on her toes like a little brightly coloured crowing bird. "I told my boy he should never have married you."

I cried my new word, bitch, and my certainty, stupid; put them together, shrieked them at her. "Stupid bitch!" It was all I could say.

"Please. Please. Out you go," cried the sister, pushing Mrs Sole. Mrs Sole turned on her, I thought for a moment she was going to scratch her. But Mr Sole put his arms round her waist from behind, lifted her up, said, "Enough's enough, Mother," and walked down the ward with her. She kicked like a child. Bang, bang went her heels on his shins. She struck back-handed with her long leather purse, but he kept on, past Fergus bleeding in the door, and out of the hospital.

"Now, Mrs Sole!" the sister said, exploding out her breath. I turned to the wall again. I did not listen. "I want to go home."

I went home not to Peacehaven, but to our rented house. I began the job of learning Fergus again. I soon grew to like him, and make declarations of love. I would not examine what I meant by that. Well, who does? I remember the time as being happy enough. I got used to his false teeth, and his sucked-in mouth when he took them out at night. For several months I would not visit his mother. Fergus walked there on Sundays, with Bobby in his pram. When I went at last we stood at arms length and were formal, and that's the way we went on. She learned to pour out words about nothing at all, and I to say, "Yes, that's true," and "You may be right." No real word passed between us again. Poor Ted Sole sat in his chair, breathing and smoking his pipe. Now and then he winked at me heavily.

Down in Wellington Felicity had her baby. Her long affair with the politician Dan Peabody came to an end and she married

Max Waring, a civil servant. My brilliant sister, Felicity, the one who would follow Dad: she married a shy ugly little man who was not very clever. It did not bother me that her baby was well on the way—that was part of her "freedom". But Max! It was many years before I understood Felicity, not her husband, was the lucky one.

But all was changing, all was unexpected and strange. There were babies everywhere: Mirth's and Esther's and mine and Felicity's. Agnes and Edith had babies in California. Sometimes when I remembered that I, the youngest sister, had had my child in the same year as Felicity, the oldest, I would be caught in a fear that everything had happened too suddenly, too fast, that there were things I should have known, and should have done, before I married. I thought again of the Black River and the Land of Missing, or I sat at the kitchen table drinking tea and feeling a yearning in me for Peacehaven and the Plumbs, and sometimes for the world, which came before my eyes in story-book shapes and story-book colours. Would I ever know it?

Then Fergus came home and said he had lost his job. For months he was about the house, fretting, and turning suddenly, and kicking things, and digging fiercely in the garden. I had two children. Bobby was the easy one. Fergus made me ache with pity for him.

We left our expensive house and moved to a little shack down by the creek. I was more at home there. I met the discomforts of the place—the tin bath in a lean-to out with the cooper and tubs, the cooking-place dug into a bank and sheltered by a beaten-out piece of roofing iron—I met them with a kind of recognition. In Beavis Street, up by Esther Meggett, I had only been playing at house.

Rebecca was born. I boiled napkins in the copper and wrung them out by hand and pegged them up to dry on a line held clear of the potato patch by a ti-tree prop. At last I began to feel I was grown up, a married woman.

I named our first two children so it was only fair that Fergus should name our third. He came up with Nelson, and was proud of himself, but I took violently against it: a military name. "Nelson was a sailor." "You know very well what I mean." So he left it to me. I chose Raymond.

He was born at St Helen's hospital in Auckland. Whenever I come across the word workhouse I think of St Helen's. That is being unfair to it. Without a place like that we depression wives might have had our babies in ditches. But in that grey city building birth somehow became grey. Again I am being unfair. But that is common with women in childbirth, and I am concerned with how it struck me then.

I travelled in by train for my pre-natal examinations. The tutor sister used us to teach her students. "Nurse Cooper, find me the head. No! Warm your hands, you ninny." And Nurse Cooper, with a tear running down her nose, felt about with her fat hands and found my baby's buttocks and head and feet. "Now, Nurse Todd. Open your legs, Mrs Sole, you don't have to be shy with us. Warm hands, Nurse Todd?" It was not kindness made her insist on that. The textbook insisted. She made them find the place, and had poor Nurse Cooper read it aloud.

When my labour pains started Fergus called in a neighbour. He rode off on his bicycle for a taxi. Two weeks the money had lain on my dressing-table, and though we had had no meat in the house in that time we had not touched it. We rode into Auckland in an Essex Super Six. "Don't have it in my car, lady," the driver said. Fergus held my hand. He has held it many times since, but that, in a way, was the last time.

Raymond's was a hard birth: for him too, I believe, although there is no way of knowing. Once the midwife slapped me on my buttocks. "Come on Mrs Sole, you're not trying." I am not an unforgiving person, but I have hated that woman ever since. When it was over I was numb and drained and torn and deeply bruised, and my certainty was not that I had given birth but that I was violated. I made a vow—it was more than that, I made a change in myself, in the chemistry of myself, in my body's cells, and if the feelings have cells, in those cells too: there would be no more doctors and nurses, no babies—no husband bringing this violation on me. I cannot alter it. I have tried.

Fergus came in. They showed him the baby. He kissed me and held my hand—but my holding was different from that in the taxi. He peered at me anxiously. "What is it, Meg? What's wrong?"

"No more babies, Fergus. I don't want any more babies."

"No, no, three's enough."

"Come on, Mr Sole, she needs to sleep."

"I'm sorry, Fergus." I knew what I was withdrawing from him. Not my body. It was more than that. He would have me no more. I would not have him.

But there was Raymond. We are not supposed to have favourites, and I said whenever it came up that I loved my children equally. But deep in me I knew I loved Raymond best. I was hurt for the other two. There had been nothing special in the pain of their births. They were unlucky—maybe lucky. I loved them with a placid protecting love, full of good feeling. It would have grown fierce if it needed to. But when the nurse brought Raymond to me in St Helen's and I put him on my breast and felt him suck, and knew us safe from that violation we had undergone, then all my bad emotions flowed across into the balancing cup, and down I came on the side of love. Over-brimming love. I can use that language.

From the next bed Mirth laughed at my face. Yes, she was there. She too had a baby on her breast: Douglas, her last. (He was Sebastian Douglas, but the boy made up his mind for the second name—and the politician he has become finds the choice a smart one.) Mirth was forty-eight. When I mentioned that recently to my daughter-in-law, Bobby's wife, who's a nurse, she said, "Good God, she really was an elderly multi-gravida." I don't think they used that term in St Helen's. But the tutors brought their classes to look at her. They were amazed at her flow of milk. Mirth took it in good part. And Willis, stumping

118

in whenever it pleased him, made hay of those snapping sisters. "You watch me blarney the starch out of them."

Mirth thrust her baby at me one morning. "Swap you. Give them a change of diet. Mine's flavoured with grapefruit." She laughed at my horrified face (she really meant to swap), and said, "You're a soft little thing. You're all marshmallows. That's what I like about you."

She became ward mother, padding about barefooted in an old army greatcoat. We confessed our troubles to her. Even the nurses confessed. Mirth wiped Nurse Cooper's tear-wet nose on the edge of her bed sheet. She waved an advancing sister away. "Don't you try and boss me, dear. I'm old enough to be your mother. You give this girl a moment. Off you go. Do your work." The sister went.

I told Mirth I was not having any more babies. She said that was all right, the woman should decide. She wasn't having any more babies either. She'd enjoyed the lot of them, but three in her first marriage and five in her second was enough. "The trouble is," she said, "Willie's such an eager little devil. I often think all the energy that should have gone into that leg he lost is being sent somewhere else. Don't worry, he's the only man for me. But this time he's going to give me time to get my menopause started." I think Willis wanted to climb in with her in the home. He probably would have tried if his sister had not been watching from the next bed.

Fergus came to see me every night. Dad came, bringing roses. "A mother, Meg. A mother for the third time. I can hardly believe it. It seems only yesterday you were born." Mother came only once. She was not well. The noise and the crowding in the ward upset her. She had had her babies at home and she thought of birth as a private business. She was driven away by the women in beds, by husbands in their boots and mothers in print dresses, and by the smell of milk and the monkey-house chatter. She kissed me and hurried down the ward, dark in her clothes, cut off from it all, and in that moment I understood she was dying. Dad had not brought his trumpet. I wrote on a scrap of paper,

How is she, Dad? He said, "Not well, Meg. I'm worried about her. But we mustn't talk about that here." He did not like the forced intimacies of the place either, but still he managed to see it as a kind of temple. Especially, he liked seeing the babies in the nursery. They blasted him with their urgency and greed. I believe he almost heard them through his deafness. "The Life Force is in that room. You can feel it, Meg." I found him rather tiresome in St Helen's.

I asked Fergus about Mother, but he had noticed nothing. "She seems all right to me. When can you come home, Meg? The kids are missing you."

"Two more days. They'll survive." I was getting tough. But a moment later my eyes filled with tears at the thought of Rebecca and Bobby. "I wish I could see them."

"Not long now, Meg." He went a little pink, but made himself say what he thought was owing to both of us. "We'll have to be careful. We'll have to take precautions." I said nothing to that. I must have looked stony. He said, "I'd better go and see Ray. It's nearly closing time."

"Raymond."

"Esther says Raymong."

"She would."

"They've all got the same initial. She jokes about that too."

"I think it's nice. I don't see any joke."

"The way R goes with Sole."

I did not see it and he would not tell me. (For more than thirty years I did not understand. Bobby told me last Christmas—a little drunk. In a perverse way, he's pleased with his name these days.) Fergus went off to the nursery and looked at his son. He came back grinning and held my hand until the bell drove him out. I gave him a letter to drop in Mr Tilley's box on his ride home. And through this act discovered the sort of love I wanted from Fergus.

Mirth had gone home. Lorna Tilley had taken her bed— Jimmy Jessop's Lorna. She came to St Helen's off the street, walked in, cramped in two, far gone in labour. They got her on

120

the table, where she gave birth to a girl. When the ward came to life in the morning Lorna found me in the bed next to hers. She turned her face away, but I got her talking, and weeping too, in no time. She would not tell me who her baby's father was. It was not Jimmy Jessop, it was no one I knew. "It happened after a party, Meg. I didn't like him much. But no one looked at me any more. I'd got so fat." She was fat enough to conceal her condition into her seventh month. Then her mother, a glass-sharp, glittering, poisonous, Christian lady, turned her out. She lived with friends, with men. They turned her out too. That was her story. St Helen's accepted her. The nurses came round that morning when Lorna was bathing and took donations for her: a nightie here, bonnets and booties and napkins. She cried when she saw them. "Nobody's been nice to me for so long."

Lorna wanted to see her father. He had been kind, away from his wife's view. But she could not write and tell him where she was. She was ashamed. In my letter I told him. I told him she and the baby were well, but that she had nothing and nowhere to go.

The next day a huge booted man creaked along the ward. He wore a Sunday suit and a collar with pointed wings. I had not seen that sort of thing for fifteen years. He had dressed for his daughter. He had dressed to offer himself. He carried his hat. He carried violets. His red ears, thick as hands, stood out from his head. Some of the girls laughed, but he was not a comic figure. Lorna cried hugely; and tears ran down Mr Tilley's face. "There, there," he said, "there, there." He patted her. They rocked in each other's arms.

It was a love that placed her in no danger. She could relax in it—grow fatter if she pleased. I did not ask what return she made, or what it was I would be giving Fergus if I took from him the sort of love Lorna Tilley had. I simply knew *that* was what I wanted—and knew as Fergus walked up the ward, clumsy and shy and red as Mr Tilley, but with a man-light in his eye, it was something I could not have. Momentarily, I hated him. He saw it on my face, and paused, and then came bravely on, frowning a little.

"What is it, Meg?"

"I'm sore." I did not see how a man could desire a woman who was torn and stitched, whose nightie was damp with milk leaking from her breasts. It seemed unnatural. It seemed a thing for beasts.

He brought me home to Loomis in Fred Meggett's car. For three more years we lived in our rusty shack. I boiled my wash and hung the nappies out over the bean rows. With the wind blowing smoke about my face and rain drumming on the iron, I boiled our meals of neck chops and spuds and turnips and corn and beans. I showed Fergus's mother I could work. I grew thin and strong as her, stringy muscles stood out in my arms. Still she would not like me. I did not care. Nothing about the Soles was of interest to me. My children were Plumbs, I said, and Fergus in his good parts was a Plumb. It was the Sole in him that moved us apart—what Alfred would have called the peasant. I called it that, in my snobbish moments, when I was attacked in my "understandings", but more often I thought of it as the animal. We got along, we gave each other a good deal of kindness, but where we had come together once in love we came now only in duty on my part, and in a dumb rage and resentment and greed—and sometimes in guilt—on his. There were times when I loved him like a child, my tenderness for him overflowed and I wanted to stroke him and hold him and cure all his troubles. He hated that.

"Meg," he said as we lay in bed one night. His hand came cautiously on to my hip. I had been nearly asleep.

"Oh, Fergus," I whispered, "I'm so tired. The children have been so naughty today," and I rolled away from him on to my side—acting sleepiness, for such things always brought me wide awake. "Tomorrow night," I murmured, and I breathed as though I had sunk into sleep.

Fergus lay still for a moment. I felt his rage. It filled the bed and filled the room and drummed under the roof. It seemed to me it would wake the children and set them screaming. I shrank under it. I became small and withered, like a dried-up fruit.

Fergus climbed out of bed. He was quick, he was full of ugliness.

"Where are you going?"

"Shut up."

He went out into the night. I ran after him as far as the door, and saw him in the moonlight dragging his axe out from the old rain tank we used as a wood store. It was only for a moment I believed he would come back into the house and butcher us all: the barest moment, a blink of pure terror. Even before he turned away from me I knew it was not possible, and a kind of gratitude came on me, and a kind of contentment, that I would be troubled no more, that he was working out his rage in some final way. He turned into the garden, and there by the silver-beet patch he attacked the trunk of our huge old wattle tree.

He chopped as white moths flew about his head. The gleaming axe and flying chips; his wide-legged stance; Fergus in pyjamas, altering us: I will never forget. The tree rang like a bell. Soon it creaked and shuddered in its head. It leaned towards the garden, and crashed at last over the bean frames, over the pumpkin patch. Its branches crushed my wash-house into the ground. Pollen smoked up into the silver night. I felt like clapping.

Fergus drove his axe into the stump. He went to the rain-water tank and turned on the tap and splashed water on his face. I got him a towel. "Thanks." He walked past me into the house and into the bedroom. When I came in he was dressing. He put in his teeth.

"Where are you going?" I asked.

"I need a walk. Don't worry, I'm coming back."

"Fergus, I'm sorry."

"Go to bed, Meg. Go to sleep." He was very calm, very slow. He smiled at me. "It's late. Raymong will be coming in soon."

I heard the gate creak and I heard him whistling as he walked up the road. I went to bed, and I went to sleep. Soon Raymond snuggled in beside me. He did not seem surprised to find his father gone.

123

When I woke, Fergus was cooking breakfast. He brought me a cup of tea. That day he did not ride out looking for work, but chopped the branches off the wattle tree and sawed its trunk into lengths and dragged them away. I took out a bucket and picked the beans from the crushed bean-row.

"I'll have to get that wash-house fixed," Fergus said.

So we lived together and grew apart. There was little drama in it after that night. I loaned him my body now and then, enough to keep a kind of contentment in him. It was a shallow thing, but he had, I think, another sort, much deeper. I robbed him of manhood, but he went out with his axe and proved to himself he was a man. He saved himself—in a way, he saved us all.

He took up cricket again and played in friendly matches. Sometimes we all went along. Rebecca sat on the bar of his bike and Bobby on the back mudguard. I wheeled Raymond in his pushchair. Now and then Dad came along and we sat on the grass and watched Fergus hitting sixers. Mother came only once. She had been at Esther's for lunch and Esther drove her down to the ground in the middle of the afternoon. No one in the teams could afford white trousers (Fergus, though, had his old Loomis cap) but I think Mother saw enough in the bowling and batting to take her back those forty years to the time of her meeting with Dad. "Your father used to play cricket," she said to me. And Dad, reading her lips, aware of her in this setting, and troubled by their lives, said, "Your mother and I met at a cricket match. Didn't we, Edie? They used to call me the steady little trundler." He tried to push away the shadow by bringing up a thing not essential to them. Fergus hit a boundary and he clapped. Mother led me off to the next-door paddock to pick blackberries. We picked into her hat, lining it first with her handkerchief. "He was very good at cricket. I'll make the children a blackberry pie." A little later she said, "Meg dear, you're not happy. I can tell."

"I'm all right, Mum. If only Fergus could find a job. That's what the trouble is." I don't think she believed me. I did not lie well.

"Open your mouth. Open. Open wide." She put a fat blackberry into Raymond's mouth.

"Greedy boy," I said.

"They should be greedy at this age."

"He looks as if he's been sucking blood. Little vampire."

"Meg, what a dreadful thing to say."

I thought so too. I hugged Raymond in apology. Mother smiled. "You're a soft-hearted girl."

"Not any more. I'm hard."

"Nonsense, Meg."

"Yes, it is nonsense. Sometimes I wish I could be."

"And not have any love left? That would be the worst thing." She was a practical woman. She spoke of love and courage and honesty as though of things in her kitchen. And when she said, "We must love one another, Meg," she was telling me something she had learned as a fact. As we picked blackberries, and fed the children the juiciest ones, she told me we must love, and we must struggle, and in the end we must accept. She told me acceptance is hardest. All this is true. But the fact is that if she managed to accept, and I'm not sure she did, it was because she believed in an after-life. Everything would be made right in that place. But I would not allow her to speak of God as she spoke of love and courage. I would have none of God, and none in this existence of an after-life. I was committed to a life of feeling, the life of now. Love I could manage, and I could struggle too. But acceptance?—accept that pain?—no. Look for an understanding of it all in the hereafter? Never! Never! I could see very clearly that it would have been something to drop into the hole left in me by the withering away of my romantic and sentimental view. But I felt too strongly the injustice of things. I felt that joys we could imagine we also had a right to.

I worried Mother, and hurt her too, that day. I told her she was foolish. But of course, soft-hearted, said that I was sorry: and I was, although I believed that in this thing (belief in God) Mother was foolish. (So was Dad, but I never found the courage to tell him.) Her hat was overflowing with blackberries. The sun beating on her head was making her dizzy, so I gave her my head-scarf, and took the hat from her, and we went back to the cricket ground. Fergus was out. He helped us through the fence. "I'll make you a blackberry pie, Fergus," Mother said. She flirted with him. They were easy with each other. Soon Esther arrived to drive her home. We sat on the warm grass for a while and picked at the blackberries like sweets until Mother covered the hat with her hands. We joked about her hardness. She saved enough to make a pie and when I went round to see her the following day she gave it to me to take home for our pudding.

We drank a cup of tea in the summer-house. Bobby and Rebecca played on the slope above the creek where I had spied on Esther and Fred Meggett. Robert kept an eye on them to see they did not fall in. We had called him from the garden behind the house. He washed his hands in the creek. "Scones, eh Mum? You'll be making us fat." We did not eat many though, we fed the children. I calculated how much less they would need for tea if they filled up now.

Mother's illness had aged her. She was sixty-four and looked ten years older. But she gave the impression of being tired rather than ill. Bone-tired: that term might have been invented for Mother. On that day in the summer-house, feeding scones into the mouths of greedy children (hungry at first, but greedy in the end), I was able to grasp her life and examine it as though it had been an object. I had not been able to do that before, though I had seen parts of it clearly enough. I had seen a surface play— those endless kitchen tasks, that seasonal activity of planting and pruning, and seen her care of Dad and her keeping of the world's life out of his study. I had known her love. But that was not all. I had known there must be more, and had never seen it. She did not speak differently that day. She told the stories she had always told. But I saw her bone-tiredness, saw death approaching, and I had a half-hour's sight of who she was. She was Edith Hamer, she was Edie Plumb—and below the surface workings of her life was a rich fullness, love and joy and con-

126

tentment, and an endless sacrificing of self and a finding of self. And disappointment and pain. But above all, love.

I write as though of a saint. She was close to that. Dad had hurt her. Dad had struck her to the heart. The others—Oliver, Felicity, Esther—carry on about his selfishness. It obsesses them. Oliver, in his pedantic way, writes to me of "Dad's retreat from the quotidian". And Felicity says that when he got off to his study with his books he was "making one little room an everywhere—but, poor old thing, in human terms he was nowhere". And even I find myself recalling his way of putting his hand to his forehead when family got too much for him and running away to Browning or Emerson. Mother stayed and coped. But this is off to one side in their life. It is not at the centre, where the others would have it. "The quotidian" was her part of the contract. She understood that with the utmost clarity. His was to seek after truth, to stand and fight. He martyred himself to his conscience, and she to him. She of course had a better understanding of it all. (That's by the way, though it makes her the wiser person.) As long as the whole thing stood upon love, she saw it as their bargain. And he failed her there. He failed in love; and Mother was struck to the heart.

Well, I grasped all this as I listened to her talk that afternoon, telling stories I had heard as a child. She gave me the blackberry pie. "We used to have blackberry picnics in Kumara, altogether, all the churches together. It was such a funny sight to see us all setting out, twenty or thirty women in their oldest clothes, carrying buckets, and a tribe of children running by their sides with billies and cans. Dressed in rags, some of them. We didn't care. They were special days. We took lemon drinks and sandwiches and plenty of cake for the children, and we enjoyed it so much, the outing, Meg, and the sun, and the *abandon* of it. We came home with our dresses torn and the children with their faces stained all purple. We looked like a tribe of gypsies (begging their pardon), and our buckets all overflowing. The next day we made jam. For the most delicious jam give me sunripe blackberries."

"There's still a few up the paddock. I'll pick them," Robert said.

"You know," Mother said, "the chimneys in Kumura were all tin ones and after a windy night they would all be pointing in different directions." And she said, "There was a boy brought the milk to the back door in the evening. He was a bit simple. One night I thought I'd talk to him a bit. I thought, Poor fellow, no one bothers to talk to him. So I asked him where he was working and things like that. And after a minute he said, 'Well, I can't waste any more time with you, I must be going.' George, your father, used to tease me about it. He'd say, 'If Joe Kent can't waste time talking to you I can't, I'm sure.'" I had heard that story many times—and laughed at it because she thought it funny. Then she told us one I had not heard. "When we were in Emslie the Church of England minister's wife died, and the Wesleyan minister's wife died. One of our elders said to me, 'Don't you die, Mrs Plumb, or folks might think the ministers are killing off their wives.'"

What made her remember that? Knowing her as I did that day, I felt it piercing me. "Oh, Mother," I said.

"What is it, Meg?"

"If only . . ."

But she was not as deep down in her life as I had been. She smiled at me. "If only, Meg? If only fisherman Jack loved Kate, and fisherman John loved me. It won't do, dear."

Soon I gathered my children and took my blackberry pie and went off home.

Winter. A cold that made our bones ache. Frost crackling like glass on the sunless bank below our house. Robert banging our window in the dawn. Mother was having an attack. I put on Fergus's oilskin and took his bike and rode through the icy rain and yellow puddles to Peacehaven. I pushed through Wendy Philson's embrace and came to Mother's bed. She lay there waxen, amber, tidied up.

"Meg, it was very quick," Wendy sobbed.

"Go away."

I kissed Mother on her brow. "Mother," I said, "I loved you so much. I'm glad you're happy now."

Of course, I only believed that for a moment. But the moment is what's important, not its shortness. I know. I felt it.

14 Felicity telephoned from Wellington and asked to speak to Robert. I told her it would cost her a fortune to hold on while I fetched him from the cottage. Besides, he was not well enough to be running up all that way. She got big-sisterish, but I laughed at her. "That won't work, Felicity. If you want to talk to Robert you'll have to come to Auckland."

"All right, I will. I'll come up next week. You can meet me off the plane. I'll telegram you."

In fact, she phoned again. "Oliver's coming too. I couldn't put him off. He wants to look at Dad's papers."

"It's a bit inconvenient. Robert really isn't very well."

"He won't want to see Robert. It doesn't suit me, either. But what could I do? Can you meet the plane?"

I drove them home in time for lunch on a mild summer day. Oliver was offended by my car.

"What did you expect? A Rolls Royce?" Felicity asked.

"I would just as soon have taken a taxi." He got in quickly in case someone should see him.

"Sir Oliver Plumb in a Hillman Imp. It'll make a good chapter for your autobiography."

"Fergus uses the big car," I said. "Tuck your knees up, Oliver. You would have been better in the front."

"Knights of the realm don't sit next to the driver," Felicity said.

"I trust you're not going to keep this up."

"Off we go." I drove home fast.

After lunch Felicity walked down to see Robert. I had warned him she was coming. They had not met for twenty-five years. I sat in the living-room with Oliver. He had climbed down a lot. Peacehaven relaxed him.

"You've kept the place up well. I approve of that. I wouldn't mind living here myself."

I must have shown my alarm for he said, a little stiffly, "Oh, don't worry. The capital's the place for me. I still exercise some influence. They need the sort of attention I bring to things. You'd be surprised, Meg, the people who call on me." He named a couple. I was surprised. I was a good deal impressed. He smiled at me. "And of course I go to Government House. We have much in common."

"I'm glad you're not lonely, Oliver."

"I could never be that."

"Are you really writing your autobiography?"

"Memoirs, Meg, they're memoirs. I'll suppress a lot. It serves no purpose to bring up certain things. I'll deal mainly with my career in the law. That is what will interest people. But you understand, when the Chief Justice—the former Chief Justice—writes of his life, he has to be discreet. He's a public figure. An elevated one, I grant you that. But there's no point in dwelling on—what shall we say, unedifying matters? I'll go through Dad's papers though. I may come across one or two things that will throw some light."

"Will you write about him?"

"No. I shall say he trained for the law. But did not practice. That has some interest."

"His trials would have some interest."

"None, Meg. They're forgotten. Let's keep them so."

I showed him into the study and showed him where the notebooks and letters were kept.

"Wendy Philson has some. But I don't think there's anything in them to interest you."

"That woman who wanted to marry him?" He must have had that from Felicity. "What's she doing with them?"

"She's writing his life."

"Good heavens! You're not letting her?"

"Don't worry, it's a spiritual life. Like your legal one. There won't be any trials. Not in earthly courts anyway."

"But our early days? When we had no money?"

"She's not interested in that. Basically, she's concerned with her influence on him. She doesn't know that, of course."

"It sounds unhealthy to me. Don't you let her in when I'm here. You'll vet what she writes, of course?"

To calm him I said I would.

"Another thing, Meg. I don't want to meet Fred Meggett. I'm not even sure I should see Esther Meggett."

"Ever again?"

"At least till this thing's over. I know a bit about it. I can't tell you, of course. But it's most unfair, the things I've had to put up with from my relations."

"We'll try to be good."

I left him leafing fastidiously through Dad's letters. When I took him a cup of tea he was deep in them, and into the notebooks. I was surprised. I had expected him to be systematic. But he was here and there—he did not know where he was.

"He really was a most dreadful man. And yet. . . ."

"What, Oliver?"

"All that intelligence. What led him astray?"

"Conscience."

"I've got that. It hasn't led me astray. He could have been someone. We could have been proud of him."

"I'm proud of him."

He looked at me. "You're just a woman."

"Thank you, Oliver."

I went back to the sitting-room. He made me laugh. I really enjoyed that laugh. I rolled in my chair. Felicity came in while I was wiping my eyes.

"What's the matter with you? I heard you on the path."

"Something Oliver said."

"What?"

"He said I was just a woman."

"You think that's funny?"

"From Oliver. I'd hate to have his approval."

She agreed with that. She laughed a bit too. Then she said, "Tell me what the doctor says about Robert."

"How did you find him?"

"Dreadful. Shouldn't he have a nurse?"

"I'm going down. When it's time. The doctor's going to tell me."

"I'll take some of the load off you. For as long as I'm here."

"It's no load. But thank you. How did you get on?"

"Very well. He's a lot more sensible than I remember. He's not exactly talkative though, is he?"

"Did you try to convert him?"

She pointed her finger. "Keep off my religion."

"I thought you had to. When you met someone dying."

"My God, the idea people have got of Catholics."

"Well, did you ask about his soul? Surely Catholics do that?"

"You're making fun of me, Meg. I won't have that."

"I'm not. I'm interested. Tell me about it, Felix."

So she did, cautiously at first, then with passion. I was not much interested in her beliefs, but she, my sister, fascinated me. The passion, the strength, the purpose—she is Dad. Of course, with her, conscience is mixed up with the doctrines of her church—she is less pure. But he is there. She has, though, something that was not in him—I never saw it—an appetite for power. She is the terror of her parish: I have it from Max, her husband, in admiring letters. Once she had wanted to alter the world; today she confines it to the Catholic world. She is full of impatience with "soft religion"—novenas and penances and rosaries. That, she says, is for Irish peasants. She wants a larger place for mind. She wants "intellectual muscle" in the teaching. *The Tablet* and *Zealandia* are full of letters from her: programmes and prescriptions and reading lists. Her priests damp her down as much as they are able. They marvel at her, admire her, and run for cover when they see her coming. (Father Pearce, shifting furniture, had asked me how "my sister" was getting on. He did not need to say which one. And he had glanced nervously over his shoulder, as though mention of her might bring her through the door.)

When she wound down at last to the matter of faith, I said, "It all seems so medieval."

"Nonsense. It's eternal."

"I don't see it."

"You can. You can. I'll give you some books to read."

"Oh Felix, you are like Dad."

"Keep that old phoney out of it. He didn't know a thing."

"Alfred used to call him Jehovah."

"My God, Meg, you've got a frivolous mind. Keep to the point."

"If you'll tell me what it is."

"I've spent the last hour telling you. Listen. Listen." She started again. I could not get away till Oliver came. (Calvinist and papist, they talk determinedly of other matters.) He sat down on the sofa and put his hands primly on his knees. "There's a smell of tobacco in the study, Meg." I went off to prepare our evening meal. Fergus drove his car into the yard. He came in through the kitchen.

"They in there?"

"Yes. Go and see them."

"I suppose I have to." Felicity talks down to him like a teacher and Oliver like a judge. When I went back he was slumped forward in his chair, arms on knees, staring at his shoes. I was not going to see him ill at ease in his own house.

"Have your whisky, Fergus. Oliver won't mind."

Oliver turned his upright head at me. "Is it too much to ask you to give up that indulgence while I'm here?"

"Far too much. Felix, would you like something?"

"Sherry?"

"Yes. Esther keeps us supplied. You get them, Fergus. I'll have a small gin and tonic. We've got fruit juice, Oliver."

"No thank you. I'll go to my room."

"Don't be silly. If you keep over there you won't even smell it. Anyway, purity's in the mind. You're O.K."

133

His family reduce him to a boy. In Wellington he might hobnob with ambassadors and statesmen. At Peacehaven he grows shrill, he trembles with that impotent rage families generate so easily in their members. "One of our finest legal minds," a fellow jurist says in his dusty memoirs. That is hard to believe when Oliver mounts his high horse in my kitchen. I would like to see the other side of him, if only to be fair. But I would tremble in his court the way he trembles among his brothers and sisters. I would grow thin as glass, you would see right through me. "What was he like?" "A stone god, an eagle," Felicity says—his rulings came like bolts from Mt Olympus. He might try for that at Peacehaven, but was soft and crêpey, like a balloon with most of its air leaked out.

"Would it be too much to ask for my meal in my room?"

"It would. We saw enough of that with Dad. If you want your food in this house you come to the table."

He went off in a huff. Felicity grinned at me. "You're a bit of a tiger."

"I wonder what he did at state banquets."

"That was different."

"I dare say."

"You shouldn't talk to him like that," Fergus said.

"Because he's Sir Oliver? Nobody takes that seriously."

Fergus cannot be sure. He had tried to laugh at the new Oliver, but could not manage. He was brought up short by a kind of magic—all that power in word and ceremony. He poured our drinks, shaking his head at not being able to say what it was he felt.

"Thank you. How was your day?"

"Not bad."

"Did you see Fred?"

"Nobody sees him. He's locked up on the top floor with his lawyers."

"Will they take him to court? Is he really a crook?" Felicity asked.

"I wish I knew."

"Come on Fergus, you must know. Maybe they'll take you to court as well."

"That's not funny," I said.

"Aren't all the directors equally culpable? Is that the word?"

"I've resigned."

"It's hard to believe you don't know what's going on."

I began to be angry. Fergus had gone pale.

"Leave it, Felicity. It's none of your business. Help me take Robert's dinner down."

"I've just started my drink."

"You can have that later."

"You *are* tough."

I served the meal and put it on a tray. "There, you carry it." But I took it from her half-way down the path. I saw she was a woman of seventy. Her breathing was not good. I had always looked on her as Felicity Plumb, twenty years old, light and quick and sparkling with cleverness. She was three score and ten. It took my breath away.

"Here Felix, give it to me. You go back. Have your drink."

"Thank you. I am a bit tired."

I watched her trudge thick-bodied up the path. What's happened to us? I thought.

It was a question I asked again on the Sunday they all came to Peacehaven: Willis and Mirth, Esther and Fred, Emerson, Robert. But of course by then it was simply a question—no revelation in it. The afternoon was cool. We met indoors. Felicity was at her best, strolling through the Zoo looking at Plumbs. They seemed to amuse more than annoy her that day. Especially withered old sagging old Mirth and her peg-legged lover. (Willis, though, has a new pink leg and wears a shoe on his plastic foot. I miss his old peg and its carved lady-names.) Mirth is doddery, and not quite right in her mind these last few years—but that does not cause us pain. She is brimming with her fulfilments. Willis squires her with untiring devotion. He has given up other women. He looks on Mirth as a wonder and sees his role as that of custodian. Perhaps in private he dusts and

135

polishes her. He conducts tours. "Felicity, come and see Mirth. She's over here. This is her. See how happy she is. Look at the glow in her cheeks. *Roses in your cheeks, love. Roses, I say.* I'll have to get her one of those trumpets Dad used to have. She's eighty now, Felix. Eighty-one next birthday. Isn't she phenomenal? Look at her eyes. There's a real sparkle there."

"Willie," Mirth said, "stand aside so I can see this lady."

"Hello, Mirth," Felicity said.

"Are you the Catholic one? What made you take up that nonsense?"

"She's got a sharp mind," Willis said.

"Terrible nonsense, religion. All you need is a man like Willie."

"She can't see past me," Willis grinned.

"Wine is for drinking, dear, not mumbo-jumbo."

Felicity laughed, there was nothing else to do. Willis took Oliver's sleeve and led him over.

"Here's the knight, lovey. Sir Oliver."

Mirth wagged her finger at him. "Why do you need medals? Monkeys don't pin medals on themselves."

"I see your point."

"They tell me you were a judge. How many men have you hanged?"

"Really—" he was shocked, "—I can't answer that."

"A terrible thing to do. I don't want to talk to him any more, Willis."

"She's got your number, Ollie. She's not done for. *Still got something left, eh love?* Course," he said, "she's not right up here—" tapping his head "—some of the time. She gets things a bit mixed up. Gets up in the night to feed the babies. *No babies left. All gone, out in the world.* And then there are times she doesn't make it to the dunny in time. She sort of forgets. But that's the way things go. She's happy as Larry."

"Hanging's a terrible thing," Mirth said.

"It's not as if I put the rope round their necks."

"Who did if it wasn't you? Putting on your black cap."

136

"Hee hee," Willis said.

"Look here," Oliver stammered; but I led him away. I saw an old man with a trembling lip and trembling hands. Dad had been breaking him down all week. He would come from the study icy and precise, but soon would turn with a fussed look on his face, as if aware of something behind him he must take notice of. "Do you know what he says?—here, I've written it down. 'By deafness you learn to hear the inaudible, see the invisible, and touch the incomprehensible.' Now what sort of nonsense is that? Of course, it all comes from denying authority." So Dad drove him back on his certainties. He needed his wife to direct them at—found me evasive—but she was dead many years. And soon he would fish another scrap of paper from his pocket and his fussed look would return. Now even Mirth, daft and doddery, could make him forget he was after all who he was.

"What a dreadful woman. How dare she say those things?"

"Never mind. Never mind." A brother he approved of was standing by the door. "Come and say hallo to Emerson."

"Yes, indeed. (Abominable woman!) How good of him to come."

Emerson has made money. He bought a glass-house when he gave up flying, and now has a city of glass, and patents on spray delivery and trickle irrigation systems that have made him the most successful tomato grower in Auckland. It is hard to remember he has flown crazy flights, that he has been the Sundowner of the Skies, and looped the loop, and walked on aeroplane wings.

He and Oliver shook hands.

"Congratulations, Oliver. I don't have to call you Sir, do I?"

"Not in the family. Although I must say I can't understand those people who say they intend to go on being Tom or Jack. What is the point?"

"Yes, yes, I agree," Emerson said. "Well, you've had a great career. We're all very proud of you." He is good at saying the right thing. He noticed once when looking at the world—a rare event—that the trick was useful, so he learned it; but listens with surprise to hear himself.

"Thank you, Emerson. That's more than some of the others have managed to say."

"You've done the family credit."

Oliver inclined his head. "It's good of you to say so. I've often thought that *you* deserved an honour. Not for that flight, of course. That was foolishness. But for all the flying you did for TEAL. I think an M.B.E. would have fitted the bill."

Emerson looked alarmed. "That's not my sort of thing."

"You're too modest."

"Someone has to be with you around." It was Esther. She had come through the door ("Essie," I hissed, "Essie") and barged her way past me and banged him on the shoulder. He ducked his head, a movement I had seen last—how it fastened on me over the years—when Dad had raised his arm to order him out of our house in his uniform. For a moment he was shorter than Esther. Then he recovered himself.

"I had no idea you were coming."

"Couldn't keep away. The Order of St Michael and St George, eh? You'll be fighting dragons. Beats me what you'll do with the maidens, though."

"Now just you listen to me—"

"No chance. What's it going to be next, the jolly old garter? How about gentleman of the bed chamber? You'll be carrying out the royal piss pot, Ollie. They say it's blue."

"How dare you!"

"I dare anything. Hasn't Meg Muggins told you?"

"Has she been drinking?" Felicity said at my shoulder.

"I'm afraid so."

"Poor Oliver. No, leave them. It's family after all. Oliver has got to look after himself."

"Fred, Fred," Esther called, "come and shake hands with Sir Oliver. Where'd you leave your horse, Ollie? Got it parked outside?"

"I can't meet your husband. Surely you understand that."

"Why not? He was good enough to meet the queen last time

138

she was out. They talked about racehorses and he gave her a tip. Come on, Fred. Get away from Fergus, he's got no gong. No offence, Fergie, you have to stand in line."

Fred came over. Whatever he felt, he covered it with a grin. "Gidday, Oliver."

"This is improper."

"Don't see why. You've retired, haven't you?"

"If you hadn't it could have been you who puts him in prison. Fergus too. What a laugh that would have been."

"She's been drinking," Fred said. "Do I have to tell you?"

"Since I got out of bed," Esther cried.

"Since yesterday morning, if you want to know. Found her out on the patio, sucking it up. I guess you all know why."

It dropped into my mind like dye in water. I felt that cloudy roiling out; and must have swayed or staggered. Felicity took my arm.

"What is it?"

"I forgot."

"Meg?"

"It was yesterday Alfred died."

"Thirteen years. Everybody have a drink," Esther cried.

Felicity tried to make me sit down.

"No, I've got to get Robert," and I left the room, and the house, and ran down to his cottage. At Alfred's funeral service I had thought I was going mad. Then Robert walked in, from nowhere. He sat behind me and put his hand on my shoulder and we listened to Alfred's friends say words of farewell. I found I was able to bear it, I should not go mad. I needed Robert now, not in anything like that desperation, but as one needs holding after some dreadful fright.

"Robert," I said, coming to his chair, "they're all up there. Are you ready?" I gave his arm a tug. It was only then I saw how bad he was.

"Help me up, Meg."

"What is it? Shall I call the doctor?"

"Help me to the table."

When I had him there he leaned over it and rested on his forearms. His breathing kept its gravelly sound of stones shaken in a tin. I fetched a glass of water and his pills and put them on the table. His head was on his fists, but he saw the bottles, with their coloured bits of useless magic inside, and he seemed to grin. Soon he pushed himself up. "Better keep old double-barrel happy." He took two pills and washed them down.

"I'll get your bed ready."

"I'm coming up. Got to see all my brothers and sisters."

"Oh Robert, no. You're not well enough."

"I'll be all right."

"They can come down. I'll send them one by one."

"I think I'd head for the bush. I'm all right. It's kind of like a wheel. It won't be bad again till next time round."

We walked along the road arm in arm. A little car was drawn up at our gate. The woman in it turned her head to watch us. She had been there when I ran down but I had scarcely seen her, and I took little notice now. I was too conscious of Robert at my side. His illness was galloping forward: it was time I moved to the cottage. I made up my mind to tell him when we got back.

Oliver had come into the garden. He was walking about in an agitated way. "Meg," he cried when he saw me, "you never told me you were inviting those two."

"It was supposed to be a family gathering."

"Yes, but Meggett! The fellow's a criminal. I can't be seen talking to him."

"Sit in the summer-house, then. Before you go, say hallo to Robert."

"Imagine if anyone got hold of this. Do you realize I'm taking the chairmanship of a Royal Commission next month? On property development! And here you've brought Meggett into the house."

"This is Robert."

"I'll talk to him in a minute. But what I'm going to do is sit down there and I want nobody to come near me until Meggett's gone."

140

"I'll hang a tea-towel out the window."

"This is no joke, Meg."

"It seems like one. Do say hallo to your brother."

"You've behaved very badly in this."

"Can it really affect you? I thought you were above such things. Where you couldn't be touched."

"In a sense I am. . . . I won't be laughed at."

"I want you to say a proper hallo to Robert."

"Very well. Robert, I'm pleased to see you."

"Hello, Oliver," Robert said. "Congratulations on your knighthood."

"Thank you.—We were at different ends of the family, Meg." It was his way of saying that the meeting was pointless. He looked at Robert severely. "But you were a victim too. We were all victims. If it hadn't been for him you wouldn't have got in that appalling mess in the war. And after. Well, it's water under the bridge. No one connected our names." He looked Robert up and down—a bumpkin, Robert, even in his best clothes—and managed a smile. "It's good to see you looking so well. Meg, I'll be in that ruin. Not till he's gone, remember."

He went away to the summer-house.

"I might leave him there all night."

"Sir Oliver," Robert said. "I don't think he liked me."

"He doesn't like anyone." But I had a last look at him, hiding behind the rambler roses in his Wellington suit. I had not known him. None of us had taken the trouble. Well, we had our own lives.

I helped Robert over the patio and into the living-room and left him with Willis and Emerson. Esther was on the other side of the room, as far away as she could get from Mirth, whom she thought of as "gaga". She was slumped in her chair—almost it seemed she ingested it like an amoeba—and was staring about her angrily. Her jar of wine in its brown-paper bag was sitting between her feet. I took a chair beside her.

"I thought I might get a phone call. At the very least."

"I'm sorry. With Felix and Oliver here, I just forgot. And Robert to look after."

"Too busy with the living, eh, to worry about the dead?"

"I haven't forgotten him. I'll never forget."

"But you won't go out of your way to remember him either."

"That's not fair."

"Nothing's fair. How about getting me a glass?"

I fetched one from the kitchen and she poured herself a drink.

"Don't you think you've had enough of that, Essie? I'll be making tea in a minute."

"Leave me out. Last one who drank with me was Alf." Felicity joined us and sat in a chair on her other side. "You won't drink with me, will you? Didn't think so. I'm stuck in a family of wowsers."

"I'm sorry I forgot. It's fifteen years."

"Thirteen. That's not long."

"I've grown into an old woman in that time."

"Haven't we all? Alf wouldn't be sixty."

"He's still alive, Essie. If you'll only believe it."

"Souls, eh? I thought you'd try that on. Well, you can save your breath. When you're dead you're dead. The lights go out. O.K.? Alf isn't floating around anywhere."

"We all have immortal souls."

"Grow up, Felix. Meg here doesn't believe it, do you, Meg?"

"I don't suppose I do. But while we remember Alfred he's still alive."

"Jesus! Fairy-tale time. For God's sake where's some grown-ups I can talk to?" She took a large swallow of her wine. Her face went pale. "I think I'm going to be sick."

"I'll look after her," Felicity said. She helped Esther out of the room. I went to the kitchen and put the kettle on. The afternoon was proving a great strain. Robert ill and Esther drunk and Oliver sulking in the summer-house. I was grateful that Mirth was asleep and that Fergus had taken Fred to the study. I went along the hall and looked at them. They were drinking whisky. Fred had his feet up on Dad's desk.

142

"Esther's lying down."

"Thank God for that."

I went back to the kitchen. Something was pressing softly on the edges of my mind. I made the tea, trying hard to let it in, but it would not come. Something to do with Fergus. . . . Then I had it. The woman in the car down by the road was Beth Neeley. "Oh, no," I said. I had enough to put up with. For a moment I thought I would run to the study and ask Fergus to go down and send her away. But then I saw it would be simpler to pretend she wasn't there.

Felicity came in. "I put her on my bed. I think she's asleep."

"Was she sick?"

"Got her to the toilet in time. Rather nasty. Isn't there anything we can do for her?"

"You can pray."

"Don't start that. You know what I mean."

"There's nothing you can do from Wellington. Write to her if you like. All I can do is keep on visiting her. It's going to be hard with Robert. I'm moving down tonight."

"To Robert's?"

"I thought he was dying when I went to get him."

"Who'll look after Fergus?"

I wish he'd let Beth Neeley, I thought, it would take a load off me. "I'll only be down there at nights. I'll spend a good part of the day up here."

"It would help if Robert shifted up."

"He doesn't want to."

"I'd stay and help, Meg. But I've got Max."

"I know. It's my job."

We carried the tea on trays to the sitting-room. Only Mirth was there, sleeping open-mouthed in Dad's winged chair. Voices came from the patio. Willis and Robert and Emerson were sitting in a row on the garden seat.

"Hear no evil, see no evil, speak no evil," Felicity said. We laughed. Willis looked up.

"Here's the girls with tea. How's my old Mirth?"

"Sleeping."

"Sleeps all day. She's a wonder."

We poured them tea and gave them cake and left them there, still talking. Felicity went to look at Esther and I took a cup to Oliver in the summer-house. He thanked me and I went back. Climbing the steps, seeing my brothers like the three monkeys, I felt they had done well: better than Sir Oliver, alone in the summer-house. They had done better than Fergus and Fred.

I poured myself a cup and sat with them. Willis began to flatter me shamelessly. It's the only style he has with women, and it has bowled them over all his life.

"Willis," I said, "do stop it. I've got better things to worry about than my appearance."

"Our sisters have always been beautiful. Every one of them. Better than film stars."

Emerson looked startled at the idea. Robert smiled, but it was an effort for him. I thought perhaps the wheel was coming round and I touched his arm and asked him in a whisper if he wanted to go home.

"Not yet. In a minute."

"Mirth's eighty-one next week," Willis said. "I'm writing a poem for her. Listen, Meg. You were good at poetry.

> "My wife is eighty-one,
> Her life is nearly done,
> But roses bloom in her cheeks so fair
> And violet scent is in her hair.

"That's as far as I've got. What do you think?"

"She'll be pleased with it. Any woman would be."

"Alf liked poetry. He'd be able to help. I've got to say something about her eyes. And her mouth. About her kisses."

Emerson looked embarrassed.

"Her kisses are what I misses," I said.

"No, Meg. Seriously. I want to please her. Here's Duggie. I'll ask him."

Duggie is their son, Sebastian Douglas, the National Party politician. I cannot be fair to him. I look on him as a traitor, like

144

Oliver, but he's not my brother and I make no allowances for him. Plumbs should not be Tories. About that I cannot be reasonable. Every time I read in the newspaper, *Douglas Plumb, the National member for Epsom*, I feel sick. When I saw him drive up that day in his flash car (no flasher than Fergus's, I admit) I gathered the tea things quickly on their trays and took them inside. I did not want to offer him a cup. I think he noticed. He does not miss much.

"She still asleep?" I asked Felicity, who was in the kitchen.

"Yes. I don't like her colour. Who's arrived?"

"Douglas Plumb. The member for Epsom."

"I must see him. The poor man's Holyoake. That's what Max calls him."

"He wouldn't like that. He wants to be the rich man's Plumb."

"Let's have a look."

Douglas was squatting cow-cocky style—one of his tricks—in front of his father and uncles. He could not place Robert and that worried him. He prides himself on his encyclopaedic mind.

"I've got it," he said, "you were the conscientious objector."

"Yes," Robert said.

"I knew I'd get you." He looked pleased with himself. "Which camps were you in?"

"Hautu. Strathmore. Shannon."

"We must have a talk some time." But he filed Robert at once in a dead file. He would be of no use.

"Douglas," I said, "here's your Aunt Felicity."

"Ah, Felicity. Of course, of course." He kissed her cheek. Douglas is thirty-two. He has his father's good looks and his mother's liveliness. Raymond, who seems to detest him, although I'm not sure, says he's very clever, he means to be Prime Minister one day and he'll probably make it. I cannot believe it. Everyone, when you see them close, even Duggie, seems too human for that. Could a Prime Minister survive with Douglas's mouth and his red Plumb hair? And especially his eyes? They are not evasive, but they're never still, they're always

145

looking out for the place he should be. They're handsome eyes, they twinkle with geniality, but they look past you obsessively for someone more important. He'll have to learn. Of course, when they've found that most important person they become still.

But enough of Duggie. He's not worth anyone's time. I don't think he is. He talked to Felicity a while, wanted to know what was amusing her (it was his resemblance to Dan Peabody), recalled her friendship with Peabody, "a clever chap", and then he spotted Oliver in the summer-house and he hared off there—proving, I suppose, that Oliver still is important. Willis had not had a chance to ask him about his poem. He looked glum. His son, it almost seems, has stolen his vitality. I've heard it said (Raymond) that Duggie has an appetite for women that would put Willis's in the shade. The old man would seem like a piker. I can't believe it. I remember his carved leg and his one hundred women.

Presently I took Robert back to the cottage. Beth Neeley watched us boldly from her car. I ignored her. I got Robert on to his bed and took off his shoes. He stopped me from undressing him.

"This'll be over in a minute. Let me do it as long as I can."

"Robert, I'm shifting down. You need someone here at night."

"Tell Fergus I'm sorry."

"He'll understand."

I waited until the attack was over. He changed into his pyjamas and got into bed. "Glad I went. Good to see Willie and Emo. Pair of clowns."

I went back along the road and got in Beth Neeley's car.

"Hello, Miss Neeley. You've been here a long time."

"Nobody asked you in. Get out of my car."

"I'm here now. What shall we talk about?"

"This is a public road. I've got every right to park here."

"Come on, dear, don't play games. Is it my husband you want to see?"

146

"He's not your husband. Why don't you let him go? I'd let a man go if I knew he didn't love me any more."

"My dear, if it was just love everything would be simple. But there's more to it than that. Fergus loves you, all right. But he's not a simple man. I wish he were."

"I don't know what you're talking about."

She was a handsome girl—twenty-five, I guess. Big and ripe, I've said it before. A meal for any man. There was more to her than that, but I was not concerned to see it. I did notice she was suffering.

"Would you like to talk to him? Shall I send him down?"

She decided I was trying to devalue him, and declared that she would take no favours from me—she wanted me simply to "get my hooks out of Fergus". She actually said it. If I had not still been full of Robert I would have been furious.

"I'm trying to get my hooks out. I've told him to go to you. Take you to a hotel if he wants."

"That's a horrible thing to say."

"Isn't it what you both want? I'm trying to help."

"We don't want anything from you."

"Except for me to let him go. I'm trying."

We were going in circles and I became impatient. I wanted to shift my things down to the cottage.

"You're a pretty girl. You don't need help from me."

She widened her eyes: Esther's trick. She had some of Esther's sparkle—but darker eyes, and a beakier nose, and a greedy mouth. Physiognomy! That was no science. She was just a stranger; a mystery I had no wish to solve.

"I'm leaving Fergus. I'm shifting out tonight. I don't care if you move in, although you'd better leave it a few more days because my brother and sister are there. But after that he's all yours. If you want him." I shook my head. I had to tell her the truth. "But it won't have a happy ending. I wish you could see."

"You're playing some trick."

"No. Fergus is free. Move in if you want."

"I'll never go into your house."

"Then take him away. Now I've got things to do. I'll tell him you're here. Goodbye."

"Don't tell him. You're an evil woman."

The word shook me. For a moment I wondered if I *were* playing some game, working this woman subtly to her ruin. As if she recognized it, she cried, "You're trying to destroy us." But that was melodrama.

"I'm trying to help you."

It was true. And I saw it was useless. My best course was to do nothing, simply be quiet.

"I hope it works out." And I went away. I got rid of my guests. Duggie drove his parents home. Felicity and I wrestled Esther into Fred's Mercedes and he drove her off. I fetched her jar of wine from the sitting-room and poured it down the sink. It almost fumed. It was like some acid substitute for blood. Oliver came up from the summer-house. He sat in Dad's chair and wanted to praise Douglas Plumb. I left him with Felicity and went to talk with Fergus in the study.

He poured me a drink.

"Fred thinks the police will arrest him soon. It's the first time he's said it to me."

"Is he very worried?"

Fergus shrugged. "There's nothing he can do. He thinks they'll leave me alone."

"You haven't done anything wrong."

"I don't think I have."

I sipped my drink. I found it easy to be honest with him. "Robert's a lot worse. I'm moving down tonight."

"I thought he looked bad. Have you had the doctor?"

"He's coming tomorrow. But someone should be there. He needs a nurse."

"Are you sure you can manage? I'll help all I can."

"I know you will. But there's someone else I think you should worry about."

"Who?" He knew at once. That, I suppose, is infatuation.

"Miss Neeley. She's been parked down on the road all afternoon. No, she's gone." I had heard her car drive away as I walked up the path. "Fergus, she's in a bad way. You got her in and you've got to get her out. She's your responsibility."

"She had no right to come here. Was she upset?" He was confused. I hated to see it. He's so impressive to watch when he knows where he's going, he goes full bore; but now he was like a lost child.

"Help her, Fergus. Take her away somewhere. You won't be doing any wrong to me."

"Is this why you're moving down to Robert's?"

"No, no, Robert's a different matter."

"Did you talk to her?"

"For a moment or two."

"What did she say?"

"Only that she loves you. Fergus, she does. Or thinks she does. Let her find out." I hoped to give him a goal. But as I'd said to Beth Neeley, it wasn't that simple. In this Fergus was not a simple man. Nor was the end of it plain. I saw the possibility of Beth Neeley unmanning him, as I had done, and saw that at fifty-eight he might not have the strength to re-make himself. My talk might be dangerous. On the other hand it might be the saving of him. I grew confused as he. It was better, yes it really was better, if I simply stayed quiet. And I thought of Robert waiting in the cottage. That was where I wanted to be.

I put my drink down and kissed Fergus on his cheek.

"How long was she there?"

"An hour or so."

"I'd better go and see her."

"I think you should."

Presently he drove away. Felicity helped me carry my few things down.

15 Fergus volunteered for overseas service in the first week of the war. He sailed away with the Second Echelon in May 1940. His ship was a luxury liner, *The Empress of Japan*. There was nothing luxurious in his attitude. He was cutting down another wattle tree.

For five years we had rented a railway house in his parents' street. Twice he had tried to set himself up in business, and twice gone back on wages. He seized the war when it came. He made himself a man. I had thought there was some life in our marriage. We were doing all right. He grinned at me when he walked in that night. "I've enlisted." The life all drained away.

We argued late, shouting at each other, but he gave no explanation, and I could not make it for him, knowing private ground when I came on it. He would turn destruction on me—no axe, no, but words not expungeable. I saved what I could.

He has not told me much about the war. As far as I can make out his group—battalion or brigade or echelon—trained at a place called Aldershot and was stationed in Kent in the Battle of Britain, ready to turn back a German invasion. Then he went to Greece, and missed the evacuation but came out in a small boat with six others. He has not said much about it, but is neither laconic nor secretive. He added a part to himself in the war, necessary as an arm or leg, but as it grew it lost its definition. He has it, but does not know.

When he came home on furlough in '44 I pleaded with him not to go back. Hundreds of men were refusing. They went absent without leave. They demanded furlough extensions. Some were tried as mutineers. Not Fergus. "I'm going back. I made a bargain, Meg."

"You made a bargain with me."

He had no answer to that. His face took points of colour, but I saw how tough he was and how removed. I gave up arguing. But if anything, he was more aware of me and gentler with me. He could not give me what I asked, but felt he had payments to make. We were almost lovers on that furlough. I kept back only a small part. I had given up the rented house and gone with my children to Peacehaven. When Fergus came home from his trips to camp I met him on Millbrook Road with a bag of clothes. He would not wear his uniform in front of Dad, but changed into civvies by the creek. Sometimes he went swimming. He shinned up willow trees like a boy and ran along the branches and dived in the leaf-strewn water, holding his underpants on with one hand. Once, in a hollow in the grass, he persuaded me to make love. I would not undress. I felt foolish and girlish and pleased, but spent the next weeks in terror that I had conceived. Soon he sailed away a second time: Italy. Cassino. He was made sergeant. He did not come home again for another year.

Robert never came home. Well, he came home after twenty-five years. When the war started he said to me, "I'm not going." He never said more than that, even to Dad. His decision was not so much conscientious as intuitive. So it could not be argued. His call-up notice came in 1940. By that time Fergus was at Aldershot and the children and I had moved to Peacehaven. I brought the letter to Robert in the garden. He read it and handed it to me. "I'm not going."

Dad could get no sense from him and had to content himself with saying, "By a divine instinct, men's minds mistrust Ensuing dangers"—dangers, he made clear, not to Robert's body but to his soul. He would have liked him to be a political and a religious objector in equal parts, and the statement he prepared for him spoke with his usual eloquence of the "necessity of a New Way of Love beyond the old religions", and of "the pagan barbarities of the imperialist war". Robert went off to face the Tribunal with its sixteen pages in his pocket, but I don't believe he had read them, and he did not read them there.

We sat on benches in a small room above Queen Street. The King, that clerkish little man, looked down on proceedings that had about them nothing of the majesty of justice. We sat through the rustle of papers and the scratch of pens. Even that dreadful question, "What would you do if you saw a German bayonetting your wife and children?"—even that took a dusty sound. Robert said he would do his best to stop him.

"How?" the chairman asked, "with a bayonet or gun?"

"I don't have a bayonet or gun," Robert said.

"If we gave you one would you use it? Your wife and children, remember."

Robert could not answer. It was plain to him that he would do anything, use any weapon, to stop a German—anyone—from bayonetting children. But he saw he had been taken off his ground and he struggled to find a way back. Dad had his trumpet pointed at him, but had heard very little. He said loudly, "Read your statement, Robert."

"Quiet," the chairman said. He asked Robert if he had a statement.

"No," Robert answered.

"And you have no argument for appealing?"

"I'm just not going, that's all. I'm not going to kill anyone."

"You must do better than this. Have you any objection to serving as a non-combatant?"

"That's the army, isn't it?" Robert said.

"It is."

"I'm not going in the army."

They stood him down. Plainly they thought him half-witted.

Robert and I rode home in the train, leaving Dad in the city browsing in bookshops. He would buy heavily to cure his disappointment.

"I can't answer questions," Robert said.

"They're not fair questions."

"Yes they are."

"Do you want to go then?"

"I can't go."

He hung on to a knowledge that came from—where? A divine source? Came as spiritual perception? Burned as revelation in the sky? Or was it in his being, was it coursing with his blood, the knowledge of this not that, of here not there, of yes and no? He was never able to make it clear.

John Willis (as lawyer) gave Alfred a message for Robert. Alfred passed it on through me: When your final papers come report to the army and tell them you're an objector. Then you'll go to an objector's camp. If you don't do that you're a military defaulter, you go up in front of a magistrate and you'll get a sentence of hard labour in prison. I wrote it all down and told Robert.

"I'm staying here, Meg. They can come and get me."

And they came: a sergeant and a constable. I sent them to Willis's place, where Robert was doing a season in the orchard. It all happened as John had foretold. Robert spent the night in the Loomis lock-up, and the next day in town the magistrate sentenced him to two months hard labour. He did his time in Mt Eden jail and then went off to a detention camp for the rest of the war.

Twenty-five years later, we sat in the cottage and talked about those times. On fine afternoons we took chairs into the garden (the wilderness), to the spot where Bluey had told his beads and Dad had sat turning philosophies over with Wendy Philson; and I drank cups of tea while Robert washed his pills down with swallows of water and talked of Strathmore, Whitenui, Terrill's Farm, Hautu. He spoke of them in a bare way, yet I was fascinated, for here were years of his life that were lost to me, and as I listened I re-created them, I breathed a life into the dry-as-dust Robert he held up to me.

He began in Strathmore, out in the pumice lands from Rotorua. The barbed-wire fences bothered him. They stood eight feet tall and were elbowed in at the top. Their strands were less than a body's width apart, meant to tear a man. As he lay in his hut at night he felt the fences in his mind. Five hundred men were at Strathmore. He felt them too, like bees in a hive, and he felt a choking in the mess hall, in the social hall, as if he were in the middle of the swarm and could not get out. The one-man huts were no hardship. And scrub-cutting, scrub-burning, was work he understood. He went out daily into the pumice lands with no complaint. But in this camp, and in Whitenui, where he was shifted, his simplicity was under heavy strain. Robert knew a lot, had seen a lot, but had not thought at all.

The camp at Whitenui was on the banks of the Manawatu River. It was smaller than Strathmore. Robert was one of only two hundred men. The main work was grubbing weeds in the flax plantations owned by the Woolpack and Textile Company. Robert was soon in a gang building a railway into the swamps. The work was useful enough, yet Robert's greatest burden was a feeling of uselessness. That was because of the fence that cut the camp off from the world; and of the men detained, so it seemed to Robert, outside time. Whitenui was no place, time made no movement there. (It was, I supplied, listening, the Land of Missing.)

Men did not go mad there, or die there, but their lives closed down. They worked in the laundries, the cookhouse, and the camp garden, they played tennis and cricket and football, read books from the library van, played records in their huts, put on a play, talked about religion and politics; but they were shadows of men. They were sentenced to a compound outside time and outside place. This is Robert's view. There must have been many who did not share it. The religious objectors, I think he tried to say, lived in another world, a parallel world, where the laws were different—the Jehovah's Witnesses, the Pentecostals, the men of the Christian Assembly. Robert found he could not speak to them. Words would not make the journey between those worlds, but rattled like gravel thrown against a pane.

In the spring of 1943 Robert stood up from his bed. He had no watch but guessed it was after nine. Soon the screw Blacktracker would be round to lock the huts. Robert put on his warmest clothes. He turned out the light and stepped outside and closed his door. He walked down the line of huts to the back of the camp. It was easy enough to squeeze under the wire. All you did was find a place where the ground was uneven. As soon as he was outside he was greeted by tiny noises, tiny movements: a sound of water trickling, the touch of a leaf on his cheek and of cold air moving off the river. It was as if his senses had come alive after being held in a stupor for two years; as if the world had begun to roll on its axis and time to move again. He said simply that he felt alive for the first time since stepping into the police car at Willis's orchard.

He struck out up the river in the direction of Palmerston North. He walked on country roads while all around the fields grew sharp with frost and the ditches iced over. When the moon came up he climbed a fence and set off over the fields. Dogs barked at him from the backs of houses. The moon told him north and east and west and he kept heading north, not in the hope of reaching any place but because he was cold, had been cold for years, and north had the warmest sound and seemed to mean beaches and orchards and somehow summer. He did not mind being lost, he was lost somewhere, not locked outside.

Morning was clear, the grass was spiky with frost. A polar chill filled the sunless land west of the mountains. Robert walked into a farm. Beyond a row of macrocarpa trees men were yelling cows into a yard. He waited till the machines began to thump. Then he knocked at the farmhouse door and asked the woman who came if she could let him have some food.

"You'd better come in."

He warmed himself at the kitchen range while she fried him bread and eggs. When he was eating, she said, "Are you the man who ran away from the conchy camp?"

"Yes," Robert said.

"You've come to a dangerous place. My husband would shoot you. I think my son would too."

"I'll go when I've finished," Robert said.

She asked him if he had become a conchy because he was scared. Robert said no. She poured him a cup of tea. "You should be scared." She told him her husband had won a medal in the first war and her sons, Jack and Peter, had enlisted in the second as soon as it started. Jack had been wounded in Crete—

that was him down in the shed milking with his father. He was very quick, but he had a plate in his skull and was not always sure where he was any more. Peter had been killed in the desert.

"I'm sorry," Robert said.

"You're not the one who should be sorry."

She asked him where he was going. North, he told her. But first he was going to find a hayshed and sleep, he had walked all night.

"Come here. I'll give you a bed. They only come in for lunch." She showed him into a small bedroom, with a bed made up and photos of football teams pinned on the walls. "This was Peter's room. No, I don't mind. Keep quiet at lunch time, that's all you need to worry about."

He did not feel safe, but saw using the room as a return he could make her. He slept in his underclothes, and woke only once, when boots clumped in the yard and men's voices grumbled through the wall. The woman came back later. She gave him sandwiches and told him where to find the lavatory. He slept again, and woke in the late afternoon. Sunlight slanted through the shelter-belt and came under the half-drawn blinds. The faces of the young men in the football teams were lit up. Some grinned happily. Others tried to be tough. He wondered which ones were Peter and Jack.

He thanked the woman. She gave him a packet of sandwiches and a bottle of tea. "There's mutton and chutney and some gooseberry jam. I hope you get where you're going."

He went down to the road, hearing the noise of milking again, and turned towards the low hills on his left and started walking. He hid when cars came by, but soon the sun went down and he felt safer. The night was clear and starry and very cold, but after his day in bed he felt warm and strong. The bottle of tea was hot inside his jacket. He hid from three cars, but later in the hills nothing came, and he strode along in the moonlight whistling tunes Mother had played when we were young. Something heavy—a truck he thought or tractor—grinding up behind him had a friendly sound. Its lights slanted over the

156

hillsides into scrub and bracken. He had plenty of time to hide, but decided to try for a lift. It came up at last, an old Dodge truck with cracked headlights and high rattling sides. Two men were in it.

"Want a lift, mate?"

"Thanks," Robert said.

"Where you heading?"

"Anywhere up there."

"Hop on the back."

He climbed up and sat with his back to the cab. A dog lying there thumped its tail on the tray. Robert patted its head. Later he gave it the meat from one of his sandwiches. He drank some tea, only warm by now but very sweet, and wondered if he should offer some to the men in the cab.

It was then he noticed the moon had turned round, they were driving away from it, out of the hills. In a moment they turned on to a sealed road. He banged on the cab and peered into it. A moonlit face grinned at him. Slick in the yellow light, a scar showed, long and wide in the close-cut hair.

Robert sat down again. He wondered if he was being taken to Whitenui or to some quiet patch of ground to be shot. Soon he recognized the road to the camp. He ate all his sandwiches and drank the last of his tea and threw the bottle as far as he could into a paddock. It might save the woman trouble. That made him wonder if he could jump off. He went to the end of the tray but the scarred boy banged the window with his fist. He showed Robert a gun. So Robert sat with the dog and patted it and hugged himself against the frozen wind, and was reasonably content. He had had a day and a night. He knew the world outside was there and he could live in it if he had the chance.

They came up to the main gates of the camp. The driver reversed hard against the wire, trapping Robert in a cage. He put his head out the window. "Hey, yer bloody twits in there, we brung one of yer yeller-bellies back."

Black-tracker came, and The Screaming Skull. Robert

157

climbed the side of the truck and jumped to the ground. They took his arms and marched him to a security hut and locked him in.

"The next day," Robert said, "they sent me to the bad boys camp at Hautu."

"What happened there?"

"Nothing much."

That was a pattern for his answers. It seems to me what happened was something like this: he learned in Hautu things that shone a light back down his life and changed the way he saw a part of it. Hautu was cold and beautiful—the country at least was beautiful, bush and birds and mountains and a stream running by the camp. The working parties went out grubbing gorse and manuka. If you watched and were quiet the land began to stir with thousands of rabbits. Trout hung in streams as clear as glass. Far away, black bush on the mountains, snow along the tops, and a line as fine as a cotton thread marking the sky. That was all right. Robert was happy with that. But at night he came back to the compounds. He woke to them in the morning. And he took from them a feeling of betrayal he had known once before in his life and forgotten about.

If Hautu had a centre it was the place known as the Red Compound. It never left Robert's mind all the six months he was there. Everything turned around it. They broke the resisters, the real "bad boys", in there. In Robert's time there were only a dozen or so. Twenty years later, in the sun of our wilderness, in the ease of our sea-grass chairs, Hautu for Robert was: ten-foot high barbed fences, two of them, a patrol track in between, a verandah right round the camp for the guards to walk on; it was the cold mad glare of floodlights through the night, and search-lights tracking lazily over the huts; it was the bush beyond the lights—lights watching the men, bush watching over all, the black still bush; and at the centre it was the Red Compound, the huts with their barred windows and frames that opened five inches at the bottom, enough for white hands in the light and white faces of men who knelt to see what the world was like.

Robert understood that Hautu was mad. It was a madness he had seen before. He never brought this into the open for me, I understood from his silences, and sentences begun but not gone on with. He said, "Dad and Alfred . . ." He said, "I knew I could never go back to Peacehaven."

"Did Dad ever know this?"

"I never told him. I couldn't tell him that. I loved him, Meg."

Dad visited him when he was in Hautu, and again when he was at Terrill's Farm. They sat in the visitors' hut and talked, and Robert told Dad he was well, he was warm enough and had enough to eat and books to read, and he got on with the men, and he told Dad about the Jehovah's Witnesses and the Pentecostals and the couple of men from the Radiant Living Church and the Christadelphians, and Dad laughed at them and wanted to know how the politicals got on. Robert asked nothing about Peacehaven but Dad did not seem to notice. He came home and told me Robert was doing all right, and the next day posted him a parcel of books.

Hautu had Robert sick with 'flus and fevers. Back in Whitenui, he went down with pneumonia and had to be taken to Palmerston North hospital. I set out to visit him there. It was early spring, 1944. Fergus was in Italy. We had begun to see an end to the war. I caught the Limited on Friday night, and sat dozing and waking through the country and the towns, through Te Kuiti and Taumarunui, through the Spiral and National Park and past the mountains, and came to Palmerston North at four in the morning. I sat huddled in my coat in the waiting room. At nine o'clock I walked to the hospital, ready with my story of having come all the way from Auckland, and please could I see my brother without having to wait for the visiting hour. They told me he had been discharged the previous day and was back in Whitenui. I cried in a chair, I was tired and cold and I needed a wash and somewhere to lie down. A nurse brought me a cup of tea. She told me there was a local train to Shannon. From there I could catch a taxi to Whitenui.

So I got on the train and I paid for a taxi, ten miles through green farms with early lambs, and I came to the barbed-wire gates at two o'clock, and the guard would not let me in. I had not made arrangements for my visit. I pleaded with him but he kept an official face and said if I liked I could put my name down for a visit tomorrow, but today it was not possible, the rules were the rules. He would not even let me leave my parcel. (I had brought honey and a cake and a bag of grapefruit from Willis.) I looked at him with hatred—a weathered man with blue eyes and a handsome face. He had a strange lilt in his voice. Now I see it must have been Rhodesian, and he the one Robert called Black-tracker. I turned away so I would not hit him, and walked up the road, and turned round and came back and made proper arrangements for my visit the next day.

A farmer gave me a lift into Palmerston North. I changed my train ticket, and ate a pie and drank a cup of tea. In a cheap boarding-house I listened to the war news. New Zealand troops were fighting on the Adriatic coast near Rimini. I did not know if Fergus would be among them, but I lay sleepless in a broken bed and prayed (not to God, I did not know to whom) that he would be unharmed. I prayed for Robert to be well and happy. The next day I got myself to Shannon and shared a taxi with three other women to the camp, and a familiar Robert, a strange Robert, stood inside the wire and smiled at me.

He was weak from pneumonia. That did not cause his strangeness. Something inside him was strange. A part of his mind I had known almost as well as my own had gone away from me and could not be touched.

"Robert," I said, "the war is finishing. They'll let you out."

"Not till the troops are home."

"But that'll be soon. The Russians are nearly in Germany."

"The Japanese war has to finish too."

"That won't be long. You'll be at Peacehaven, Robert."

"I've got to go where there's no barbed wire." It was perhaps the completest statement he had ever made, and I did not understand it.

160

"There's no barbed wire at Peacehaven. It's your place, Robert."

He said nothing. He began to talk to me about his friends in camp. Bert Chambers had a gramophone in his hut and a collection of classical records. Bert was an orchardist from Loomis, Willis had helped him when he planted his trees. It was funny, Robert said, how many of the men in the camp came off farms and orchards. And Dick Jacobs—Dick had gone under the wire a month ago and they hadn't caught him yet. He had been sailing a yacht in the Pacific Islands when the war broke out, and he just kept on sailing. The French picked him up and handed him over to the Australians who passed him on to the New Zealanders. Now he was gone and it looked as if he'd made it. (Robert grinned at me from his sea-grass chair. "Remember I told you once about Dick Jacobs? He was Dick Webster, the bloke who bought my bach. He sailed his launch up the creek one day and I was building my jetty. He just about run his boat in the mangroves. Reckoned I brought it all back, the wire and all. He'd been up there ever since, changed his name. He was a good bloke, Dick.") And there were two brothers he'd got to know. Parminter was their name. They came off a farm in the Wairarapa, and they thought it was the Ark. Everything was damned outside the Ark. That was why they would not fight. The war was the start of the wrath of God.

"Crackers," Robert said. "But they reckon it's a good farm."

"Don't go there, Robert. Come back to us." But I saw he was gone. For the rest of my visit I sniffled in my hankie and dabbed my eyes, and Robert patted my shoulder, and I said things like, "Please don't, I'm all right," and "I know you'll do what you have to," and "We love you, Robert." I badly needed to sleep; and second class seat or no, I slept all night on the Express going home. I put Robert from my mind—or rather, I let the strangeness in him become Robert, and that was something I could not understand or soon be bothered with. I loved him as though he were dead.

When the European war ended the government allowed the

C.O.s a weekend leave. Robert went with the Parminter brothers to their farm. He liked it there and went back in March 1946, when he was finally released, and lived there five years, pushing the craziness of it to one side. According to Dad, who went to see him once, the Noah on that Ark, Tom Parminter, decided Robert was a sort of Christ. (That did not make him boss though.) I asked Robert about it, but he just grinned.

"They were all screw-loose. Nothing wrong with the farm though. That was all right."

16 My children ran wild at Peacehaven. I never knew where they were on those fifteen acres. I had grown into it, now they had their turn. Watching them, I imagined a pathway for myself into their lives: I knew places they believed were known only to them. There were dangers: shadows fell on me. From my bedroom window I saw Becky, fourteen that year, leading her boyfriend by the hand through the rhododendron trees above my bank. For a while I said, no, no, I won't interfere, but I could not stop myself and I crept down. There was a hideous creaking in my mind, time strained its joints. But there was nothing going on, no Fred-and-Esther work. Rebecca and the boy were eating apples and talking about tennis. She went red when she saw me.

"Come on, Mum, stop spying on us."

"I'm sorry dear, I just. . . ."

She seemed to understand I was caught on some barb from another time and she smiled at me with pity and laid it clearly down that things had changed.

"Buzz off, Mum. This is our place now."

She was a physical girl, tough and quick. Back in the house, I smiled with pleasure at her understanding. Because of her forehand drive and her somersaults and handsprings and her burping at the table I always underestimated her mind. Her affections too; perhaps her needs. Others filled them. She has been the happiest of my children. After her infant and her growing-up times, I can remember her hugging me only once. She was nineteen. She burst into my kitchen like a wind, the door smacked the wall and bounded back and crockery rattled in my cupboards. "I'm in, Mum, I'm in." She hugged the breath out of me and danced me round the kitchen. A better mother would have known at once: she had been chosen for the New Zealand basketball team to tour Australia.

I am getting ahead of my story. And I do not mean to write about my children. They had no path to that centre my generation of Plumbs turned about. I would not have wanted them there. Raymond saw more than the others, but knew enough to follow them into the world. He has lived his life as a Sole, not as Raymond Plumb, which I heard him once wishing for as his name.

Dad saw him as a Plumb. But then, he saw a number of people as that, Wendy Philson especially. Wendy though was not happy to be just an honorary Plumb. I shall be fair to her and say she loved Dad. In her way. And being already his companion, his disciple, his lover (in a narrow sense, though she would have said it was broad as the sky), she saw no reason why she should not be Mrs Plumb. I have said already sexual feeling is in her nature. She would have enjoyed loving Dad and becoming mother to new Plumbs.

I saw it all when I came to Peacehaven. I knew what was gone from Dad. I knew he had no strength now to take up life with a woman. Wendy should have known it, but she could not get properly rid of self (though that had been the goal of most of her strivings). So I worried. I had no need to.

"Meg, come in a moment. I've got something I need your advice on."

That was enough to make me put down my broom. I went into his study and sat on the stool.

"Life is funny, Meg." He did not hear my reply—"There's

163

not much in it makes me want to laugh"—but wagged his head and tapped his desk with his fingers. "Misunderstandings arise. The human mind is so imperfect. We can make it a clear stream if we try hard enough, but there are all these tributaries coming in. Muddy streams. It's most annoying."

I agreed it must be.

"The spirit, Meg. How to free the spirit from the flesh."

"Is this what you want my advice on?"

"Women's business, Meg. What do you think of Miss Philson? What's your opinion?"

"She's all right."

"Come my dear, you can do better than that."

"Why do you want to know?"

"I find myself in a difficult position. Wendy has been useful to me. No, no, it's more than that. I've grown very fond of her. As a daughter, mind. You don't object if I see her as one of my daughters?"

"Not in the least."

"It never crossed my mind she would want to be more. You know how good she's been. She's helped me in more ways than I can name. But Meg . . ."

"Go on."

"I don't understand women. Your mother was the only woman I understood."

"Go on about Wendy."

"It seems she wants to be my wife."

"I've known that for a long time. She's not going to be happy as secretary when she thinks she can be more."

"Well, she is more than secretary."

"But less than wife?"

"Oh yes. Oh yes.—Meg, she *will* look at me."

I was sorry for him. A seventy-year-old man should not have to put up with being sexual prey. I told him he must make Wendy's position clear to her.

"I have, Meg."

"That she's a muddy stream?"

He smiled—the nearest thing to a grin he was able to manage. "You mustn't take my flights too seriously. No. She is, of course, a very gifted woman. She has a good mind—very clear. If she could only keep the other thing out."

"Do you want me to talk to her."

"No, no, it's my duty. But Meg, you see—I can only love your mother. That's the truth of it."

I returned to my sweeping. I hummed as I went along and grinned to myself. I should have known Dad better. The man who had met his church head on and the state head on was not going to cave in to Wendy Philson—though she was a tricky proposition. She came to me in the kitchen. I thought she was going to hit me, but I kept my ground. I had got to the point in my life where I wasn't going to run.

"You're my enemy, Meg. And your father's enemy."

"Not in the least."

"You've interfered in something you don't understand."

"Some meeting of souls, you mean? I'm afraid it was one-sided."

We went on like that for a while. She had become a big woman, broad in her body, and physically she frightened me a little. But I grew sorry for her. She was a woman going after love and missing her clutch. She was in pain, she kept on turning, looking for a way, but could not find it. She stepped back all the time on her special ground.

"You can't destroy what we have. We are man and wife already. We are soul-mates."

"I'm happy for you to be that."

"We don't need blessings from people of your sort. We're above you, so far above you'll never understand."

"I'll make you a cup of tea, Wendy."

"We don't need bodies. We're on another plane."

"Then stay on it, don't pester him. He's an old man. Talk your ideas with him. He's happy with ideas."

"You don't understand happiness."

She stung me with that. "Perhaps I don't. But I know the sort of happiness you want. You want to be in bed with him."

She came at me. "We could have wonderful children, don't you see?"

"Soul-babies?" I laughed. "You're a stupid girl, Wendy. They fill their napkins too."

She sat down at my table and wept. She made a puddle of tears on the polished wood. I served her tea, and she blew her nose and thanked me. I had not meant to beat her so finally.

I was cross with Dad for several days. I went down to the empty cottage, and thought of Wendy packing up her love, carting it away, carting away her years of devotion to him, going off with uselessness at the centre of her life. I got myself in a state and I sat at the table and wept as Wendy had done. I told myself this was what men did with women, used them in one way or another and tossed them aside. I was angry at the part he had made me play. Yet thinking of them married, I saw how impossible it would be.

"Meg, my child," boomed a voice from the door.

"Who is she? What's she doing here?" another voice said.

"She is our landlord's daughter. What's this I see? Tears? Let me dry your eyes, child. You're too pretty for this." Bluey Considine advanced on me with a glued-up handkerchief in his hand. Behind him came a little black-dressed hunchback, stumping on a surgical boot, grinning—or was he snarling?—with a pink mouth like the mouth of the snake Robert had held up to me in California.

"I don't like women in the house, Bluey."

"Meg is special. She is the Reverend's daughter."

I had managed to put the table between me and the dreadful rag he offered me; and I managed to say, "What are you doing here? Dad's at the house."

"We'll be going up to see the Reverend. But when I noticed the door open I thought I'd show Roger our new abode. This is Roger Sutton, my good friend."

"Will she come here often, Bluey? You know how women interfere."

166

"Now, Roger. She'll make us puddings, won't you Meg? I can taste them already."

"Has Dad rented you this place? He never told me."

"He has his mind on higher things. Painful descents, Meg. We mustn't ask a man like the Reverend to bother himself with the world. But yes, it's ours, Roger's and mine. Just down the road from you, my dear. The dinners we'll have, eh Roger?"

"I do the cooking, Bluey. No visitors. Remember our agreement."

"Ah Roger, relax boyo. You're in the Reverend's country. Life is different here." Bluey was nervous though. He knew my dislike of him, as he had known Mother's, and he wanted to be settled in before I could upset things.

"Which bedroom will you have, Roger? You can choose."

"When did Dad arrange this?"

"Why Meg, he wrote me a letter. I had it yesterday. It came like a benediction. No, we mustn't use that language in the Reverend's country. Meg, it came like the offer of a five-course meal to me. If you could have seen the place we had you'd understand. A tin shack in Freeman's Bay. Stairs like an engine-room ladder, and Roger with his boot. And the lavatory—I won't offend you, Meg. Now listen, listen." He bent close to me (Sutton was inspecting the bedrooms), and in his Irish beery eye was a toughness I had never seen before. "You can see how it is with Roger. You can guess the care he needs."

But Sutton, club-footed, hump-backed, never moved me to compassion in the twenty-five years I knew him. Bluey now and then did, and this was a time. I said, "Oh, bring your stuff, but don't expect any puddings," and I walked out of the cottage, promising myself I would never go back. If Dad wanted Bluey as neighbour, Dad could pay with his time. But I knew it would be no pleasure to him. Bluey was a burden he had carried half his life. It was no act of selfishness having him there.

So Bluey's voice sounded in the study on afternoons, and Sutton fought his battle against convolvulus and did very well. He enjoyed hating me. He needed a woman around. Now and then I took a pudding down.

One day Esther walked into my kitchen. She sat down and asked for a cup of tea. Fred had driven her round, she said. He'd come to squeeze some money out of Bluey Considine.

"What money? What are you talking about?"

"Not in the world, are you Meg?"

"Yes I am. Further than you think. Has Bluey been betting?"

"He backs slow horses, the silly old bugger. And then he doesn't pay up. Fred's gunner have to twist his arm."

I was excitable in those days, I was turning all ways, in a rage I could not fasten on any object. But Fred!—here was something. It seemed I had a sight of all that was wrong. I ran down there. I came into the kitchen at a run. I had taken Esther literally and expected to find Fred torturing Bluey in some gangster way, and Bluey crying for mercy, and I was prepared to jump on Fred and beat him with my fists. I was not prepared for anything so casual as Fred sitting on the table swinging his foot or Bluey in the sofa, spooning up mouthfuls of rice pudding and plums. Only Sutton was right. He faced Fred like a terrier. He shook Bluey's shillelagh in the air. Fred was calling him a tough little rooster. When he saw me, he said, "Not another one."

"Get out of here, Fred," I said.

"Meg, Meg," Bluey boomed, "Mr Meggett and I are talking some business. I'm thinking of putting money into his firm."

"Get out before I call the police."

"Police?"

"Don't mention those people. They're terrible people, Meg."

"You be quiet. How dare you bring bookmakers into my house?" I meant on to Peacehaven, into our lives; and meant bring ugliness into the world. They could not follow me, and who can blame them? Fred, shocked as much as Bluey by my mention of police, tried to say he was only collecting a debt, but I would not be stopped. I grabbed Sutton's shillelagh and waved it at Fred. I told him to get out before I hit him.

"You're off your rocker, Meg."

"Go on. And take your wife with you. I don't want to see her."

"I'll tell her that."

"You do. Tell her she can come back when she learns to behave decently."

Fred left, and I rounded on Bluey and Sutton, I stamped my foot. "You too. Go on, both of you get out."

Sutton looked as if he would fight and Bluey huffed a little, but they went when I banged my stick on the table.

"She's mad, Bluey."

"She's upset. Come on, Roger. The poor girl wants a little time to cry."

They left me in the room, with its mutton smell and its framed racehorses, and I did not know where I was. I gripped the table edge and closed my eyes. I thought I was fainting, and I knew I was lost. Always I had found that serenity Mother had made in me, and rested there, but now it was gone, I turned but could not find it. For many years I had kept the image—kept it as a kind of explanation—of a small room at the top of stairs. I went in and bolted the door and was in *my* place, where no one could come—a white room with a clean bed and a ewer set and fresh water and outside a sunny garden with birds singing. I washed my face with water, I was new. But now I could not even find the stairs or see the door, I ran for them but they were gone, there was nothing there, and I fell, down, down, becoming thin as air—and Bluey was right in a way: I wanted time to cry—I wanted all the rest of time to cry. I sat on the sofa, let my tears run out, and felt they were blood running down my cheeks and my life was running away. I let it go.

Esther came for me. She took me to Peacehaven and put me to bed, and she and Mirth nursed me through the half year of my breakdown—an easy name, it annoyed me as I got better. And "got better" is wrong too. I simply gathered up pieces I could find of myself and started on a way they allowed me to go. I behaved acceptably; was, as one of Esther's Americans said, "an O.K. gal". But I knew I was robbed, and damaged by my loss. I waited to be whole for many years. People liked me better. I learned to smoke and drink. Dad was the only one who saw that

I was less than I had been.

Esther was determined that what I really needed was "a good time". She dragged me off to parties with Bob and Al and Spike and Tony Cucchiella. I had to be dragged, their voices reminded me of California; but once there I smoked my Lucky Strikes and drank my wine. An O.K. gal, in the words of Spike O'Dowd. I was sorry for Spike, loud and very young and always a step or two behind the others, but could not get Mother out of my head. Vulgar! Bob would just have got by. He did not chew gum.

Bob fell in love with me. He was a pleasant boy and I had come back far enough into life to be mildly flattered. That was all. I tried to be good to him. He was full of experience he could not digest, and saw me as the older woman, "wise in living" (the Americans are like that), who would help him come to terms with it. That is a way of being loved few women can cope with. But as I said, I was good to him and let him kiss me—nothing more. He said he would be killed when he got back to the war. Looking at his face (I had told him it was handsome and he said it was "kinda Boston"), I believed him. I saw how something as fragile as this, made of stuff like bone and flesh, must fall to pieces, war or no war, and I had no reason to doubt his fore-knowledge of the time. I put my own face in my hands as though I were holding it together and I felt tears running into my palms. I had these minor relapses, small "breakdowns". I turned and got away from Bob, not wanting him to see.

I think it was that night Esther got him to her bed. She had always liked him best and had only been filling in time with Tony Cucchiella. Soon he was telling her she was "wise in living" (Good God!). His face, he admitted, was "kinda Holly-wood". Her son Adrian, born in 1944, is Bob's, I'm sure. So Pittsburgh Irish genes got left in Loomis. When Spike wrote to say Bob had died on a beach landing in Iwo Jima, Esther sat still for a long time with the letter in her hand. Then she said, "What the hell did I expect? It was just a fling. Get me a glass of plonk, Meg." She would not let me kiss her.

Esther's Americans were privates and corporals. Fred mixed

with captains and majors: crooks in uniform. He called them "smart cookies", and that's what they called him. Everyone made a buck, the American way. Fred saw the war as machines, not men. He asked himself what would happen to all those trucks and jeeps when it was over. He asked his majors and they grinned and wanted to know what he thought.

There's a story that Fred leased a ship and sent it round the Pacific Islands buying G.M.C. trucks. He got them at a few pounds each and brought them back to New Zealand, where he sold them to farmers, mostly returned servicemen, at profits of two and three thousand per cent. Nobody seems to know whether it's true, and Fred just grins when he hears it. What is true—the newspapers made a huge story of it—is that he bought war-surplus trucks and jeeps from the government for twenty pounds each and sold them a few months later for four hundred pounds. Fergus clipped the reports of the Royal Commission hearing into the scandal. Looking at them, I see that Fred bought fifteen hundred trucks. The tyres and tubes alone were worth more than the whole price he paid. He stripped the power winches off some and sold them back to the government for eighty pounds each. "Scrap" he bought for eight hundred pounds was full of ball races and starter motors and generators. Fred claimed he took a great risk. He had no idea the demand would be so great. When it was pointed out he had made a gross profit of eighty-six thousand pounds and a net profit of at least fifty thousand, and acquired twenty-five thousand pounds worth of new capital assets, and that he still had sixty percent of the trucks to get rid of, Fred replied that he had the right, in the ordinary way, to get what the public was prepared to pay. Nobody quarrelled with that—not in the courtroom; and most of the people I spoke to had made a sort of swashbuckling hero of Fred. The politicians, the public servants, were the ones to blame: idiots they were, and maybe crooks.

Trade in surplus kept Fred busy for several years. Then he turned his eye on Loomis. Loomis was ripe for plucking—or, as he puts it, ripe for development. Don't ask me why no one else had tried it. These things wait for men like Fred, and others spend the rest of their lives talking about the chances they missed. They saw Loomis waiting there, but something held them back. Nothing held Fred back. Half a chance was all he ever needed. "Vision, gents," he says (uneasy with the word). I call it nerve. He's the boy who sticks his hand in the jar and steals the lollies. To hell with the risk! It's plain why people admire him and will keep on admiring him even when he's locked up. He does a lot of damage and some good, but they're not interested in that. He's not much interested himself.

Fergus watched him enviously. Back from the war, Fergus had changed, but other things were the same. He was working as a plumber, and trying to get enough together to start out on his own. He circled round Fred, sensing his chance lay there. He was too proud to ask favours, but when Fred set up his own construction company and started putting up blocks of shops on the Great North Road between the Loomis bridges, Fergus went to him with a plumbing tender Fred couldn't turn down. All Fred had to do in return was put up the money to get him started. I did not like it. I did not like any connection with Fred. But Fergus argued it was a plain business deal and once it was over he'd go his own way. That was how it turned out. I saw Fergus happy, growing in the post-war boom into *Fergus Sole, Plumber*, employer of three tradesmen and an apprentice. He spoke of overheads and tax. I thought it a game he played. He still went off each day in his working clothes and when I called at his jobs there he was on his back under a sink. He spoke to his men in their Middle East slang: *shufti* and *maleesh* and *bint*. I did not think he would grow into a boss.

Meanwhile, Dad grew old, he grew very old. He said about old age, "It's hard work, Meg. After this dying will be a treat."

His favourite place was the summer-house. He sat there writing in his shiny-covered red or black notebooks. He wrote nothing long. He had twitted me once for having nothing but "thoughts". In his old age thoughts were all he could manage. He always had a book with him, and many times what he scribbled down belonged to others: chiefly his favourites, Whitman and Emerson and Browning. He wrote a funeral service for himself. Even that was made up of quotations. He handed it to me in a notebook of its own. *Funeral Service of George Plumb*. It began: I have light; nor fear of the dark at all. I recognized that: Browning. Further down was a piece I did not know:

> Thy thoughts and feelings shall not die
> Or leave thee, when grey hairs are nigh,
> A melancholy clave;
> But an old age serene and bright
> And lovely as a Lapland night
> Shall lead thee to thy grave.

Dad had put a question mark beside it.

"But it's lovely," I said. "I'm going to leave it in."

"Still sentimental, Meg?"

"But Dad—"

"I want the truth."

"It is the truth. You're happy now, aren't you?"

"Oh, happy enough."

"And anyway, you've put in stuff from the Bible."

"There's a lot that's good there, Meg. All right, keep it if you must. There's another one further down."

He asked me to have it typed out. "No parsons reading it, mind. I want one of my sons."

"Which one?" Not Oliver. Not Robert. Certainly not Alfred.

"You choose. Don't bother me with that."

In his last year he wrote the story of his life. He put thoughts aside, and book-dipping aside, and looked at himself, with a fair amount of knowledge and not too many evasions—perhaps none, perhaps he came to places and was genuinely blind. Yes, that is it. He wanted the truth. I do not know where he found strength to begin, but strength to carry on came from his visit to Robert on "the Ark". He told of that visit; and of his disastrous meeting with Alfred. He said in the end he was ready to die; and he signalled his readiness by taking up a new notebook and scribbling borrowed thoughts again.

"What's he copying?"

"Whitman," Raymond said. "It seems a bit unfair on Uncle Alf."

"How do you mean?"

"Well, Whitman was—you know. It sticks out a mile."

"Raymond!"

"He liked women but he liked men too. All that stuff about beard and brawn and fibre of manly wheat. I don't think Grandpa sees it, though."

Everybody was wanting to criticize him. Alfred had smashed his trumpet. He seemed almost naked without it, he had lost some of his strength. Felicity mentioned Samson shorn, with his eyes put out. She had no sympathy. "Serves him right. You can't switch the world on and off when it pleases you. Alfred saw that."

Dad sat in his chair by the winter fire. The only way to talk with him was paper-chat. Everybody had that privilege now. Bluey came up and wrote in his copperplate hand, and sometimes forgot himself and blarneyed away. I heard him from the kitchen. Dad did not mind. I think he even picked up a bit of it. Most of their talk was about the old days—John Jepson, Edward Cryer, the wharfies' strike in Thorpe and Dad's trial for seditious utterance. They kept off religion. Once, when Dad was dying, I came in and found Bluey sitting by his bed holding his hand. I wished Raymond could have seen it.

At the end Bluey, who had been such a burden always, was Dad's most welcome visitor. I turned Merle and Graydon away and made Wendy wait if Bluey had called. Wendy tapped her foot and looked dangerous. "He can't like that old soak. You're a weakling, Meg. I'd soon throw him out."

"He goes much further back in Dad's life than you."

"What does that matter? The future is all that counts."

"Dad hasn't any future."

"You deliberately misunderstand. Well, never mind, I'll see he's not forgotten."

The Butterses took their disappointment better. They had

each other. They came to their mentor hand in hand with a new report on Oneness, and if he was not available went away to take a little more of it. Sometimes I let them in with Wendy. That annoyed her too, but it gave me the opportunity for telling all of them that time was up. Dad found them a strain. He would sometimes close his eyes and pretend to sleep.

Oneness, George, soon you will know, Merle wrote.

"He'll know," Graydon said.

"Not if you two don't give him some peace," Wendy said.

Oh the joy of it!

"Melting into God."

"They sound like a pair of ice creams."

Indeed we must believe that we have seen, when light suddenly dawns on the soul.

"Plotinus," Wendy said contemptuously.

"We've known it. He's known it too."

"He has. I give you that. He's known it in several lives."

"The future life is what counts."

"Agreed, agreed. But what would you know about it?"

"What we have seen."

Merle wrote, *George, now you are close, what can you tell us of the future life?*

Dad roused himself. "One world at a time."

Wendy pounced on the paper and scrawled, *Thoreau!* and Dad looked annoyed.

"Wisdom is transferable, Wendy. It belongs to no one man." He closed his eyes.

"He's tired," I said. "Everybody out."

"He's pretending," Wendy said. "He just wants to get rid of these two."

"He's communing. We know, don't we?" Graydon said.

"Everybody out."

I got them out of the house and went back to Dad.

"Please, one at a time Meg, not three."

I can keep the lot out if you like.

"No, no, they've been kind to me. But don't mix them

together. I don't know where I am."

They all believe in Oneness, don't they?

"They don't know what they believe. None of them. And Oneness is all very well—but Meg, I want to see your mother."

Willis and Emerson came to visit him. Esther came now and then. As a young woman, she had entertained him. He had seen her grabbing at pleasures, but knew that she was happy and generous. Now he saw her standing soul-less in the human world, turned into stone like a troll. I told him he was wrong, but did not press it. His extravagance came from sensibilities a little out of control in his last days. Good and evil pressed on him. He told me that all his life his knowledge of the evil in man had made him tremble with fear and loathing, just as his knowledge of the good had uplifted him. Orthodox theologies, he said, have a place for evil—that is one of the greatest of their attractions. We must resist that easy way. But that leaves us facing evil alone. He had never discovered how to fight it except to fight, in himself and in the world. He believed good was stronger. Faith in the end was his strongest weapon.

His dying though was not a time of battle but, for most of it, a tranquil running-down. He enjoyed Willis and Emerson. He laughed with them. Felicity paid a visit and was good. She kept her impatience down. I saw the way she must have been with him as a girl. She found pleasure in returning to it. And Dad lifted himself in his pillows, laying down Man's destiny to this strongest child. I was a little jealous.

Emerson came one Saturday morning in spring and took me for a ride in his Gypsy Moth. It was the aeroplane he had flown from England to Australia twenty years before. He was a well-known pilot now, a captain with TEAL, flying four-engined seaplanes across the Tasman; but real flying, he said, could only be done in small planes. He had tracked his Gypsy Moth down, found it mouldering in a barn in the Waikato, and bought it for a few pounds. He worked on it and now it flew again.

"Come on, Meg. I want to see how she goes with a passenger."

"You can get plenty of passengers."

"I want one of my sisters."

"Take Felix."

"Not me," Felicity said, "I'm too old for joyriding."

"Aeroplanes crash," I said.

"Not when I'm flying them."

"The Sundowner of the Skies," I joked. I wanted to go. I would be terrified, but I felt something might lie on the other side of that. And I could not turn Emerson down when he looked at me in his eager way.

"Come on, Sis."

"Yes, go on," Felicity said. "You need a break. I'll look after Dad."

We drove to Ardmore aerodrome. I put on a flying helmet and goggles. "No stunts, promise me."

"Bank left, bank right, land and take off." He crossed his heart.

He helped me into the front cockpit. A mechanic swung the propellor, and it was a wonder to me how something as solid as that could dissolve in a blur. I had never flown, but as we raced shuddering over the grass, and lost our weight, and the earth slipped into the wrong dimension, wonder kept me turning my head and crying back at Emerson. There was no place for fear. Thin streets and tiny cars and houses with cardboard roofs, lead cows and a tin sea, hills patted smooth by hand: all wrong, and recognizable to my special sight. Human kind seemed impossibly brave, inhabiting a crust of fields and streets through which they might fall at any moment into space. It seemed Emerson would be able to fly his aeroplane to the edge of the world and dive under it and we would find brown earth and the roots of trees.

Slowly as we droned along I lost this sense; miraculous perspectives shivered into ordinary. Emerson leaned the plane over to the left and right and I saw fields and hedges and milking sheds and small towns. Suburbs went by, racecourses, volcanic cones with houses up their sides. We flew over Mt Eden and looked in the crater. Emerson pointed ahead.

"Loomis?" his mouth seemed to say.

"Yes," I yelled.

We flew over the mangrove swamps at the mouth of the Whau creek and over the farms of Te Atatu. Emerson wheeled the plane and we followed another creek into the land. Children in coloured canoes waved their paddles at us. I saw a waterfall splashing into a pool. The brown salt water changed to green. "Moa Park," I cried. There were the diving board and the swings and the roundabouts and the pirate ship rocking on its axle. We had had our school picnics there. On that green strip by the creek I had come second-to-last in the egg and spoon race.

"Esther's place," I pointed. Shining-new, shining with glass and clinker-brick, it stood in the trees above Moa Park, pointing its glossy face at the town of Loomis. Emerson took the plane across the hill and swooped down waggling his wings. He banked at the bottom, almost touching the tree tops, and again we beat our way round. I saw birds flitting in the branches like sprats in water. Esther ran out on to her patio. She waved; a square foreshortened figure. The next time we came round she was back with a tea-towel in her hand, and a man with her. I saw the sun gleaming on his bald head. "Alfred," I screamed. His arms went up and down like railway signals. Emerson took the plane up high until we saw the sea again. He dived at Alfred and Esther. We went straight down at them. I did not scream, for I trusted him, but the world narrowed, shrinking like the pupil in an eye: park lost, then trees, then lawns, then the roof of the house, until the patio was left; and Esther and Alfred, faces white, dish-flat, on bodies short as tree stumps. They scuttled one each way. We zoomed past the chimney, we rocketed over the trees, and Emerson climbed, grinning, his joke over. He waved lazily at the two on the patio—they were clutching each other—and turned the plane along the line of the creek and our visit was done. I watched them, Esther and Alfred, I waved at them until a hill swung round and hid them from sight.

We followed the creek. I saw Loomis, the golden mile—

Meggettsville—and the railway settlement, where widowed Mrs Sole lived in her numbered house, still working herself to the bone, and saw the bridge by Millbrook Road, and then we were following the road. The white dust shone, the pools of the creek flashed yellow. Emerson leaned the plane this way and that, as he had leaned his motor bike on our night ride.

We made a wide circle round Peacehaven. Like Esther's house it stood on the side of a hill, but it seemed more to have grown out of it than to have been put down there. The terraces of lawn and garden made shallow steps up from the creek and the house under its hedge of trees carried on that natural-seeming rise and levelling-out. Over the creek was Merle and Graydon's castle, and Bluey's cottage in the wattle trees. Sutton shook his spade at us from the garden. He was angry at our noise. Bluey filled the door and put up his hand to shade his eyes as we crossed the sun. We ambled past Peacehaven, close and low. Dad sat wrapped in blankets in a chair by the French doors. Fergus must have carried him out before going to the cricket. Tea things stood on a table at his side. Felicity was pointing. I'm not sure Dad saw us.

Emerson climbed. I turned and made a fierce no with my mouth. He must not dive at Dad. He shook his head, pretending he hadn't meant to, and he took the plane across the orchard and the lawns. We came almost on eye level over the summer-house. Dad was ready and he waved at us. He was wrapped in blankets like a doll and had a blue woollen cap on his head, pulled over his ears. As we climbed away and turned for a last look I kept that little patch of blue in my sight. It was bright as a flower. We went up and I lost it. Loomis was under our wings. The creek and Millbrook Road ran side by side. As we droned over shrinking houses, I had again a moment of special sight. I was aware of Dad at Peacehaven and of Alfred on that patio two miles away. I saw their closeness and their pain. I saw like a bow in the sky the joining of them that would never break; and felt, like the sky we floated in, their distance from each other. I felt it like a distance between us all.

Emerson took us high. We coasted down to Ardmore aerodrome like a car down a hill.

"Come again one day, Meg."

"Once is enough. But I wouldn't have missed it. Thank you, Emerson."

By the time I got home Bobby and Raymond had lifted Dad back to bed.

"You were like a bird, Meg. It was miraculous."

"The noise," Felicity complained.

"He couldn't hear it."

"The story of his life. He just looks up and sees a great white bird."

"That's not fair."

"What are you girls talking about?"

"Tea," Felicity yelled; and wrote, *Tea. What would you like?* on his pad.

"An egg, I think. Boiled four minutes. Only your mother boiled my egg properly."

"Orders, Meg. Into the kitchen, girl. I'll hold his hand."

When I came back Dad was propped high in his pillows. His eyes were bright. Felicity smiled at him, nodding sharply and keeping quiet. He told her about Woman's Task in the Coming World. I put his tray in front of him and he said, "I've got good girls."

He lived into the new year. Labour was out; Fraser and Nash were out. Dan Peabody had lost his seat in Thorpe. Sid Holland was Prime Minister. New Zealand had what Dad called "a ruling party of cannibals". That was not one of his better shots. Since Labour had brought in conscription in the war he had lost all interest in politics and looked on parliament as a monkey-show.

January, 1950. I came into his bedroom and found him dead. He looked as if he had died peacefully. His face was more friendly than stern. It was faintly querulous. He did not look dead. His hands on the turned-down sheet had the look of resting. I covered them up. I went out and phoned my brothers Emerson and Willis. I phoned Esther and sent a wire to Felicity.

She and Oliver came up for the funeral. I showed Oliver the service Dad had composed. He said it was a disgrace. Felicity sniffed and said it was about what she had expected. But Willis, pleased to be chosen, read it in a bold and musical voice. He read it better than he sang *Danny Boy*.

> So be my passing!
> My task accomplished and the long day done,
> My wages taken, and in my heart
> Some late lark singing,
> Let me be gathered to the quiet West,
> The sundown splendid and serene,
> Death.

Yes, I thought, that's close enough. It wasn't quite like that, but it will do.

17 He had said Alfred would not survive him long. Is four years long? In Alfred's life that time was full of turnings this way and that, yet in another way it was just a breath.

John Willis was dead. No one took his place. That does not mean Alfred lived alone. He was seldom without a young man. Sometimes he had two or three in tow. They were not all his lovers. His house in Herne Bay became a centre for homosexuals. Alfred, at forty-five, was an elder of his tribe. He gave a roof, he dispensed wisdom; he took, I suppose, love when he could find it. Once he told Esther he had saved half a dozen lives at the very least, and saved the sanity of more young men than he could count, and one or two women. Saving his own was more difficult. Loneliness, in the midst of those young men, and drink, and hatred, were his troubles.

After Dad's death I went through the books in his study. Felicity and Oliver had taken some—Oliver the rare and valuable ones, Felicity said—and I chose others I thought Willis and Emerson might like. Esther refused books but took a painting. I posted Robert Dad's copy of *Walden*. One day I pulled from the top shelf a little selection of Shelley's poems. Bobby had left home to teach in the country and I was choosing books I thought he might like. As I climbed down the steps to put it on the desk I noticed several brown spikes poking from the pages at the top. They snapped when I touched them. I opened the book and found half a dozen pine needles inside. At first I thought Dad had tried to press them like wild flowers. Then it came to me that here, half-way through *Prometheus Unbound*, Alfred had stopped his reading one day, and marked his place, and climbed down from his tree; and that day or the next Dad had discovered him and turned him out.

I opened the book at the front. *To Alfred Plumb from his father. April 1922. Poets are the unacknowledged legislators of the world.* Alfred had scrawled his name at the top of the page. I put the book on the desk beside Bobby's pile and went on with my work, glancing at it from time to time. Mother must have found it in his room and put it on Dad's shelves, where it had stayed for twenty-five years.

The next day was Saturday. I wrapped the book in brown paper and walked into Loomis, where I caught the bus to town. Esther had told me Alfred's address. I took a taxi from the terminus. It drove through Freeman's Bay and Ponsonby and I thought this was just the place for Alfred—it was seedy, beaten-down. But Herne Bay was a surprise. Houses like Peacehaven, flowering trees everywhere. The gardens seemed tropical. I asked the driver to put me down at the end of Alfred's street. I meant to come up gradually on his world. I had the idea that the whole of a homosexual's life was sex. When they were not actually "at it" (Rebecca's phrase) they were getting ready, or recovering from it, or circling round each other, passing signals and intriguing. So I banged the gate at number 9 and walked slowly up the path, sniffing flowers, talking to the birds.

The house would have delighted me if I had been able to see it properly. It was like a wedding cake covered with fancy icing— fretwork, finials—yet it had a simple look, almost an austere look. On later visits I saw that Alfred had managed this by having the walls painted white and the roof stone-grey. The house was solid but light, frivolous but pure. I approached it along a red scoria path, sure it was a deception. John had left Alfred "rolling in it", Esther said; but here was a lack of ostentation, a signalling of wealth, I thought of as aristocratic. There had to be a mistake. Alfred could not be here.

Someone was playing the piano in a room along the hall. The music had the purity of birdsong. I waited for it to finish, but it kept on. At last I knocked. The player cut off with an angry chord. A young man came to the door. "If you're from some church we're Catholics here."

"No," I said, "I'm looking for Mr Hamer. Alfred Hamer."

"Is it business? He doesn't like being disturbed."

"No, no, it's a friendly call."

"Oh. Well. What name shall I say?"

"Mrs Sole. I'm his sister."

"Ah, one of the sisters." He looked at me with a friendly alertness. "I'm not sure he'll want to see you but I'll ask. Don't go away."

Alfred came cautiously down the hall. "Well, well," he said, "well, well." They were Dad's words, spoken with Dad's intonation. The small bald man was a Plumb through and through. "Meg, this is a surprise. I'd given up all hope of getting you to visit me."

"You've never invited me, Alfred."

"I thought you'd run a mile."

"Well . . . here I am."

"So I see. You'd better come in. It's lovely to see you, Meg." He kissed my cheek and took my hand, and pulled me over the doorstep. And seeing my fright, he gave a quack of laughter.

183

"No one will hurt you. There are no monsters in the thickets here. Only poor Bruce. You probably heard him playing. Bruce will make us a cup of tea, won't you Bruce? Or perhaps you'd rather have wine?"

"Tea will be nice."

"Tea will be naice. Try the wine, Meg. Burgundy from Burgundy, not Loomis creek. Come on, come on." He led me up the hall and into a room so bright and airy I felt I would float away. I looked around for something to hang on to.

"Sit down. Grab a chair."

"What a lovely room."

"You like it?" He smiled at me. I think he almost blushed. "This is my work. This is what I do instead of poetry. Come on, I'll show you. I'll show you my whole house."

We went back to the verandah and started from there. He had reason to be proud of it. If he had not had money he could have made a living as a decorator. Where I had expected darkness there was light—there was light even in his bedroom, even though the coverlet on his bed was midnight blue. I took that as a touch of defiance. There were mirrors everywhere, flashing light, opening into worlds from which my own meek face suddenly blinked out. There were paintings and photographs, beautiful and cruel young men, with their faces naked. The kitchen settled me—"clashing" colours stood side by side in harmony. I was learning something. But in the end—after bathroom, sun-room, guest-room, lounge again ("don't use that word")—I was not happy. There were signs of grubbiness, and a museum stillness, and I saw the house as something he had done and finished with. He seemed a little bored by the time we sat down. He was more enthusiastic about his wine.

"How do you like that, Meg? New Zealanders don't know what wine is. I don't waste this on Esther, you know. You're privileged."

"I love those curtains, Alfred. I just love them."

"Those? Swedish. I've got a friend who imports stuff. He gets my wine for me too. 'Tisn't easy."

"Could you get me some?"

"I don't know, Meg. . . ."

"I mean the curtain material. You can keep the wine. It's too sour for me."

He was shocked. "I give up. I give up hope for all New Zealanders. Here, give that to me, I'll drink it. Make her a cup of tea, Bruce."

Bruce ("I'm giving him a roof, Meg. Don't be nervous.") made me lemon tea and then sat at the piano, picking out notes softly and smiling at us with a sly goodwill.

"He wants to play. He's got a passion for music, haven't you Bruce? Apart from that he's a nosey little devil. All right, give us a tune. Show us how good you are."

While the boy played, Alfred sipped his wine (sip sip, sip sip) and topped it up and studied me. He suffered moments of love and hostility. Time had damaged his face, but expressions stay the same. He had loved me once and his love kept on, but I came out of Dad's world and he hated that.

I clapped when Bruce finished playing. He gave a professional nod. Alfred said, "You've showed off long enough. Leave us alone now. Go and mow the lawns. Earn your keep."

The boy showed no resentment. Cool in his blue shirt and belted slacks, insulated in his youth and skill, he was not touched by Alfred, who suddenly seemed petulant and seedy.

"I'll tinkle here. Don't mind me." Bruce smiled. "I'll play you something else later on."

"Bloody little skite." Alfred hauled himself into the other corner of his chair, turning his back on Bruce and facing me. "Well, what did you come for? What have you got in your little parcel?"

"Something of yours."

"Be careful, Meg."

"I thought you'd like to have it. It's something you left behind."

"I left nothing behind."

"Here." I offered the parcel. "It won't bite." But I had made a

185

mistake. His mind went rushing somewhere. I saw a burning on his skin and a pushing behind his eye.

"It's just a book. Please? For me?" I tried to charm him. What else could I do?

He forced his breath out with a tearing sound. "You're a stupid bitch."

"Don't swear at me, Alfred." I began to be frightened. "I'm sorry. I'd better go home."

He came out of his chair, springing frog-like. "Give that to me. Give it to me now."

He snatched the book and tore the paper off. The little green Shelley, gold embossed, fluttered in his hands like a bird.

"See the pine needles? You must have been reading it in your tree." Against his rage it was nothing. He shivered for a moment. His eyes took on an oily sheen. I tried to see where he was going. But he was quick as water. His feelings slid about like butter in a pan. I thought he might tear the book to pieces. But a gloating satisfaction came on him at last. "Meg, ha ha, we'll see. Bruce, where's my fountain pen?"

The boy fetched it from the mantel-piece.

"Alfred, Dad was proud of you," I said.

"Ha! Thank you, Bruce. No, don't go away. This is for you, my dear." He wrote on the fly-leaf, under Dad's inscription. "There you are. Show Meg."

Bruce made a face. He handed me the book. *To my dear young friend Bruce Barnhill, from his fellow twilight dweller Alfred Hamer, born Alfred Plumb. April, 1950.*

"Tells an interesting story, that page. Here, I'll put some wisdom in. A gem. He was good at gems. Bring it here, Bruce."

He wrote: *On the other side of the river is a boy with a bum like a ripe peach, and Alas! I have no boat.* "There. A good bit of life in that, don't you think? I'd like to see how poets would legislate for that."

"I don't want to have it, Alf. This is your game, not mine."

"You'll keep it if you want to stay here. Go and tinkle on your piano. A bit of crying music, please. Meg wants to cry."

"I do not. I'm going home."

"Go then. Go on. No, wait. Tell me what you thought you were doing."

"I was trying to stop you being unhappy."

"By bringing me a book from my sainted dad?"

"You can't hate him all your life."

"Can't I? You watch me. She's got a Jesus complex, Bruce. She wants to heal the world."

"Leave her alone. Have another drink."

"A Jesus complex, Meg. No, that's a bit on the firm side. What you've got is a female thing. All these emotions you pour out, it's as if you're bleeding all the time. So undifferentiated. It's almost biological, Bruce. I suppose it's got something to do with menstruation."

"Shut up, Alf. You make me sick sometimes."

"I make him sick! Go and tinkle, you little pansy bludger. That's why I keep you here. And don't you lose that book."

Bruce went to his room and closed the door. Alfred sighed. He poured more wine in his glass. After a while he took out his handkerchief and wiped his face. "You've had me sweating, Meg."

"I'm sorry I made you quarrel with your friend."

"That? That was no quarrel. You should hear us sometimes."

"I think I'll go now, Alfred."

"Good idea. The day's a bit of a wreck."

I telephoned for a taxi. While I was waiting in the hall Bruce put his head out of his room and whispered, "He's drinking himself to death."

"But only on the best Burgundy," Alfred shouted.

Bruce looked startled. "He's half deaf, you know. He's psychic." He shot back and closed his door. A moment later he was out again. "He drinks whisky too."

"Betrayal, Meg," Alfred called. "But I don't mind. He does it out of affection."

When the taxi sounded its horn he came into the hall. "Goodbye, Sis. Come again. But don't bring any books."

"Do you really want me to come?"

"Oh yes. Apart from John there's only been Esther and you. Bring me a rose from Mother's garden."

"We're pulling them out. And the orchard too. We're selling that."

"Bring me one before they go. But no emotions. O.K.?"

"Yes. O.K."

"I'm sorry about my shouting. It wasn't for you."

I became a regular visitor at his house. Fergus did not like my going there but I explained it was a family duty. That was a lie. Unless Alfred was too far gone in drink I enjoyed my visits. I never lost my nervousness of homosexuals. Touching between them, words of affection, made me uncomfortable. I was afraid they might start enjoying their sex lives in front of me, like dogs. Alfred was amused by my discomfort. Only once or twice it made him angry.

"We're people, Meg. There are other things in our lives."

I did see that. Music was more important to Bruce than sex. I grew fond of him and missed him when he went to study in London. I did not like any of the others so much, and they did not care for me. My nervousness did not amuse them. There were men there like estate agents and bank managers, and young men like rugby footballers—young men who were rugby footballers. None were as beautiful as Bruce and none, as far as I knew, were talented. I could not understand them desiring each other.

I understood the girls better—Ailsa and Pauline and Kay. Alfred explained there were no sexual connections amongst those three. That made me a little more easy with them. But when Ailsa came in one day with Joan, her lover ("butch", Alfred said; the meaning was plain at once), I almost had to leave the room. Later I came to like her very well. She was an artist. I went to one of her exhibitions and bought a painting of two little girls, one with Ailsa's face and one with hers, building a castle in a sandpit while their mothers gossiped, drinking tea. It troubled me a little, but the girls had faces smoothly white, one plain,

188

one beautiful. I saw that they were living by some inner rule or logic. I saw they were themselves. But while I tried to explain that to Joan, I found myself caught on her difference; I imagined her and Ailsa doing things to each other, and I looked at her as though she were an animal in a zoo. She saw. I'm not sure why she bothered with me after that.

My usual day for visiting was Saturday. I never stayed to the parties. Tea remained my drink. Once it fell to me to answer the door and explain to a pair of Jehovah's Witnesses that we were all good Catholics in this house.

"You did that very well."

"I've no patience with them. How can they believe that stuff?"

"Easy. Belief is easy. Look at Felix."

"More nonsense," I said.

"At least the tikes have got some style. They please the senses. Shall I nail a crucifix on the door? One with lots of blood?"

Once when Felicity was up I took her with me to Herne Bay. It was a dangerous thing. I took the precaution of telephoning first. Alfred was pleased, and apprehensive. As our taxi took us through Ponsonby, I reflected on the complex of feelings in him. I saw how their strain against each other must stretch him almost to a breaking point.

"Don't talk about Dad."

"I'm not daft."

In fact, she was cleverer with him than I could be. She praised his wine. She got him talking about mother, and growing up, and his university days; and, at last, about his discovery of his nature. I was on edge. I expected Dad to rear up at any moment. But they trod around him without seeming to know that he was there.

"Didn't you ever like girls?"

"Oh yes, you bet I did. I liked anything beautiful. When one of Meg's little friends took down her knickers and showed me what she had—I'm not making it up, Madge something,

189

Meg—anyway, I thought it was a lovely little place. But boys were lovelier. There was never any question in my mind. I could look at myself, Felix. Living proof."

"What about now?"

"Now? If a woman made a pass at me I'd run to the ends of the earth."

"So you really are one?"

"The genuine article."

He was flippant about his agonies. He had us laughing with talk of his "runaway organ"—even I laughed—and his lusting after boys on tennis courts. "They were so pure in their whites. That was part of it. God, I was confused." He had known he was real but thought he was possessed. Later he had thought he was a freak. Then he discovered from books there were others like him. But where? Where?

"They must have been in my class at school. They must have been thick on the ground at university. I know for a fact they were. But I never found them. I can't work out now why they never found me."

John came along. Alfred did not like the look of him. But John knew Alfred. One day he took him by the hand and said, "Isn't it time you found out who you are?"

"What are you grinning at, Meg?"

"He sounds as if he'd been reading *Bab of the Backwoods*."

"What?"

"Never mind. What about that lipstick you wore?"

"Ha! My transvestite phase. Lasted half an hour. I was never one of those. John showed me who I was."

John was his great love. He never found another. It was bad luck for him that he came on it first and came to promiscuity second. The other way round would have been better. He lived with John for twenty years and when John died Alfred had only the experience of love to carry with him into his twilight world. He kept his loneliness to himself. He became an elder of his tribe.

While we talked a woman came in and sat down on the squab

190

by Alfred's chair. She was dressed in scarves and bangles and bright bits of cloth. Dresses were down to mid-calf that year, with waists of elastic. There was nothing of that for her. Her dress came to her ankles. It was belted with a piece of plaited leather hung with Pisces, Taurus, Scorpio etc., in brass and zinc. I thought she was probably trying to look like a gypsy, though her high-bred English face gave her little chance of that.

Alfred introduced her as Sybil.

"We're in for an oracle," Felicity whispered.

It was less than that. Sybil read handwriting. "She's done me," Alfred said. "Tell them what you found, Syb."

Her voice was rich and trembling—her most attractive part. "He is seeking a great love, but it eludes him. In his past there is great love and bitter sorrow—"

"Keep off that. Stick to what's up front."

"He is destroying himself. Unless he finds a love that cures him—"

"She doesn't mean earthly love, she means divine."

"Time is short unless he discovers that."

"She thinks I'm for the chopper." Alfred drew his hand across his throat.

"I see violence, Alfred. Take my warning."

"She won't say what sort."

"Because I don't see what sort. But it's there. Not far away."

"Good, isn't she? She's a real performer."

"He doesn't take me seriously. That's one of the penalties of my gift. And the pain of seeing too much."

"What do you think, Felix?"

"What should I think?"

"Let her try you. Come on."

"I will not."

"It's not a sin. You wouldn't have to confess it."

"It's got nothing to do with that. I won't be a party to confidence tricks, that's all."

"How about you then, Meg? I'll pay."

191

"Oh no." The woman made me nervous. She had hit on some truth about Alfred, and that showed insight, whether it came from handwriting or not. I was disturbed by her prophecy and wanted to be left alone with it. Alfred brought a pencil and pad. He put them on my knee.

"Come on. Give it a birl. There's no dirt she can dig up about you."

Sybil pushed her squab close to my chair. "Just write what comes into your head."

"I don't believe in it," I complained. I wrote my name and address.

"Oh come on," Alfred said. "Something with a bit of meaning in it. She's not just reading your character you know, she's telling your future."

"If I write something with meaning it'll give her a clue."

"This will do," Sybil said. "In fact, this is perfect. I need some quiet now."

Alfred shifted her squab into the corner by the piano. "She goes into a trance," he whispered. "The handwriting starts to tremble and then it speaks to her. Course we can't hear," he grinned.

"You don't believe this nonsense?" Felicity said.

"She's a pro. This'll cost me a quid. So we'll play along. You've got to admit it's a pretty good performance. Look at her."

Sybil, in the shadows, in what might very well have been a trance, black and red and green and gypsyish, did appear to me a person who might possess some occult power. Felicity snorted. "Let's go outside." Sybil gave a small sigh. I thought it had a gloating sound. I was not happy leaving her with my name and address.

We sat on the lawn underneath a flowering cherry tree. Petals fell on our shoulders. Soon Joan and Ailsa joined us, and one of the managers came in with his boyfriend. I wondered if spring and flowers and singing birds worked a magic for that kind of lover. Joan winked at me.

Later a starved-looking boy came up the path. He turned when he saw us and made back for the gate. I saw a grey bandage on his wrist. Alfred called his name and ran after him. For several moments they talked in the shade of trees by the garden fence.

"He cut his wrists," the manager said. "Alfie's good with these kids. If anyone can put the poor little blighter right he can. It's dangerous though. Alfie takes too many risks."

I did not understand. Joan explained, "They're so unstable, these boys. They're like quicksilver. It would be easy for one of them to turn against him."

"Attack him, you mean?"

"No, no. Tell someone. It could end up with the police."

The boy came back with Alfred. He sat down awkwardly and kept his silence. He had warts on his neck. It was always a puzzle to me to discover homosexuals could be ugly.

I wandered in the garden, picking flowers. Down at the end of the road a white railing marked the edge of a cliff. Yachts lay becalmed on a pearly sea. Nature was indifferent, I thought. Coming back, I found Joan waiting for me. "I know what you're thinking, Meg. He helps these people but nobody helps him."

"He's so lonely. And he's drinking so much."

"We try, Meg. We do try. But there's this thing he won't let us talk about."

"Come on, Meg," Alfred called. "It's time we saw what Sybil's dreamed up about you."

The woman had come out of her trance and was enthroned in Alfred's chair. She spoke in a voice that seemed to come out of caverns, but what she said was ordinary enough. She told me I had been a happy child. Family was my emotional ground. She told me I was lucky in my husband. Heart ruled me, not head, suffering therefore could not be escaped, but happiness for me would be intense. Sentiment though was a danger to me. I had let it cloud my love and distort my view of the real world. Sentiment, she said, was an illness I suffered. Even those ruled by the heart must strive to achieve clear sight.

"That's pretty good," Alfred said, "that's not bad at all."

"Anyone could tell that just by looking at her," Felicity said.

"Ah wait, give her a chance, you haven't heard the prognostications yet. Come on Syb, give us a bit of gloom."

Sybil lowered her eyelids. There was something reptilian about her. She seemed to sleep.

"Now don't play hard to get."

"The future is not clear."

"That doesn't surprise me," Felicity said.

"I was working in a fog." Her eyes flicked open and fixed on Felicity, making it plain who was to blame for that. Then they came to me, changing on that quarter turn from spite to melancholy. "But I saw a great tragedy. And then I saw one come and teach you to see."

"Do you mean one with a capital O?" Alfred asked. He grinned at me. "You don't feel religion coming on by any chance?"

"What sort of tragedy?" I had strongly at that time a knowledge of the body's fragility, and with it precise visions of dreadful events. I saw my children crushed and burned and torn.

Sybil turned her eyes on Felicity. "I could not see. Unbelief brings a darkness down."

"Mumbo-jumbo," Felicity said. "Come on, Meg. I've had enough of this woman. We'll go home."

"You didn't see any of my children in danger?"

"Oh Meg, she's a fake, can't you see?"

"Relax, Felicity," Alfred said. "Give old Sybil a chance. She's just an honest working girl, aren't you Syb? Don't spoil her act."

Sybil said, "I know when I'm not wanted."

"Oh stay. Have a glass of wine. You can do some of the others. Do Joan. I'll pay."

So Joan wrote down her name, and we trooped out to the lawn again and sat under the cherry tree drinking wine and lemon tea. Soon our taxi came. Felicity hugged Alfred. She told him to be good, and he crossed his fingers, grinning, and promised he'd try.

In the bus going home she lamented the waste of so much good feeling and good sense. I did not think it wasted. I had seen how useful Alfred was and how well loved. I talked about his loneliness and his drinking. Neither of us could think of a way to help him.

Esther was the only one who could help. He loved her far above me.

18 Esther, in her palace above Moa Park, was going through a bad time. She did not love Fred, but it had little to do with that. They had given each other licence to "play around". He had simply shrugged his shoulders at her Yanks. If he knew the boy Adrian was not his he gave no sign. Esther and he were "buddies"—she said "mates"—in a confidence trick they played upon the world. At least, for Esther it was a confidence trick. She never understood where the money came from, and seemed to believe that as long as she kept on grinning and "whooping it up" things would get better all the time. She did not know she had an emotional life.

Fred passed out of that world while her back was turned. Fun drained out of him. He settled down to make money seriously. His experience in building and letting shops in Loomis convinced him there was a fortune to be made in commercial properties. He saw what he had done small he could do large. Meggett Enterprises became his life. I do not mean that business was all of it. He found a kind of propriety in letting his appetites go.

It was some time before Esther discovered she was alone. Her "good times" kept on for several years. Then she began to see that good was gone, they were no more than noise. Fred was somewhere else, her buddy no longer. His girls did not worry her even then. But to be outside the trick he played on the world, that money-gathering trick, was to be without her habits of twenty years; her certainties, her resting place, her home and hearth; things that she had never known she had.

She turned to Adrian, to Alfred, and to drink. Her care of her children had been rough at the best, and very much off and on. Now, for the younger, it became obsessive. Fred had no part in Adrian. Her retreat into love for the child—I'll call it love—punished him; although I doubt he noticed. His focus could no longer be shortened to take in domestic events. He had his own construction company putting up buildings large and small, not only in Auckland but all over the North Island. And he was involved in mortgage gearing—borrowing huge sums of money, shifting them here and there, and coming up in the end with returns for himself of twenty and twenty-five percent. It was legal, but it was risky. Fred took the risks. People began to say he was a millionaire. Once the word would have made Esther squeal and throw a party. Now she said, "What the hell, it's his not mine." Fred too made a sour face: trying to make out there was something special about a million was just a way of tying a man down. He didn't know how much he had, he paid an accountant to look after that sort of thing.

Fergus's career had been going well too. He waited for what he thought a decent interval after Dad's death and then suggested we pull the orchard out and subdivide the land as building sections. "I know how you feel about the place, Meg, but no one's looking after the trees—it's not worth even picking the fruit. The land's going back. We could really make a packet out of it. The way I see it is, we bring a road in from the back, right down to the creek, and make a turning bay there. . . ."

I thought about it for several weeks. Bobby had gone to do his country service, Rebecca was shifting to a flat in town, and Raymond, after less than a term, was talking about giving up university and training as a journalist. He had an attachment to the orchard, but it was romantic rather than practical. No one had given the trees proper care since Robert's time.

I went walking there in the dawn. I had to decide. Fergus had waited long enough for his answer. I looked at the bearded trees, with bare branches and sweet apples high up. Dew gleamed in spider webs. The little stream coming down to the creek oozed through patches of swampy ground where tea-red water lapped about my gumboots. Brambles stood in banks as tall as houses. This had been elf country once. Now it was nothing special.

I walked in the hollow where Alfred and John Willis had made love. I felt no fear, though always before I had approached with a shiver, half-expecting to find something hideous there. It was an unattractive place. Gorse and bracken stood in clotted lumps. On the far side pear trees rose clear of the undergrowth. They were hung with brown withered-looking pears. I waded into the bracken and found the rotting quince stump with my feet. I stood on it. Dad had forced Robert to chop down the tree. I thought of his behaviour with impatience, nothing more. It was as if I had held my nerve: figures haunting the place were only fence posts; moans and cries of passion were the wind. I saw the orchard in Fergus's way: land "going back". It gave me a lonely feeling. But then I thought sensibly that if my life at Peacehaven was locked in me the orchard as it had been was there too. So let the bulldozers come, let houses go up and new people move in. The place might just as well be used. I walked down to the house and announced it to Fergus. He was pleased with me. I was glad to have made him happy. Later in the morning I wondered if I had shrunk or grown.

The bulldozers came the following summer. We let the trees dry out, then made a huge bonfire. It looked as if a building was on fire. I walked up with Fergus after work and stood by the embers. All around, the land was scraped to its clay. A tar-sealed road and concrete footpaths ran down to the creek and surveyor's pegs marked quarter-acre sections.

"Forty-three new houses, Meg. That's something."

"You can do the plumbing."

"I'll do more than that. I'm going to build them."

"Won't that take a long time?"

He laughed louder than was necessary. "Not with my own

197

hands. I'll set up a company. We'll go in for house construction in a big way."

"That'll take money, Fergus."

"Sure, sure. I've got that all worked out. . . ."

He had talked to Fred. The new company would be part of Meggett Enterprises. Fred would have the controlling interest in it. "But I'll be the manager. I'll have the say," Fergus said.

"So what you'll do is use these sections to buy yourself in with Fred?"

"He's going places, Meg. I don't see why we shouldn't tag along." I tried to break in but he shushed me. "I know what he's like, you don't have to tell me. But I'm the one who knows about house construction. As long as we're making money he won't stick his nose in. We'll have our shares in it Meg, and my salary too."

"You were happy as a plumber."

"That was small stuff. This is my chance to get in with the big boys."

"Is that what you want?"

"I can't stand still. You'd like some real money, wouldn't you? You'd like a better house?"

"I'm not leaving Peacehaven."

"It's getting pretty crummy, Meg."

"Spend some of your real money on it. I'm not leaving."

The argument shifted its ground. I gave way on the construction company but would not give an inch about the house. Fergus nodded and grinned. "O.K. It's a deal."

So Fred Meggett sucked my husband in. The new houses went up and Fergus was happy. He drove around in a flash new car with *Sole Construction* painted on the door. He was off to Hamilton, to Wellington, to Christchurch, even to Sydney. When Meggett House went up in town Sole Construction had a whole floor and Fergus an office as big as our sitting-room, with a secretary posted at the door. He never tried to live Fred's sort of life. He liked to dig in our garden and go to the cricket. His idea of a real break was a weekend fishing trip with friends; and
198

letting his hair down—he had nothing against it—a party, a few beers, jokes in the kitchen. Fred sucked him in but did not spoil him. I admired Fergus. Sometimes I wished we could be more than friends.

Esther declared him too good to be true. She was sure he had a secret life and she joked with me about office girls and dives of sin. Alfred found it easier to believe in him. He had named Fred's world The Sties and Fred King Porker. Fergus became The Pig Immaculate. The name made me angry. I reminded Alfred of his own wealth, which he had done not a hand's turn for. "True," he said, "but I pretend to no virtues. Fergus does. Well, he doesn't pretend. But you do, don't you Meg? And you're just a fat little piglet, really. You've got your snout in the trough."

"None of us would please Dad any more." That shut him up. He poured himself another whisky. We were at Esther's place, at the patio table, on a summer afternoon. At the bottom of the hill Moa Park vibrated with children. The wooden moa nodded at the gate and the pirate ship showed its Jolly Roger in the trees. We could see a stretch of river, with coloured canoes paddling back and forth. Fergus was in Sydney, setting up a deal in prefab houses. Fred was "away". The three of us, three Plumbs, well fed, discontented, self-pitying, sat at the brick table making ourselves silly with strong drink. Now and then Esther jumped up and ran inside to see Adrian, who was in bed with the mumps.

"She fusses over him too much," I complained.

Alfred shrugged. "He's all she's got."

"She's spoiling him. He's unbearable enough as it is."

"Are you scared she'll turn him into another queer?"

"Nonsense. I never said that."

"You're thinking it though. You really can't stand us, can you? You come among us as though you're kissing lepers."

"That's not fair."

"What you'd like is a little magic pill you could slip in my drink. Make me normal, eh? I'll tell you Meg, you'd be killing me."

"You've had too much to drink. We all have."

"What have we got but drink, you and I? And that poor old wash-tub in there. We might as well enjoy life while we can."

"That's not true. I've got a lot more." And I meant it. "I don't even like this stuff. I'm only trying to keep you company. But why should I bother?" I pushed my glass away.

Alfred laughed. "Good old Meg. A drunkard through compassion. You're a real original."

"I'm not a drunkard. Please Alfred, do we have to talk like this?"

"My little sister wants me to be nice. O.K., I'll be nice. I really do love you, Meg. But I hate you too. You look like him."

"So do you."

"I know. Look. Look,"—touching his round Plumb forehead and his cheeks. "And look, I'm bald. Look at these, I'm going deaf. What a revenge he's having. But I've got one trick left. I'm alive, he's dead."

"You're so nasty, Alfred. Sometimes you make me want to vomit."

He put his head down. I thought he was going to cry. He stayed like that a long time. I saw how far he had let himself go—black fingernails, grime in his scalp. I began to think I smelled him: a smell of clothes worn too long, and a dunny smell. I saw him purely, as my brother, whom I loved, and I began to get up and go round the table to him.

"Don't talk to me like that. I've got nothing left."

"I know. I know."

"Don't touch me." He pulled away. "You don't have to touch me, Meg. I know you and I are all right." He stood up and went to the French doors. "Pour me another whisky while I'm gone."

Soon, through the house, I heard him piddling in the toilet. He had never learned to close the door. Mother had followed him there and pulled it shut, averting her eyes. I wondered what he would say if I did that.

Esther came back. "Where's Alfie?"

"In the dunny."

"Dunny, Meg? You are getting crude."

"How's Adrian?"

"Suffering, the poor little bugger. He wants to get up."

"And you'll let him, I suppose."

"I will not. What's the matter with you? Have you and Alf been quarreling?"

"He's drinking too much."

"You can't stop that."

"I can't stop anything. Nor can you. I thought you could once, he's always been closest to you, but it's too late."

"You are getting morbid. Alfie's all right. I don't know what he sees in those boys, but that's his worry. Where is he? Where are you, Alf? I'm trying to keep him away from Adrian."

"What?"

"Well, you know, he's a good-looking kid. It must be a temptation."

"That's ridiculous."

"You can't be too careful, Meg. I wouldn't want Adrian— you know?"

"But Alfred's his uncle. Adrian's a child."

"And Alf's a pansy. I've got to be realistic."

"But Esther—" She was gone into the house and I followed her. I could not believe this. But there she was at Adrian's bedroom door, hooking her finger at Alfred and saying in a merry voice, "Come on out of there."

Alfred was sitting on the bed. He did not understand. "Hold on, I'm telling him something."

"Out, Alf." She took his arm and pulled him to the door. "You go to sleep, Adrian."

"I'm talking to him. He's not sleepy, Esther."

She took no notice, but got him into the hall. Then she closed the door. She turned the key. "That room's out of bounds."

Alfred understood. His high-coloured face took a yellow tinge. Water came from his eyes. He whispered to me, "She's not serious, Meg?"

"She's not. She's just being crazy."

Esther said, "You can look Alf, but you mustn't touch. Them's the rules."

His nose began to run. "I'm a homosexual, not a paederast. Meg, Meg—" he turned to me—"I wouldn't touch him."

"Come on, we need some more hooch," Esther said briskly.

"Adrian's my nephew."

"She's crazy, Alfred. She's not well. She doesn't know what she's saying."

"I know, all right. I've said my piece. And now we know where we stand. Come on Alf, wipe your silly face. You look a sight."

Alfred ran out of the house. I followed him and caught him at his car.

"Alfred, she didn't mean it. Please come back."

I pulled him by his arm but he jerked free. "I've got to get out of here."

"Come back with me. I'll make her apologize."

He got into his car and closed the door. "How? . . . How? . . ." I don't know what he was asking. I tried to tell him I would see him tomorrow, phone him tonight. But he looked at me in a way that held no recognition. He was gone out of my world.

"She loves you, Alfred. She really does."

He drove away. When the car had turned behind the trees I went a dozen steps back and screeched at Esther on the patio, "You bloody fool." I could not bear to be near her. I got in my own car and drove home. When she rang me later I banged the phone down. I could not bear her—stupid and destructive and self-indulgent. I thought that very likely she had killed Alfred.

That night I rattled around in my big house. It seemed to be full of ghosts. From the verandah I looked at the Sole houses over the creek. I had grown snooty about them—raw and ugly on their scraped-down sections. Tonight they were huddled in a cosy way, in company. I tried phoning Alfred. Ailsa told me he had not come in. They were waiting for him. Bruce was home on a visit but the party could not start till Alfred came. Parties were never the same without old Alf. I spoke to Bruce. He told me not to worry. Alfred had all sorts of haunts. He'd be home before long with his tail between his legs. "Come in tomorrow Meg and I'll play you a concert. This piano's got cobwebs in it though. It's a real mess."

"Bruce, he was upset. And he'd been drinking."

"Don't worry, Alfie doesn't do silly things."

I rang Esther. Adrian answered the phone. He said his mother had gone to bed. That meant she was drunk. I asked if he was all right and he said he was great, his mumps had gone down and he was making a feast. Uncle Alf hadn't turned up again.

I sat on the verandah, drinking tea. The lights went out in Merle and Graydon's house. Down in the trees Bluey's cottage was dark. In one of the new houses people were playing cards at the kitchen table. Loud music came from further up the street. The singer was Johnny Ray, Rebecca's favourite. His howls rang along the creek and tightened like a lassoo round the houses. In a back garden a man was digging a hole.

At midnight I made my last call to Herne Bay. The party was subdued. They had rung around and no one knew where Alfred was. Everyone was going home, Bruce said. He would leave the light on for Alfred. The silly old dear had probably found the hairy beast somewhere.

I lay in bed and tried to read a book, but could not make one sentence follow another. I played over accidents he might have. I saw fire and deep water and high cliffs and a plunging car. I cancelled Alfred's deaths by calling them up.

I was wakened by the sun shining on my face. A thrush was singing. The fears and dreams of my night pushed to come back, but met the sun, the day, the singing of the bird. I got up busily and made tea and toast and boiled an egg.

I was spooning up the last of it when the telephone rang. "Bother," I said.

"Is that you, Meg? This is Bruce. Meg, something's wrong. The police have been. They wanted the names of Alfie's next of kin. Meg, are you there?"

"Yes."

"They asked all sorts of questions. What was he doing last night? When did I see him last? Meg?"

"Yes?"

"Next of kin? Why would they want that?"

"It means he's dead."

I took it like a knife driving into me, but took it calmly. When the detectives arrived I was waiting at the door. I told them I had seen my brother last at four o'clock yesterday afternoon. I told them he had been drinking and was in an emotional state. In return they told me he was dead. They tried to say it kindly and would not tell me what his injuries were or put a name to the way he died. A man walking his dog had found the body at six o'clock that morning in the trees at Moa Park. Alfred had been assaulted: that was all they would say. They asked me if there was someone here, my husband perhaps, who could make a formal identification. I told them Fergus was in Sydney. "Well . . ." they said.

"No. Oh no. I couldn't. Did they hurt his face?"

"His face was damaged, Mrs Sole."

"You'll have to try Willis. Or Fred. Fred Meggett will do it."

And Fred, in fact, made the identification. He had come home to find police in his house and Esther hysterical. The doctor was trying to get a sedative into her. He rang me when he came back from the morgue. Although he tried to sound mournful I heard the cheerfulness in his voice. He was always happy when he was up and doing. The way it looked to him, he said, was that Alfred had gone into Moa Park and tried to pick someone up and whoever it was didn't like it and kicked him to death.

"Kicked?"

"'Fraid so, Meg. Kicked him all over, really. Not very nice. His face—"

"Stop. Please. I don't want to hear."

"Sorry. You've got to know some time. Do you want me to ring the others?"

"I'll do it. They're my family."

I rang Willis and Emerson and Felicity. I rang Bruce; Bobby; Rebecca; Raymond. When the conversations were done I wrote to Agnes in San Francisco and asked her to get in touch with the others. (I could not remember some of my sisters. Edith, Florence: who were they?)

Willis came late in the afternoon. He cried, and drank Fergus's beer. His grief washed round the house in salty waves. Emerson arrived. He chewed his lips and sat dejectedly in a chair. I sent them home.

I was alone at Peacehaven. It grew dark. I did practical things but the house grew haunted and I had to leave. I went down to Bluey's cottage. Sutton put on his boots and went for a walk. I told Bluey what had happened. I sat there for an hour while he patted me, made me tea. He rumbled his distress and wiped his eyes and blew his nose. I confessed I had never been able to get used to Alfred's homosexuality and I cried that his life had been wasted.

"Ah Meg, dear girl, where's your charity? Alfred was a good boy. He was all right. Love him, let the rest go." He told me Sutton was a homosexual. "For twenty years he's wanted to be my wife. I would have obliged him. Roger loves me, that's the truth of it. But I just can't get my pecker up with a man."

Sutton passed me crabwise in the gate. He gave me a grin of contempt. "Bluey's mine."

I hurried back to Peacehaven. The night was black and the stars sparkled like glass. I stopped on the drive. The soft noises of the creek made me think of Dad: streams symbolized the spiritual quest, and stars that Perfection we should one day attain. Alfred though, for all his verse-making, had seen streams as streams and stars as stars. I could not bring them together. Between them was only grieving and hatred and pain. Yet their lives had depended on each other.

I went on up the drive and across the yard. Light from the open door fell on the steps. How was I to take my brother's death into my life? It seemed that it might kill me. I did not want to die and I did not want to live. I ran up the steps into my kitchen. I looked around for something that might save me. There was nothing. I walked across the room and I walked back. I plucked at myself with my fingers. I looked at them. Were they part of me? I laid them on the wood of Mother's table and tried to find a way of going on. Alfred was dead, gone through a pain and horror that might just as well have been inflicted with knives. How could I take that into myself?

Peacehaven creaked and shivered. The tap dripped into the sink. Cats raised their dead howls in the night. I sat down. My fingers slid on the table—the polished wood. I found a way to run, and I ran there. That smoothness grew on me like a skin. I hooked my legs childishly in my chair. I anchored myself and placed my cheek on my hands. In a grizzling voice, I complained of my sorrows.

Presently Mother came and touched my cheek and stroked my brow.

19 Fergus flew home in time for the funeral. I rang Bruce and told him he could come if he wanted to.

"Have you worked the music out, Meg? Can I choose it?"

I had no idea what form the service would take. I asked him if he had any suggestions, thinking that homosexuals, like rationalists and humanists, might have a service of their own.

"Maybe if some of us say how we felt about him?"

We agreed that he should work things out, leaving a place for Willis and Emerson.

On the morning of the funeral I read in the *Herald* that four youths had appeared in the magistrate's court charged with Alfred's manslaughter. "Fergus, look how old they are."

"Manslaughter," Fergus said. "I thought it was murder."

"Fifteen. Sixteen. They're not grown up."

All the way to the crematorium I could not get the picture out of my mind of boys killing Alfred. I saw them as fat and happy, dressed in navy-blue shorts and grammar school caps. I had been calm since my night at the kitchen table, but those sweet-sucking boys unbalanced me. I had seen only their ages and failed to notice one was a steam-presser and one an electrical apprentice and two were unemployed. They grinned at me from the cold air in the crematorium chapel. There was a hideous dislocation between their faces and the solemn music. I sat in the front pew with Fergus and Willis and Emerson. Fred had not come and Esther was under sedation. Bruce and Joan and Ailsa and two of the managers and the boy who had slashed his wrists sat opposite. Bruce spoke. More music played. One of the managers spoke. I thought I should go mad. Did none of them see there were things that could not be borne? Life must stop. The moment was coming when I would stand and scream.

Then Robert walked into the chapel. I felt him in the door, and in the aisle, and heard him breathe as he entered the pew behind me. His hand came to rest on my shoulder, and I sighed, and in the space of a second remade myself and accepted life. I do not wish to play the moment up. It was quick. It was, I suppose, ordinary. But I know I was on the point of going mad; and because Robert came and put his hand on my shoulder I did not go mad. I have lived fairly easily since. I have toughened myself and let a good deal go.

It was not so easy for others. The boy who had slashed his wrists stood up. His cheeks were wet with tears. Light from the stained glass windows coloured his warts red and yellow. "Alfie saved my life. He showed me who I was. I'll never forget him." Fergus moved uneasily. I patted him on his thigh. The boy sat down and Bruce put music on. Then Willis stood up, clumping his leg on the floor. He had wet cheeks too. He spoke about Alfred as a boy. A good deal of it was invention. Willis had been away at sea. I think he believed it though. He spoke of tree huts and building mud dams in creeks, and evenings round the piano while Mother played, and a church picnic where Alfred tried the lucky dip and won a kewpie doll, which he gave to his sister

Meg. Like me Willis was a sentimentalist, but it was fitting in him. I was pleased someone was speaking for us and that Alfred's friends could see we loved him. Nobody seemed to mind when he said it was a great tragedy that Alfred had never known the love of a woman.

The coffin slid away on rollers. We filed outside and stood on the slope of the hill, with headstones and crosses stretching away to the pine forest over the valley. "Come home for a drink," Fergus said. But the homosexuals said no and said goodbye. They drove away in a large red car—"Bentley," Emerson said—belonging to one of the managers. I have not met any of them again. Fergus relaxed a little. He repeated his invitation, but we decided to go to Willis's. Fergus, his duty done, went off to work.

Mirth made us lunch. My brothers talked, lying in the sun. We made a fuss of Robert and asked where he had come from. He said he had read about Alfred's death in the paper, and watched for the funeral notice and caught the train down to Glen Eden that morning.

"Down from where?"

"North. I've got a little place."

His brothers did not press him. They had never pressed each other. We girls had always been the demanding ones.

In the middle of the afternoon Emerson ran me to Peacehaven for my car. I left a note for Fergus and I picked Robert up and drove him home. I saw the creeks and sawmills for the first time. Robert led me into his house in a diffident way. "It's not much, Meg." He had been there for two years and was just starting to get things the way he wanted them. It all looked scruffy to me, but I did not say so. When I had been there a little longer I began to see how things might be. He was going to renew the roof. When that was done he would throw a lean-to out the back for a bathroom and wash-house. We walked down to the river. An old dinghy was lying bottom-up on the bank.

"I'm caulking her. She'll be as good as new. There's plenty of fish out there."

"The jetty doesn't look safe."

"I'm putting a new one in. That's my job for next summer."

We had not talked about Alfred; but I began to speak of him as we walked up the section. I told Robert about my visits to Herne Bay—about Bruce and Joan and Ailsa and the boy who had cut his wrists.

"They all loved him. His life wasn't wasted."

"Of course not."

"Did you see how old they were—those ones who killed him?"

"Yes."

"Will you come with me to the trial?"

"Do you want to go, Meg?"

"I have to. I'm trying to understand it." I did not tell him he had saved my life. But I knew I must do something for myself. If I left the thing unended it might come back one day and take some shape that would destroy me. I had to see the boys and take them with Alfred, Dad, with Bruce and all the others, into my life. I did not try to explain it to Robert—had not explained it properly to myself—but said to him, "Come with me, Robert. There should be someone from our family."

When I drove home that night I had his promise.

The case came up in June. I met Robert off the train in Loomis and we drove into Auckland and parked by the university. We walked along to the court past Government House. The trees and the paths settled Robert down after the dangers of our drive through the traffic. I felt my tension reduced too, and though I was going in a few moments to hear the story of Alfred's death I felt the danger to me recede. We joined the crowd outside the Supreme Court. I heard one man—I took him for a lawyer—lay a ten shilling bet with his friend that Alfred's killers would get off. "I'd have those boys spruced up and looking clean. I'd have them like a bunch of wing three-quarters."

That was just the way they were. They were scrubbed and innocent. The electrical apprentice had an impish look, and the steam-presser—Peter Parker, six months out of school—was blue-eyed, pink-and-white, cow-licked by his mother. They sat in the dock through the trial, shoulders back, while the facts came out, and it was plain that other forces must have been at work. I knew as soon as I looked at them guilt would come down on Alfred. Even Reeves, the prosecutor, could not leave him alone.

He spoke with affectations of care and precision. I did not care for him. He was like an amateur actor playing the lawyer, and his interest went only as far as his role. I thought how absurd wigs and gowns were, a prop to vanity. The judge was Mr Justice Stavely. A harmless little cocoa-drinking man blinked out from underneath his wig. Alfred, I said to myself, none of this has anything to do with you. But that changed. Through the medium of Reeves's voice Alfred's last hours began to thicken and stand up before me.

Witnesses had noticed him in Moa Park from four o'clock onwards. He had watched children playing in the pirate ship. He had hired a canoe and paddled about inexpertly. People using the diving-board had had to shout at him to get out of the way. There was evidence to show, Reeves said, that the deceased was in an emotional state and that he had been consuming liquor. He was seen in the trees drinking from a bottle. In this condition, with his judgement impaired, he had fallen prey to four young men who had gone to Moa Park with the express intention of hunting down a homosexual and assaulting him. The statements of the accused, Reeves said, would make it plain that they had found a person they thought to be a homosexual—"they refer to such a person as 'a queer'"—that they did assault him, and he died.

I held Robert's hand. This was not just two hours of time Reeves was describing, this was a whole life coming to its end. A part of us was contained in it, of Dad and me and Esther, and Robert too. Esther had done to Alfred what Dad had done thirty years before—pushed him out of his family into the dark. This time he had found no John to save him. At some point—after how long in *his* time?—he had noticed someone moving on the edges of the dark: a boy with grinning mouth and crooked teeth. He had swum to that human shape through an element as empty to him as water, and stood by him, and said his name was Plumb. Yes, Plumb. He was trying to get back into our family.

The boy, the decoy, thought he was saying Plum. (The name had an unpleasant sound. The judge wrote it down.) They met in the lavatory at the back of the pirate ship. Alfred gave the boy a drink from his bottle. He made indecent remarks to him. That is true. But Alfred was crying for help. He spoke whatever words he thought were expected.

Reeves called a woman who had seen the two walking—"skylarking a bit"—through the park towards the place where Alfred's body had been found. After that no one saw him, except the four who killed him in a clearing in the trees.

Late in the day Reeves called a pathologist, Carmichael. This man described his work much as Fergus would have done. He was flat and practical. He had examined Hamer at 7.45 a.m. on March 16 and formed the opinion that death had occurred between 5 p.m. and 9 p.m. the previous day. Hamer had two broken ribs and contusions on his chest and abdomen. In addition he had a fractured jaw and a fractured nose and a fracture to the base of the skull—the bony plates above his eye sockets. There had been considerable bleeding. There was a pool of blood over the right eye and a pool of blood and urine in the fold of the cheek and gums. In Carmichael's opinion the cause of death was haemorrhaging of the brain associated with a minor fracture of the skull and a severe fracture of the nose.

"What could cause such fractures?"

"A heavy blow or blows."

"With the fist?"

"That is certainly possible."

The defence lawyers were up then, one by one, and it seemed to me they were blaming Alfred for having a thin skull. Parker's lawyer in particular kept after Carmichael. Wasn't it true, he asked, that the bony plates above Hamer's eye sockets were very much thinner than in a normal skull? (He was a clever man, his

"normal" made it plain that Alfred's was a homosexual skull.)
Carmichael said yes, they were thinner. Paper thin? the lawyer
asked. That, Carmichael said, was an exaggeration. But he
agreed it was possible the haemorrhage would have been less
severe had the bones been thicker. The lawyer gave an angry
smile. Having a thin skull, he seemed to say, was the sort of
trick one would expect from a queer.

He was the only lawyer to ask Carmichael about the urine in
Alfred's mouth. His concern was to show that Alfred had not
drowned in urine. The rest of the body, his clothing (though
clothing was a matter for the police), gave evidence of having
been splashed with that substance. It was likely then, the lawyer
asked, that some of it had arrived in the deceased's mouth by
accident, misdirection? Carmichael said he could not answer
that, but the lawyer had made his point; and the judge, with the
air of a man who has heard enough unpleasantness for one day,
called a halt to proceedings.

As I drove Robert back to Loomis I asked him if Dad had ever
spoken with him about the way he had been troubled by a
knowledge of evil. It came down on him like a physical thing,
like a black fog, cutting out light and warmth, and he was aware
that powers hating life sat watching him. They could see in that
element. "There's a place in us Meg that belongs to them and all
our lives they're trying to get in. A room in our hearts. But we
control the door. We are the ones who open it and close it." That
empty place, he told me, is man's hatred of himself. He told me
of his meeting with Sullivan, a murderer, on the West Coast.
Sullivan had killed many men, most by strangling and stabbing.
In him that space had been filled. And evil, Dad went on, had
got into him, into George Plumb. It got in on the day he drove
his son Alfred Plumb away. "I held open the door. They
came in. There was a dreadful shrieking. I heard it all through
me."

I don't suppose he meant it literally. He was standing evil up
to look at it, and standing up responsibility too.

"No," Robert said, "he never told me. Poor old Dad."

"Robert, I think I can go by myself tomorrow. I can manage."

"Are you sure?"

"Yes. Yes." I stumbled on for a bit, saying that Alfred's life had ended before the blows were struck. We were a part of that. What happened in Moa Park was a part of those who killed him. I could face that perfectly well by myself.

For its final three days I sat at the trial alone. I did not take all the arguments in—what was the point?—but watched Parker and his friends for a sign that they understood what had happened to them. I knew I was expecting too much of boys. It had taken Dad twenty years to understand. I heard Parker's lawyer call them "lads", and saw them sit up straight and look like lads. I watched in hope that they would understand they were not that.

A few days ago I went to the Public Library in Auckland and looked up the newspaper reports of the trial. I found that a good deal happened while I sat there lost in my hope for those boys. Policemen came to the stand. They read statements they had taken and the lawyers questioned them. One boy, Fredericks, the electrical apprentice, admitted punching Alfred's face while his friend, Tucker, held him by his arms. Alfred fell on his hands and knees, making a gasping noise. Fredericks kicked him in the chest and this made some money fall out of his pocket. Tucker picked it up and shared it with the fourth boy, Moore. And Parker—"I needed to go. I just got the idea." Tucker pulled him away before he had finished. When they left, Alfred was lying on the ground grunting. They ran to their car and drove away.

I remembered the part about Parker. I remembered Alfred's grunting. It took his humanity away. He was an object lying on the grass, making animal noises, splashed with urine that might just as well have been his own. There was no pity in the room, but a trembling of disgust and a shrinking away. Parker's lawyer felt it: he said nothing. Later he seemed to suggest that Parker's urinating was in the nature of a prank. Boys had always done

213

that sort of thing—piddling up walls to see who could go highest.

They made their final speeches. That was on the third day. I heard very little. The prosecutor said that Alfred, "the unfortunate man", had a right to live in spite of his shortcomings. He spoke of the four boys as "a pack". But it seemed to me the jury preferred the defence view—they were "lads". No one saw what they really were. No one told them they were lost, and yet might save themselves.

Fergus had made a fire in the sitting-room. We sat up late talking about the trial. He could not believe the boys would be acquitted.

"They will be, Fergus. Their lawyers had all sorts of arguments. No one knows who made the punch that killed him. It was like a dance."

Fergus was shocked. But I meant a puppet dance, a sort of wooden turning into the event and out of it. I could not explain it to him.

"What happens tomorrow?"

"The judge sums up. And then the jury goes out."

"Do you have to go, Meg? You can read it in the paper." He believed I was punishing myself, and was afraid I would have another breakdown.

The court was crowded next morning. I managed to get a seat at the back. I caught only glimpses of Parker and his friends. They were as well brushed as ever. The judge was cross and tired. He must have worked late on his summing-up. One of the curls on his wig had lost its stiffness and hung half-open. To me he looked like a woman at her washing, quite worn out. He went over the arguments on both sides and showed the jury all their parts again. Aiding and abetting kept him a long while. It was impossible to tell whether he believed the boys were guilty or not. His voice had a lifeless fall. I wondered if he had come to understand nothing that he said was relevant.

The jury went out before lunch. I bought myself some sandwiches and went into Albert Park. The sun was shining after

214

rain. I dried a seat with my handkerchief and sat looking down Victoria Street into the city. The sky had a pearly glow that reflected off the streets. It seemed to me I was in a clean and windy place, looking down the long trough of my life. I apologized to Alfred. None of my activities, and none of my thoughts, of the last few days had been in any way a memorial to him. Alfred was gone. All that could be said now was that we were brother and sister, and that I had loved him, but not enough. I watched the people hurry through the streets. It's common at such time to look down on them in a god-like way and see them as ant creatures, scurrying about their bits of business; or to take a sense of their pain, and suffer the illusion of carrying it and of saving them. One is Jove or Jesus. I've been both in my time. But on that day I had a better sight and did not take shapes blurred with my feelings for real things. People bent into the cold wind in the street. Trams ground through the intersection. A pattering of rain came over the trees. I sat there taking it in. Horns blew crazily. Students ran up the steps, turning their winter faces to the sky. I did not want to make something of it. Man's love? Man's hatred of himself? I ate my sandwiches.

I went back to the court several times. The jury had come out of their room for direction on some point, but I missed that. From four o'clock I waited on the court steps. They were ready to come back at a quarter to five. Parker and Fredericks and Moore and Tucker climbed up from somewhere in the depths of the building. They had washed their faces and combed their hair. A drop of water gleamed in Parker's cow-lick. The jury filed in and found their seats with a gritty shuffling. Their foreman was a bald rosy man with a gold watch-chain on his belly. Four times, in a round convincing voice, he answered the clerk's question: "Not guilty."

A rumble of content sounded in the room. Parker gave Fredericks a dig with his elbow. The judge discharged those two. He remanded Moore and Tucker to face another charge. That puzzled me until I remembered they had shared the money that fell from Alfred's pocket. That was theft, and so they would be charged. It struck me as mad and I gave a little laugh.

"Good, eh?" said a man beside me. "I knew they'd get off."

I drove down to the Post Office and telephoned Fergus. I told him I was neither surprised nor angry, but he thought I was simply being brave. He told me to hurry home. He would race me out to Loomis and have a drink ready for me, and then he'd fry a steak.

"Thank you, but I've got to tell Esther. And I want to see Robert."

"Meg, you've done enough. Come home. You'll make yourself ill. I'll go and tell Esther."

"No. I'll be all right dear. I might be late, so don't wait up."

"You're sure you're not upset? I can't understand that verdict. It's a bloody disgrace. Even a homosexual . . ."

"Yes, Fergus. I'll see you later. Don't worry about me."

He had looked forward to propping me up, but then was relieved not to have the trouble. I thought about our life together as I drove to Loomis. Although the things that had filled it had drained away, through my fault as much as his—was it anyone's fault though, was not some law at work?—there was, it seemed to me, enough left to make it worth going on with. We would never make each other happy. He lived so much in the regard of men, and so much in his own private regard that took in notions of manliness and honesty and courage, inexpressible though they were by him, that little room was left for a third place in his life, a place for me. We took from each other the comforts of proximity and habit, and in extraordinary times supported each other more out of affection than from duty. If asked we would have said we loved each other, and believed it true, though neither would have been able to say what we meant by love. So we had a marriage. I say that in no cynical way. All the same, I did not want Fergus on that night.

I went the back way down to Moa Park. It was dark by the time I turned off the road opposite the blue-eyed wooden moa and drove up the scoria drive to Esther's door. I was not looking

216

forward to seeing her and for once hoped Fred Meggett would be home.

Adrian let me in. He said his father had not come in for tea. The woman who did the housework was washing the dishes. Esther, wrapped in an eiderdown, reclined on a sofa pulled up to the fire.

"Meg," she cried when she saw me, "Get my wine, will you? That bitch in the kitchen won't let me have any. That's not her job. I'm going to make Fred fire her."

"I want to talk to you first."

"Not about Alfie. I don't want to talk about him."

"The trial's over, Esther. It's all finished, dear."

"I can't face talking about it without my wine. Get it for me, please. Come on, Sis."

I went to the kitchen and asked the woman where she had hidden it.

"She's not supposed to have any. That's Mr Meggett's orders."

"I'll take responsibility."

I took the wine back to the sitting-room and Esther poured herself a tumblerful.

"They were let off, Esther. The jury found them not guilty."

"Fred said they would. Anyhow Meg, we both know who killed him."

"Nonsense. If I thought you'd done it I'd tell you. All you did was behave like a silly fool."

The wine helped her speak with clarity. "I know what I did. So shut up, little sister. You always were a do-goody little thing."

"Listen—"

"I will not. Who needs your guff any more? What I need is my vino. And I need Alfie. The only way I can have him is by knowing what I did."

I let her go over it. Adrian came in. She caressed him absently. She had switched off her love for the boy at Alfred's death. She patted his hair and allowed him every bit of food he

217

asked for, and gave him no other care than that.

"Can I have that chicken leg in the fridge, Mum?"

"You've just had tea."

"I'm still hungry."

"All right. All right. Go and get it."

"Esther," I said, "I'm going up to see Robert."

"Who? Oh, him. Fred told me he'd turned up. You always liked him. I'll tell you Meg, Alfie was in love with me once. We used to kiss. His sister! He never said, but he wanted to go to bed with me. I always knew when some boy wanted that, and he wanted it. God, I wish we'd done it. God, I wish we had."

"He still would have been a homosexual, Esther."

"I'm not talking about that. You're such a stupid bitch. Let me fill my glass. I'm sick of everyone. Of everyone. All I want is Alfie."

I stayed with her until Fred came home. He frowned at the wine. "Did you give her that?"

"Yes."

"Well,"—he shrugged—"what the hell? I hear they got off. I suppose you're sore about that?"

"Not particularly."

"I can't work you Plumb sheilas out. Jesus, will you look at her! She was good-looking once."

"So were you. At least I suppose she thought so."

"I've got something better. Don't you forget it."

"Money, Fred? It's never worked with me."

"You're too bloody dumb. Both of you are dumb."

I laughed at him. His cheeks went red and swelled up. "I'm glad those kids got off. I used to do some queer-bashing myself."

"I'm sure you did. Goodbye, Esther. I'll come and see you soon."

Driving north in my little car, I considered the waste of her life. She had made a greedy demand on it, but there were certain immutable things that would not be turned to her satisfaction. Now she had come to grief on one of them, and because in all

218

things she had been immoderate there was no controlling the event and her life was a waste. I did not see a way for her to restore any part of it. Fred would be no help. He was a devourer too, more ruthless than greedy. I saw a long future for Esther. She would hang on to life, not in any hope, but for its bodily gratifications. I supposed I would take her on, up to a point; take her like a retarded child; but I would not let her spoil my life.

Robert's bach was dark. I let myself in and felt for a light switch, then remembered he used a Tilley lamp. I felt in my bag for matches and struck a light. The little room came into view, velvety in the dimness. Here, I thought, was the home of a man who made only proper demands. For a moment I was righteous on his behalf. Then I told myself to stop pushing at things. I tried to light the lamp but it was too complicated for me. I lit a candle and looked in Robert's bedroom. His bed lay white and simple, neatly made. Pyjamas striped like a peppermint stick were folded on a chair. I opened the back door. "Robert."

Not since I was a child, listening in the dark, had I been so aware of silence. There was no human sound, no animal or insect sound, no rustle of leaf or sound from the earth or river. There was only a winter stillness, winter silence. It made me almost faint with happiness. The cold, and the black night, and the huge stars were a benediction. I set off down the garden. The flame of my candle fluttered, so I cupped it in my hand. Wax ran on to my fingers, hot as blood. I saw a moving shadow that might have been a cat. Trees with great depths in them moved by. A clucking and a flutter came from the fowl house.

I went along Robert's jetty and stood on the end. Foam patches moved on the water, floating up-river. The old dinghy was gone. Robert was out fishing and would row in on the tide. I sat down, blew my candle out, and pulled my coat around me. I waited there. Every now and then I closed my eyes and rocked in a kind of unthinking contentment.

Presently I heard the sound of whistling. It was *The Vale of Tralee*, one of Willis's songs. After a while it stopped. I heard only the sounds of the boat: rowlocks, water splashing. A dome of light moved along the top of the mangrove bank. Soon the dinghy nosed out and turned towards me. Robert had fastened a lantern to a pole fixed on its prow. The night enclosed the boat on a disc of water. It seemed to mould a yellow ball about the figure bending at the oars.

Ten yards away he turned. "Is that you, Meg?"

"Yes. Hallo. Isn't it late for fishing?"

"I went out about five to look at my nets. Had to wait while the tide turned."

He brought the dinghy in at the side of the jetty and hauled it half-way on to land.

"What have you got?"

"Flounder. Have you had tea, Meg?"

"No."

"We'll cook some." He shifted a sack from a wooden box in the boat and showed me his catch.

"Lovely. You're out of breath."

"She's a long row."

"It didn't stop you whistling."

"You heard that? Sound carries in the dark. You take the lamp."

We walked up through the garden. I told him the trial was over.

"What happened to them?"

"They're not guilty. Incredible, isn't it?"

"They'll have to live with it, Meg."

"Oh, they'll manage that. No trouble."

"You can't say that."

He lit the Tilley lamp and stoked up the range. "Put the kettle on, Meg. I'll do the fish."

We sat down to our meal, and we talked into the night. We remembered things about our childhood that we had never spoken of, and I think it was the same for him as me: we gave them shape and put them safely away.

He wrapped me two flounder in newspaper and brought the lamp to show me to my car. I drove home down the road to

220

Loomis. Drawn along by my yellow lights, I too seemed to be in a world moulded by the night.

Fergus was asleep. I kissed him on his forehead and slipped into bed.

20 Through the spring and summer I have been possessed by what Dad would have called a *furor scribendi*. I am not the only one suffering in this way. Up in her witch's castle Merle Butters scribbles in blank verse to the dictation of her Japanese lover. And over the creek in Peacehaven Wendy Philson labours day-long at the story of George Plumb. She's still in the note-taking stage, but soon (in several years) she will be ready to take her place at his side, recording selected adventures on the Odyssey of his soul. So we go on.

Mine has been a tale of deaths. Rebecca, Mother, Dad, Agnes (in spite of the attentions of a San Francisco Fire Department resuscitator squad). And of course Alfred. Sutton has died. (Outside of my pages Bluey has died. Fergus's parents have, as he puts it, passed on.) And now I come to the death of Robert. Yet I go on thinking of mine as a happy tale. It seems to me to have more of life in it than of death.

I will take it up from the night I became Robert's nurse. He woke several times.

"You've shifted in have you, Meg? Does Fergus mind?"

"No. I think he'll be going away for a while."

"Business?"

"Something like that." But I told myself to stop playing the nurse. Washing him and seeing to him physically was enough. For the rest of it I must be his sister. "He's got a girl-friend and I think he's going away with her."

"I'm sorry, Meg."

"I haven't been a very good wife to him."

"Will he come back?"

"I've no idea."

"Will you take him?"

"I think I will. But I'm not sure. I don't want him *creeping* back."

"That doesn't sound like Fergus."

"Beth Neeley's just a young woman. I don't think she's twenty-five. I'm frightened of what she'll do when she finds out Fergus is sixty."

"She must know that."

"In some ways. And then of course Fergus is a puritan. I don't think she's one of those."

In the morning I went to Peacehaven and helped Felicity and Oliver get ready to catch their plane. Fergus had not come back. I hoped his night had been a happy one and that morning would not waken his conscience. I worried about him sleeping without pyjamas.

"Where's Fergus?" Felicity asked. "We should say goodbye."

"Gone to work. He starts early on Mondays." I did not want to go into explanations, or have Oliver score another failure to a Plumb. "You'll have to ring a taxi. I want to be with Robert when the doctor comes."

"Good. Good," Oliver said. He was spared another ride in my Hillman Imp.

When they had driven away I went back to the cottage and did my housework. Robert had dressed himself. He felt a little better, but something had altered in his mind. He seemed smaller this morning. A new look of quiet was on his face.

The doctor came at mid-day and spent a long time with him in his room. When he came out I told him I had moved down and would be nursing Robert from now on.

"I was going to say it was time."

"He was bad last night."

"Yes, well—" he looked at me cautiously, "the disease can accelerate you know, and I think it's doing that to some degree. But there are steps in the mind sickness can take."

222

"He's getting ready to die."

"If you can persuade him that he needn't give up . . ."

"Robert accepts things. He'll fight as much as he has to. And die when it's time."

"Well, well, I don't have an opinion about that. At this stage he needs a bronchodilator. I'll arrange that. There'll be more sputum, I'm afraid. But what I'm frightened of is congestive heart failure."

"Heart failure?"

"No, it's not an attack, it's just a condition. If that comes he has to have complete bed rest. He can't lift a finger. You might need to hire a professional nurse. But of course, we may avoid it. Now I want you to look out for—cyanosis. Do you know what that is?"

"Blue fingernails?"

"Any bluish discoloration. Skin. Fingernails. Watch out for headaches. Watch out for fevers. If you see anything you don't like give me a ring. I'll come as often as I can anyway."

"Can I take him visiting?"

"Not too much. We don't want any strain."

I called at his surgery in the afternoon and picked up the bronchodilator. It gave Robert a lot of relief. The doctor also tried him on mist inhalations. He seemed to enjoy those. "We used to do this in the kitchen. What was that stuff?"

"Friar's balsam."

Fergus called and took away his things. I heard his car go up the drive, but decided not to interrupt him. He knew where I was if he needed me. I went up when he was gone and found a letter on the table. He hates writing letters. He cannot reveal himself. Even when he wrote from Italy he kept to stiff accounts of his health and the weather. In this letter he had tried very hard:

"Dear Meg, You were right about Beth being my responsibility. But if I go to her I've got to stay. It can't be just an affair—that's not my sort of thing. It's got to be divorce and then a remarriage. ["Good God," I said, "he's going to keep

223

her waiting."} I've promised her that. But naturally she doesn't want to wait. So we're going to start sharing a place straight away. ["Thank God for that."] I can't see you again. No matter what you say I've treated you badly.

Well, chin up Meg.

Yours sincerely,

Fergus.

P.S. I'll be the guilty one in the divorce. Beth doesn't like it, but I owe you that."

I laughed and put it away. I hoped that whatever happened would not be too painful for him.

He made arrangements to have his mail picked up, and for the lawns to be mowed so that I should not have that expense. I kept our separation from everyone but Robert. Others found out soon enough. Esther was angry with me. She would have excused my letting Fergus "take off for a dirty weekend", but losing him altogether was another thing. She wanted me to put detectives on him, show some fight. "He's got troubles enough," I said.

The children sent me letters. Fergus had written to them, saying he was to blame. None of them accepted that. Raymond, in some pain, blamed Life—but did not go so far as to mention its Dark Hand. Bobby said we were a pair of silly bloody fools, he'd always known it. All the same, "splitting up" was probably for the best. The wonder was we hadn't done it before. Rebecca offered to come if I needed her. I answered that I was all right, and Fergus was all right as far as I knew, and I told them they should get on with their lives.

Winter came and Robert seemed to be holding his own. It was important he should pick up no infection in his lungs. The doctor was not keen on my taking him out. But Robert fretted in our little house. He tried to make a start on painting the kitchen but the fumes were bad for him and the exertion too much. I turned over some garden to put winter vegetables in. The most Robert could manage was to push a few seeds in the ground—broad beans and carrots—and the sound of his breathing after that frightened even him. So I took him on visits

224

to Willis and Emerson, and talking to his brothers he was happy.

One day we picked Willis up and drove out to Mangere, where Emerson had his tomato farm. We saw glass roofs shining in the sun as we approached. Willis said, "There's more than last time." I think he disapproved. Emerson's glass metropolis was too far from nature. It probably struck Robert that way too, but he said nothing. I thought the place entirely right for Emerson. It had an airy quality, the whiteness and the space of upper air.

Every time we called on him he showed us everything. So we made the tour again, and saw the irrigation controls and the spray controls and the boiler room and the packing room, and last we stood at the door of each of the ten vast glittering sheds where the crops were grown. Some were empty, with only pipes like plumbing on the brown earth, others had young plants, and three or four grew pieces of tropical jungle, love apples. I felt the hot wet air, and smelled the peppery smell of spray and the smell of crushed tomato leaves, and would not let Robert put his foot inside the door.

"She looks after me, Emo. But it's quite a place. Quite a place."

Emerson blushed. There is something of lover in him where his brothers are concerned. He took us up to his house for a cup of tea. It's a pink stucco cottage, Spanish style, with two black vertical lines over the door. They make the narrow porch frown. Inside, the rooms are small and dark. It's not an adequate stopping-place for a man who has flown over jungles. He should build himself a house of glass.

Emerson lives in his kitchen but he opened the lounge for us and we sat on wooden-armed chairs with their seats puffed up like balloons. Framed photos of Mum and Dad stood on the mantelpiece. Robert went close to look at them. They were photographs taken in Thorpe about 1905. Emerson was a boy then and Robert and I not born. Dad was safe inside his church, though making noises, and Mum in the St Andrews manse, that house she had loved in her life second only to Peacehaven. The

Reverend looked stern, a little angry, a little as though he had just smelled something bad, but his wife was smiling gently and had that look of faint surprise turning into delight that came on her face when she had found some perfect rose in her garden.

The sentimentalist in me will not die. Once it had the shape of my whole life, but now it's a dried-up thing, light as a bat, hanging upside down with its feet clawed tight on my ribs. Occasionally it gives a flutter and squeak. I watched Robert with the photographs. He took them to the window to see them better. Willis came to his side: two men with the round Plumb face and the Plumb bald head.

"She was a good-looking woman."

"She was a beauty. Look at this old so-and-so, ready to take on the world."

"Bugger," I said, and took out my handkerchief.

"What did you say?" asked Emerson, coming in with tea.

"Nothing. Here, let me pour."

He put down the tray. "I'll show you jokers something." He went to his bedroom and came back with a piece of cardboard the size of an exercise book. "Take a look at that." He laid it on the coffee table and we crowded round. It was a photograph from the *San Francisco Chronicle*, dated July 18, 1915. Emerson had pasted it on cardboard.

Pastor, 10 Children Seek Home In California. Denied Free Speech In New Zealand.

And we all smiled out.

This is not a convention of children. It is merely the family of the Rev. George Plumb, a Unitarian Minister from New Zealand. The happy group came from that country because the clergyman denounced war and was denied free speech. Here is the family, snapped by a Chronicle photographer upon arrival here by the liner Marama. . . .

My smile was uneasy. California was not my land. But Esther sparkled, Agnes, Edith, Florence had looks of delight. Rebecca had a thoughtful smile. The boys all grinned. They had been told to say cheese. Only Mum and Dad and Felicity made no show of pleasure. Dad had a sharp eye, a speculative look. In

226

other photos I have seen he manages the appearance of a visionary. But arrival in this new land had him worried. Felicity was worn out. She had spent two weeks chasing lively children over three decks of an ocean liner. No wonder she could not sparkle. And Mother, in lace choker and cameo brooch and feathered hat, Mother was at her most ladylike. She looked slightly down, as though at something very small in stature, and her coolness survived fifty years and the furry paper. Newsmen were an intrusion on our life, she found them vulgar. In her hand she carried a posy of violets.

So the Plumbs came to California, and I looked at them with long sight and what cameramen call, I believe, a wide lens. There was Rebecca, who would drown in three years time at New Brighton beach, thousands of miles away in the other hemisphere. And there was Alfred, a beautiful child, curly haired, wide-eyed, with pictures, one would say, alive in his head, and his future simple, crystal clear, like a cup of water to be drunk. He would die at a place called Moa Park, cast out from his family, beaten and kicked by a boy in the grip of evil. And there was Esther, practising her eyes on the cameraman and drinking up life. I saw her broken. And Robert, freckle-faced, more stolid than his brothers. A solitary life waited him, four years behind barbed wire, and death at fifty-four from a disease that destroyed his lungs. Mother, Dad, Agnes, Felicity. And me. Me. Me! Pain grew in my chest, tears flooded my eyes.

"Weepies, Sis? Come on," Emerson said.

"Damn it. Damn it. I thought I was over this."

"I'm not there," Willis cried. "It isn't fair. Why did I get left out?" He was trying to clown me out of my grief, but with a preternatural understanding I was aware of the disappointment in his cry. Life had not given Willis all he had wanted.

Robert slapped his hand on Willis's pate and moved it as though ruffling curls. "Poor old Willie, he always did want to be everywhere. You should have been ten men. Don't you remember, you were away at sea loving all those ladies?"

"I'd sooner have been with you lot. Hey Meg, wipe your eyes

and I'll tell you about Carmelita from Rio."

"I've heard that one. She stole your underpants."

"No," he cried in delight, "that was Bonita in Port of Spain. Carmelita was a great big girl—"

"You take milk and sugar, don't you Willie? Emerson, put that photo away, it'll get tea on it. Do you want something, Robert?"

We recovered. We passed the rest of the afternoon in a jokey manner. Emerson told us flying stories and Willis, signalling his conquests with rude mouth-organ chords, told us about his ladies and the sea. "But you mustn't think there was anyone like old Mirth. She's still my best girl." He blew a sweet enduring middle C.

Loaded down with tomatoes, we drove home. Willis got out at his gate and limped away. I put Robert to bed and heated some soup. He could take only a few mouthfuls. I was up to him half a dozen times in the night. "Too much laughing, Meg."

That did not stop us going again. We picked Willis up and drove there the following Sunday.

When Wendy Philson heard Peacehaven was empty she asked if she could stay one or two nights instead of driving all the way back home. That way too she need not take Dad's papers out of the house. I was pleased to have someone there. I told her she could stay as long as she liked. When Robert and I strolled in the grounds on fine afternoons we saw her through the study window, head down at Dad's desk, her pencil going nineteen to the dozen. At other times she just sat with an ecstatic look on her face.

"She's communing with him. Do you feel him in the air?"

Robert grinned. He could not manage walking and speech together.

"I feel him. I feel Mother too. Wendy wouldn't like it if she knew she was about. Not up to the spiritual mark, I'm afraid.

Poor Mum." I laughed. "Well," I said, "it's actually got nothing to do with Wendy, that's her game. I've had them like a buzzing in my head ever since they died. I don't need Wendy for that. Or old Merle either."

Robert paid his visit to Merle on a wet July afternoon. We had to fit it in between three and four o'clock. "I don't have much time," Merle said on the phone. "Mr Fujikawa is very demanding these days. He's suffering from the cold."

"You mean," I said, "there are seasons where he is?"

"I've told you my dear, when he visits me our weather takes over. Mr Fujikawa wants me to book on a Pacific cruise. I think I should go. I hate to hear him coughing."

She tried to turn me away at the door but I pushed my way in, saying Robert was not well enough to be left alone. The truth is I was curious. Mrs Peet, the medium, had promised to call and if she found the occasion right would try to make contact with Dad. Merle took us to her drawing-room—she's the only person I know to use that word now—and we sat down and waited for Mrs Peet to arrive. Robert's breathing was louder even than the crackling fire. I half expected it to dislodge the china Pans and shepherdesses, the Venetian glass vases, from their ledges and shelves about the room. Merle seemed a little dismayed.

"Mr Fujikawa doesn't care for loud noises."

"We'll go before he comes," I said.

"In a sense he's always here. He's always just a short way round the corner. You needn't look Meg, that's not funny. I believe, Robert, that one day Mr Fujikawa will come right through. He will join us on this side. That will be the most important event in man's history. And I of course will be his wife. Ah, here's Mrs Peet." She went to answer the door.

"Are you all right?" I asked Robert. "We can go soon."

"I'll make it. Old Merle's a dag."

Mrs Peet had brought her sister, Mrs Thomas. They were stick-thin tall gaunt women with long jaws and long noses and beautiful liquid eyes. Mrs Thomas did the talking for them. The other, Mrs Peet, simply inclined her head on its too-thin neck, and gave a far-away smile that had in it so much of artifice I felt like applauding. But when she spoke—and she spoke to say, Yes she would love some sherry ("If it's dry")—I looked at her more sharply. I knew that ginny plum-cake tremolo—and in a flash had Sybil, belted Sybil, in her flowing robes and zodiacal signs, reaching out her hand for Alfred's pound note. She had obviously prospered. Rings on her fingers now, with genuine stones, and, unless I was mistaken, a hand-tailored frock and hand-tailored coat. The gypsy was gone. I felt delighted, almost as if she had declared some part of my own life a success; and in that mood was prepared to let her have her way with Dad.

"Do you still read handwriting?" I asked.

"You must be mistaken. I've never read handwriting."

"But when we met—"

"We have never met. Merle, this isn't dry sherry. I can't drink this."

"You should have medium dry," I laughed.

They looked at me blankly—even Robert, who usually understood my jokes. I let it go. I was still pleased with Mrs Peet. Merle asked anxiously if she felt the signs were right for—you know?—was she receptive? "I'm not sure that all of us here will give you quite the right sort of ambience."

"Oh," I said, "I believe in Mrs Peet. I really do. And Robert's got an open mind, haven't you Robert?"

"I hope so," Robert said.

Mrs Thomas gave us a fastidious sidelong look. "She can't work if anyone breaks the circle. She'll get a migraine. I'm not sure I should let her take the risk."

"Oh please, we'll really try hard."

Mrs Peet gave her far-away smile, but made a languid sign with her hand, and Mrs Thomas said to me, "There is of course the wee matter of fee."

"I'll pay. I'll pay. How much?"

"After, please," said Mrs Peet, frowning for the first time. I said I was sorry.

Merle blacked out the room. She lit a lamp and placed it on

230

the sideboard. The air became heavy with shadows.

"Why the gloom? I thought it was all light on the other side."

"And we are in darkness," Merle said. "The weather is ours."

"I hope they'll be wearing their woollies."

"Meg," she warned severely.

"I'm sorry. Do let's go on."

We sat at a round mahogany table inlaid with a sun and crescent moons, and laid our hands on its surface with our little fingers touching. I was thrilled and a little afraid. This was just as I had found it described in so many novels. We waited a long time as Sybil (I'll call her that) prepared herself. Her face became more horsey, more refined. The room, the shadows, the sinking fire in the grate, Robert's breathing, the faces of the women, the delay that went on and on, all worked on me and put me into a state of light hypnosis. I was ready for Dad. Without warning, Sybil's head slumped on her chest. Her heavy ear-rings dangled by her nose. Shudders ran through her body and penetrated to our fingertips. Her breathing became almost as ugly as Robert's. Then she raised her head. Her face had taken an unearthly glow. Her beautiful smooth eyelids gleamed like pats of butter. I felt a stab that Alfred was not here to join me in admiring her. She grinned secretly, clicked her bony teeth.

"Who wishes to speak with me?" Sybil asked in Dad's voice—Dad asked in Sybil's voice? I cannot decide which it was.

Merle must have signalled to Robert for I saw him shake his head. She pressed her little finger on mine.

"Is that you, Dad?"

"Meg. I have been waiting."

I wanted to ask him what he was doing in such company. I also wanted to ask had he met God. In the end I said, "I hope you're well."

"I cannot stay long, Meg. Ask what you want to know."

"Is Mother with you?"

"Your mother is happy."

"Have you met God?"

Sybil gave a little jerk and through the gloom I saw Mrs Thomas frowning. Robert had a grin on his face.

"You must not ask about the great mysteries. Knowledge would destroy you. But I say, have faith."

"I can't."

"Is the leap too great? The world is flimsy. It has not sufficient substance to hold you back."

But I thought of flesh and thought of blood. I thought of love. Substance was there.

"Will Fergus come back to me?"

"Ah." Sybil/Dad sounded pleased. "If you love him sufficiently he will come."

That was nonsense, and I almost said so. "Can you explain?"

"You must not ask for explanations, child."

"Why not?"

"Because I do not wish to give them." That was in his style.

"What did you think about all the time when you were in your study and Mum was in the kitchen with twelve kids?" But I thought, Good God, I'm giving ammunition to this woman, and I said, "I'm sorry, I take that back. How's Alfred getting on?" I threw it lightly in; but my heart gave a terrible lurch and my knowledge of where I was, and even who, fell off balance. Whatever it might be for others, this could never be a game for me.

"He is well," Sybil said. "He has seen his errors. Here what was crooked is made straight."

I gasped at that—her impudence. It cured me of distress and I flashed with anger. Robert came to my help. He coughed and fished for his handkerchief. The circle broke. Sybil clacked her mouth shut. I thought she might have bitten through her tongue. She made an empty sound, a grieving moo, from deep in her. Mrs Thomas pulled her like a child into her arms.

"Don't you know that's like a punch on the face?"

"I had to get my handkerchief out. Meg, I'll have to go."

"You'll all have to go. Mr Fujikawa wants to come through," Merle cried. "Yes darling, yes, too many people. I'll get rid of them."

"How much?" I asked. "It used to be a pound."

Sybil groaned on her sister's chest.

"Ten," Mrs Thomas snapped. "Guineas, please."

"Good heavens." I had to write a cheque. "Merle, thank you. It's been interesting."

Then we were out on the porch, with rain beating over our heads, and Peacehaven ghostly in a mist.

"What did you think of that?" I said to Robert.

"They were a pair of twisters. Merle's all right, though. Mr Fujikawa's real."

I drove him home and got the range fire blazing, and we sat in the warm kitchen drinking cocoa. At five o'clock we heard on the radio news that Fred Meggett had been arrested and charged with fraud. "Now there's a message from another world." I worried about Fergus and thought of running up to Peacehaven to use the phone. But I waited till after tea. I got Robert to bed, and said I would be gone for half an hour. I drove around to Moa Park to see Esther.

She was by her fire, glass in hand and wine jar at her feet. She welcomed me with a screech. "Adrian, get her a glass. We'll drink the bastard down, Meg. I knew we'd get him in the end."

"No thank you, Adrian," I said.

I looked at him to see how he was taking it, but all I could see was an extra watchfulness in his eyes. Old eyes, boardroom eyes. I've heard it said Adrian is on his way to becoming richer than Fred. He buys old houses in Mt Eden and Newton Gully and crams them up to the eaves with tenants; and, they say, collects his rents himself, every Thursday, in his Jaguar. A fat young man in a yellow waistcoat and gold watch chain. "Not bad for twenty-one," Esther crows. Adrian has never had anything to do with his father's business. "Too many risks." Fred calls his son, contemptuously, a percentage man.

"Have they locked him up?"

"Out on bail. But that's not for long," Esther cried. "We're all sitting here gloating. Even Porky's gloating, aren't you love?"

I looked at the old man on the other side of the fire. He was huge and loose in his chair, all folds of skin. He was like a giant sack half-emptied. His ancient sunken face was shaking with mirth.

"You remember Porky?" Esther said.

"Oh yes." Fred's father, Porky Meggett, had been our butcher when Loomis was a country town. I had not seen him since his shop became a Mighty Meatery. "How are you, Mr Meggett?"

The old man rumbled and shook. "You've heard about my boy? He's gone and done the biggest fraud of 'em all. He'll go down in all the history books."

I asked Esther what had happened to Fergus. She gave a snort. "He's small fry. They're not going to worry about him. It's the big boys they're after. All Fred's mates. They're going to lock 'em up and throw away the key."

"Who did they arrest?"

"Fergus is all right," Adrian said. "They got Dad and Tarleton and Gundry and Sloane. That's all. But I think Fergus is going to have to close up. The bottom's falling out."

"You know where Fred was when they arrested him?" Esther cried. "He was with his floosie. Ha ha ha. In the middle of the afternoon. In the sack. They had to wait while he put his underpants on."

"Who told you that?"

"Adie. Fat boy here."

Adrian went pink. "They did arrest him at her place."

"He upped a girl when he was only twelve," Porky Meggett said. "I took the skin off him but it didn't do no good."

Esther filled her glass. "Come on Meg, don't make me drink alone. Not on a night like this. Let's all drink. We'll drink to the great man's downfall. Downfall! Hee hee, that's good."

I let Adrian bring me a glass and I sat on a squab pretending to sip, watching Esther gulp down glass after glass. She pulled the most hideous faces. She hated the stuff but could not live without it. I thought it a pity her pleasure in Fred's arrest could

234

not take the place of wine. It was hard to say which was making her drunker.

"I've been salting cash away, you know that Meg? I've got plenty. I'll stay up when he goes down. This house is mine. In my name. That was his idea—a tax dodge. But it's mine. Ha ha. He thought he could walk on water but he's sunk."

"Fred'll come back. You watch," Porky Meggett said.

"He's sunk. He's bloody sunk. Down with his ship. Toot toot. Gurgle gurgle. Ha ha ha."

I stayed until she fell sideways and began to snore. Adrian helped me get her to her bedroom.

"I'll manage. You go away."

I pulled off her dress and rolled her stockings down her pudgy legs. Anger made me rough. I had to get out of there. I rolled her into bed and covered her up. I kissed her forehead. "Hi, Sis," she moaned, "where did you come from?" I ran out of her bedroom and out of her house and sat in my car and smoked a cigarette. Then I drove home to Robert. He was sitting up in bed, using his bronchodilator.

"Not you too?"

"Is she bad?"

"Yes. Yes. She's a mess."

"What about Fergus?"

"He's all right. They left him alone."

I sat with him a while. He tried to talk about Esther and Fergus, but all the time he could not help looking at his disease. He was wondering when it would kill him. After a while he said he felt like sleeping. I turned out his light and went to my room. I got into bed and lay awake for a long time thinking about my life and all our lives. I did not try to make any sense of them, I simply turned them over. Robert's breathing sounded in the cottage. Esther, Robert, Alfred, Fergus, me, Mum and Dad: then again, in a different order, with old faces, younger faces: they rolled as though on a drum, came up foreshortened, smiled fat-cheeked at me, and rolled away. It seemed to go on all night. They seemed to go on turning in my sleep. I had a headache

235

when I woke in the morning. I took three Disprins with my cup of tea. Forty, fifty years ago, I had gulped my family down, grown drunk on them. I supposed I had been drunk on them all my life. Now I wished I could vomit them up.

In the afternoon I had a visit from Jack Short. He hung about the door, unwilling to come in.

"How's Fergus, Jack?"

"He's well, Mrs Sole. As far as I know he's well."

"He's not staying up too late at nights?"

"I don't know what he does at nights. I don't think—I can—really discuss that with you."

"Come in, man. I won't bite." I sat him at the table. "Now, I suppose you've come about a divorce?"

"I know nothing about that, Mrs Sole."

"Call me Meg. Have a drink, Jack. No? Well, a cup of tea?" He turned that down as well. The mention of divorce had unsettled him. He saw himself in an improper relationship with me. He spoke fast.

"The truth is that Fergus—you've heard about yesterday? Meggett being arrested? Fergus is all right, they're not going to proceed against him. Well, that's only proper. He hasn't done anything wrong. But the truth is—everything's gone down a hole. We're fighting to save what we can. And Fergus—well, Fergus is short of cash."

"Does he want a loan?"

"No, no, nothing like that. What he asked me to suggest to you—well, the house is your joint property, you see?"

"He wants to sell Peacehaven? The cheeky blighter."

"He knows how you feel about the place, Mrs Sole. He truly does. . . ."

"You bet he truly does. Well. Well. Sell Peacehaven, eh?" It appealed to me. I pursed my lips and nodded my head and walked about the room. Jack Short sat there, watching anxiously. I put the kettle on. The sun was going down behind the trees and Robert came in from his chair in the garden.

"How would you feel if I sold Peacehaven? I'd have to live

here for the rest of my life."

"It's your place, Meg. You know that."

"You don't think I should hang on to it? For sentimental reasons?"

Robert had turned inwards to his disease. He seemed to be having long conversations with it. His eyes looked deep as wells. I saw him struggle to come back, and suddenly I was distressed for him, and I put my arms around him. "It's all right, don't worry, I'll make up my own mind. You just go to bed."

Jack Short had watched all this with horror. "I think I'll just go—"

"Sit down. I'll get to you."

I took Robert into his bedroom and helped him to bed.

"Sell it if you want to," he said in a vague way.

"Don't you worry about it. Shall I get the doctor?"

"Not yet. Not yet."

I went back to the kitchen and made tea. "There you are, Jack. How much does Fergus think we could get for it?"

He named a price.

"That's low. I suppose he wants a quick sale?"

"I don't think you'd get any more, Mrs Sole."

"I can get a thousand on top of that. Fred Meggett told me what it was worth one day."

"Yes? Well—actually, we do have a buyer. He can settle tomorrow if we say yes. He just needs to have a quick inspection."

"I can sell the place in half an hour."

"You can?" I had said something improper again.

"Do you want to wait or shall I give you a call?"

"Look, Mrs Sole—"

"I'm not interested, Jack. We sell at my price, to my buyer. Otherwise it's no deal."

When I had got rid of him I looked at Robert again. He was lying on his bed with his inward look. I said I would be out for a short while but he did not hear. I put on my coat and went up to Peacehaven.

"Wendy, how would you like to buy this place?"

"Me? You'd never sell. Not your father's house."

"It's too big for me. And I need the money."

"Money," she cried. "But this is Peacehaven, Meg. George Plumb's house." I was betraying him. Then joy took over. "I've dreamed of it. I dream of it every night. Oh Meg, thank you, thank you. I'll look after it. You can come whenever you want."

"There are some conditions." I wanted her to buy the furniture too. I would own Dad's books and papers, but they would stay in the study. She would let in any Plumb who wanted to use them. And she would let me visit the house when I chose, and walk in the grounds. But I wanted that, I told myself, for pleasure, not to come home. All that was left to me of home was myself.

"I want the Buddha."

"Oh, I wanted that."

"Well, you can't have it. I'm sorry."

"I hope you won't disturb me when I'm working." But joy still dazzled her. She did not argue at my price.

So I set things moving and stood aside, and Wendy became the new owner. Fergus wrote a note thanking me. He said he was well and hoped I was the same. Winter went on and Robert sank deeper into his illness. He had, most times, the look of hearing whispers in his mind. On sunny days I got him into the garden and once or twice took him walking as far as the summer-house. "This needs repairing," he said. He did not seem to remember building it.

In August I began to notice an increasing ruddiness in his face and a blue coloration in his lips.

"Heart, Mrs Sole. It's what I warned you of," the doctor said. He mentioned hospital and again I said Robert would not go.

"He may need oxygen."

"Can't we get that here?"

"If you don't mind the expense."

"I don't mind. I've sold my house."

He suggested a professional nurse. Robert would have to stay in bed. He must be fed and bathed and clothed as though he could not lift a finger to help himself.

"I can do all that."

"A nurse would do it better."

In the end we agreed I should have someone in each afternoon to bed-wash him. He recommended a woman called Mrs Petley, who looked jolly and smiled a lot but rarely spoke a word. She always seemed to be rushing off and I learned she had seven or eight other patients to wash in her afternoon. But she did her job well. Robert liked her. Sometimes I heard the murmur of her voice coming from his room. I arranged for her to come in for an hour two mornings a week so I could do my shopping.

One day I stopped at the Post Office and telephoned Fergus. The phone rang and rang but no one came. I tried Jack Short and he told me Sole Construction Co. was closed. He gave me a number where I might find Fergus. I half expected to hear Beth Neeley's voice, but Fergus answered.

"Fergus," I said, "it's Meg. I'd like you to do something for me."

"If I can." After his surprise he was very formal.

I told him about Robert. Nervousness made me tumble things out. I spoke about enlargement of the ventricle, and right heart failure, and dyspnea and cyanosis, and respiratory failure—all the words the doctor had used to me. I told him Robert was dying and would not get out of his bed again.

"He should be in hospital, shouldn't he?"

"No. He doesn't want to."

"That's not the point—"

"It is the point. He'll die wherever he goes. He's got a right to choose."

He was silent. "I see what you mean. But it's hard on you."

"Maybe. I knew what I was getting into, though."

He asked me what I wanted him to do. I said that Robert needed a hospital bed, one with a head that jacked up. I thought Fergus might know where to pick up a second-hand one. And I had thought he might be able to make an over-bed table in one of his workshops—but Jack had told me they were closed up now.

"I can do it. Leave it to me."

"I can pay, Fergus."

"You don't need to pay. I think I know where I can get a bed."

"Thank you."

"I'll get started on the table right away."

"Thank you."

"I'll send them out by carrier."

"All right.—Goodbye."

"Goodbye, Meg."

"Oh Fergus, the table will have to be on wheels."

"Yes, I know."

"He can lie across it, you see. I can pad it up with pillows for when he gets tired sitting up."

"That's good."

"Goodbye then, Fergus."

"Goodbye, Meg."

I hung up. I was trembling. I did not know whether it was from need of him or love. I had said I did not need him long ago; and told myself love was just a word. But if it was not these, why did I tremble? Why did I lean on my elbows over the phone with my thumbs pressed in my eyes to keep back the tears? Soon I managed to think of other reasons. I had not slept properly for months, and tiredness always made one emotional. Fergus was in another country, another life. I took my handkerchief out and dried my eyes; I promised myself I would hold to that view.

The bed and table arrived later that week. I had to get Willis and Emerson to help me move them into Robert's room. After that he was more comfortable. He slept a lot. He no longer seemed to look in at his illness. He and it had made a kind of marriage, but somehow Robert had come out on top, the one who earned the money and paid the rent. He looked out now at the world with an interest almost childlike.

The world, though, had shrunk to his little room—twelve feet by nine. I left the curtains open so he could see the peach tree

240

and the lemon tree by the creek. The peach tree was breaking into blossom—blossom on its red new twigs and close on its ash-grey trunk. Each unbroken bud was like a pink lolly. Deep in the lemon tree yellow lemons gleamed with a waxy look. I had picked the outside ones, and as I leaned into the tree, bending my way round the prickly branches, I saw Robert propped up high in his bed, smiling at me. "All those colours, Meg." I put a branch of peach blossom in his room. "I didn't think I'd make it into spring."

Bad weather came again. I had to keep his curtains closed for warmth. He asked me to bring the wheat-field and the hay-field prints to his room. I propped one on a chair and one on his bed.

"Who painted those?"

"Someone called—I can't pronounce it."

"I wouldn't mind being there. You can almost taste the water in that jar."

"It might be wine."

"Whatever it is you can taste it."

He kept them all day. "I like those girls." "Look at those quail go up." "You can tell how sharp that scythe is."

He wanted them back next day so I hung them in his room and often when I went in I found him watching them as though they were fields outside his window.

The doctor had said he should not talk, but I did not see the sense in that. I sat with him many hours, sometimes at night when he could not sleep. We talked about our childhood, pulling things out of the past as though from a penny bag of broken biscuits. Neither of us knew what we would find. It almost became a game. Sometimes Robert even tried to laugh.

When Emerson and Willis called the game became an orgy. I did not enjoy that so much. I could feel us straining. Robert seemed to be humouring us. I had the feeling that he was in the room but also at a distance. His illness and his knowledge of his death worked in him like an extra sense, putting him beyond us. I was not aware of it when we were alone, but when Willis sat there rocking his pink foot and snoring tunes on his mouth organ, and Emerson, a little flushed with emotion, leaned forward and recalled another event—one I would have thought him far too wrapped up in his motor bike to have noticed—then Robert began to flicker in my consciousness, in and out of reality, and I strained like a man lifting weights after recollection and sent my girl's laugh pealing round the room. When they had gone I always gave Robert an hour alone.

October came. The rains stopped. A real spring began. I kept his windows open. The scented breeze came in and played round his face. I do not think he could smell it, any more than he could smell the rot from his lungs. The doctor put him on cortico steroids and they gave him relief. But there were times when I thought his struggle to breathe (not to get air into his lungs but to force it out) would kill him. I thought it would burst his heart. He spent hours lying over his table. That was the only position that gave him comfort. He lay so still that several times I thought he was dead. Now and then he fell into a state of semi-consciousness. It seemed to serve him in place of sleep. I put my face down by his glassy eyes. They seemed to presage annihilation. I could not believe in that. "Robert," I whispered, "can you hear me?" Usually he came back and said my name and held my hand.

He died one morning when I was out shopping. Mrs Petley met me at the door. She had a greedy look.

"Come in, dear. Let me take those groceries." She put them on the table. "Sit down. Take the weight off your feet."

"I don't want to sit down."

"I think you should. I've got something to tell you."

"Robert," I said; and at once felt incredibly stupid. I seemed to regress to a childhood state. Giant shapes I could not understand came pressing in. It was only for a moment. In that time Mrs Petley forced me into a chair. I jumped up.

"There was no pain, Mrs Sole. He died very peacefully. A model death."

I walked without hurry into Robert's room. She had lowered the head of his bed and pulled a sheet over his face. I was not

242

ready for it and I said loudly, "Robert?" I folded the sheet back to see his face. She had closed his eyes and combed the tufts of hair above his ears, and bound his jaw up with a cloth. She had no right. I wanted to undo that knot and take the cloth away. Instead I looked at him. I sagged against his ridiculous bed. Mrs Petley leaned past me and twitched the sheet neatly over his face. She turned me round and walked me into the kitchen.

"I'll make you a cup of tea. Then I'll have to rush."

"I don't want tea."

"You should, Mrs Sole. Death is always a shock."

"I've been expecting it." I smiled at her. It forced her back a step.

"Is there someone you can get to sit with you?"

"I don't need anyone."

"In that case I'll get about my business. I laid him out. At times like this I don't like to talk about money. . . ."

"I'll see you get paid."

"Thank you. I'll call in at the doctor's as I go through town. He'll want to get down for a death certificate."

"Yes."

"He shouldn't be long." For a moment I thought she was going to overcome her dislike and kiss me. But she nodded and said, "Sympathies," and took herself off.

I waited till the sound of her car died away. Then I went to Robert's room. I looked at his mummy shape lying on the bed. I had meant to fold the sheet back. I had half-intended taking the cloth from his jaw and ruffling his tufts of hair. I had thought I might open his eyes and close them for myself. I did none of that. I looked at the sheet marking the points of his face—forehead, nose, chin. He had slipped beyond any act of possession I might make, or act of love. He had lost all definition and had gone out of my time. I did not touch him.

I went back to the kitchen and put the kettle on. After a few minutes it started to sing. I left it there. I went to my room and closed the door. I sat on my bed and wept for Robert, and for all of us.

243

21 Emerson was fretting to overtake the hearse. We followed it at forty miles an hour, past the mangrove creeks and busy sawmills. The morning was sunny and blue. Willis sat in the front with Emerson. Felicity and I were in the back.

"Calm down, Emerson. It's a funeral procession."

I had brought a bunch of stock to put on the grave. They were tumbling from their paper in my lap—milky white and a dozen shades of lilac. Their perfume was spicy and light, rubbing on our skins and enlivening us.

"Have you got the service, Willis?" It was the third time I had asked. He grinned and patted his pocket.

"I think it's right there'll be just us," Felicity said. "Just his brothers and sisters. No one else."

"There might be one other. I dropped a note to the man who bought his bach."

"Oh. That's a pity isn't it? The notice said private interment."

"He was in camp with Robert."

Emerson twitched his shoulders nervously. "I was meaning to say, I had a phone call too. From a bloke who said he and his brother were in Shannon camp. He said they'd like to bring their father along. I didn't feel I could say no."

"So much for a quiet family service," Felicity said.

"It can't do any harm. Robert might have liked it," I said.

"And he might not."

"Don't quarrel, girls. Not on this day," Willis said.

We followed the hearse along the thin sealed road by brown drainage canals and hedges of toi-toi and fields of fat spring grass. The little red-roofed town came into view, with the harbour beyond.

"What made him choose this place?"

"He found it when he was drifting round."

We drove through the town and wound up a metalled road to the cemetery. It lay above an arm of the harbour, cut off from the fields by a paling fence. Trees had been left to grow in it. Here and there roots broke up through the ground and pushed the old headstones askew.

The hearse was at the gate, while a man dressed in a sports coat and tie struggled to unchain it.

"That's Dick Webster. Robert's friend."

The hearse drove through and stopped in the shade of a tree. Emerson parked in the grass at the side of the road. Dick Webster came over. He told us he was sorry about Robert and thanked me for inviting him. He had come to town in his launch and walked up from the wharf. "The bach is in good shape, Mrs Sole. I'm looking after it." He was still uneasy.

While we talked an old Ford car red-spotted with primer paint rattled by and pulled up in the grass. A notice on the rear window said: *God Speaks*. Three men and a woman got out and made a circle by the gaping doors: thick granite-seeming men, and a woman bony as a starving child. They stood dark-grey, aloof, still as broken columns, stone angels. I realized they were praying. Dick Webster stared at them. "Bloody Parminters." He went red. "Pardon my language. I'll go and help with the coffin." He went down to the hearse, where the undertaker's man was waiting by the raised back door. Emerson and Willis followed him. They started to roll out the coffin.

"Did he say Parminter?" Felicity asked.

"I think so."

"Robert lived with them in the Wairarapa. Religious cranks. They've got a nerve."

The prayer finished with a slow raising of heads. The Parminters seemed to come out of a trance. The old man, the patriarch, felt his way into the car. I saw he was blind. The woman helped him nervously, moving her skinny limbs like a stick insect. She took a humble seat, dimly alert. The two younger men tramped down the verge to us, raising dust from

245

the seeding grass. Their awkward suits and ties were ridged with fold-marks.

"Is this Bob Plumb's funeral?"

"Yes," I said. "Are you the ones who rang my brother up?"

"I'm Ralph Parminter. This is my brother Wallace. Bob used to live with us on the farm."

"On the Ark. Are you still there?"

"The police drove us out. Them and the reporters. We live at Warkworth now."

"How many? Just the four of you?"

"We're all that's left. And our wives."

"Believers still?" I asked. "Still on the Ark?"

They did not answer that. "Bob was one of the Chosen Ones. He was the Vehicle. My father would like to say the words over him."

I looked at his countryman's face and his great hands poking like snapped-off roots out of the narrow sleeves of his black suit. He and his father and brother had turned Robert out from a home he loved and set him wandering, but I could feel no hostility to him. I smiled and said, "That's not possible. But if you want to share our service that will be all right."

"Bob belongs to us."

"Rubbish," Felicity said. "You're a bunch of loonies. Go away. You're not wanted here."

"Quiet, Felicity. I'm sorry, Mr Parminter, but we are the next of kin. You can join us if you like."

Ralph Parminter shook his head. Breath whistled in his nose. "No, you're mistaken. We've got Betty here. She was his wife."

"That woman in the car?" Dimly through the glass I saw her skinny shoulders and thin hair, and face with its bulbous forehead and mongoloid eyes. "Who married them?"

"My father."

"Is he licensed? Do you have a certificate with you?"

"He's licensed before God."

"That's not good enough, I'm sorry to say. I'll tell you what. We'll have our service first. After that if your father wants to say

246

some words he can.—Be quiet, Felicity.—How does that seem? We'll be gone and you can say what you like."

The brothers looked at each other. Ralph went to the car. He leaned in and talked with his father. The old man's blind white eyes were luminous in the shadows. Ralph came back. "As long as we go last."

"Oh, yes."

"We'll come down when you've finished."

"I hope you're not going to say any mumbo-jumbo," Felicity said.

"Felicity, please. Whatever they say, it can do no harm."

"They'll insult his memory."

"Robert can't be hurt. Now come on, please. I'm sorry, Mr Parminter."

Emerson and Willis, with Dick Webster and the undertaker's man, were carrying the coffin down through the trees. We followed them. Willis had taken off his hat and put it on the coffin. When he came into sunlight his bald head shone.

"Look where he's put his hat," Felicity said.

"Do stop complaining. Isn't this beautiful? I think I'd like to be buried here."

Red cattle were grazing in fields sloping down to the shore. Seagulls screamed and squabbled over the crablands. Out in the river mouth two men in a dinghy were checking set-lines fixed to a buoy. On the other shore, behind drab-green mangroves, Robert's bach, Dick Webster's bach, stood in its garden and orchard.

I showed it to Felicity. She was more interested in Willis's hat. "For heaven's sake take it off there. Here, I'll carry it." She frowned at me. "They're like the Marx brothers."

"Robert wouldn't mind."

"Stop being sentimental."

The accusation startled me. I had thought I was simply pointing something out.

Willis turned his head. "Don't quarrel, girls." Tears had started running down his cheeks.

"That's all we need," Felicity muttered.

The men put the coffin down by the grave. They looked at me.

"You'd better lower it in. Then Willis can read the service."

The undertaker brought some tapes from his pocket and showed the others what to do. A gravedigger, resting on his shovel by the fence, walked over to help. It was just as well. Willis looked unsteady.

When the coffin was in the ground the undertaker left. The gravedigger went off to a far corner and rolled a cigarette.

"Willis, can you manage?"

He took out Dad's service and started to read.

"Lord, Thou hast been our dwelling-place in all generations. Before the mountains were brought forth, or ever Thou hadst formed the earth and the world, even from everlasting to everlasting Thou art God. Thou turnest man to destruction, and sayest, Return, ye children of men. For a thousand years in Thy sight are but as yesterday when it is past, and as a watch in the night. . . ."

His voice grew stronger. He read through to the end. Some of it did not fit. Dad had prepared it late and Robert had not lived into old age. It did not seem to matter. And God? And immortality? That did not matter either. Who can tell?

When Willis had finished he took out his mouth organ and played *Danny Boy*. Felicity grew stiff with indignation. I patted her arm. The last wail of the tune died away. Emerson scattered a handful of earth on the coffin. He had probably seen it done in the movies. The sun-dried granules of clay pattered down like rain.

"Is that all?" Felicity asked.

"Unless you want to say anything."

"Not me. Not here. I'll have a mass said for him."

"What about you, Mr Webster?"

He shook his head.

"Thank you for coming." I put my flowers at the head of the grave.

248

We walked back to the trees. The Parminters passed us, coming down. The two sons, in their black suits (as ancient as Robert's clothes had been), walked on either side of their father, holding his arms. Betty came behind, with her eyes looking about. Her green head-scarf had yellow horseshoes on it. She smiled at us in a scared way. Willis stepped across to speak with her but the old man heard. He freed himself and swung round. His white eyes glared through us. "Betty, come!"

We watched them go down to the head of the grave. The gravedigger was approaching but Ralph Parminter waved him off. The old man stopped. His voice boomed in the air, the same Old Testament voice my father had been able to turn on. "Lord! Lord, hear me!"

"Or else," Felicity said. She looked as if she might march down and drive them all away. I held her arm.

"Lord, we come before you to intercede for the soul of one who strayed from the paths of righteousness. Hear us, Lord. We are your Chosen Ones. . . ."

"Bunkum! Bunkum! How can you allow it?"

I led her through the trees, wondering why she could not accept whatever happened on this day. I felt again the extraordinary happiness I had felt in the garden in San Francisco when Felicity had come out and told me we were going home to New Zealand.

At the car I shook hands with Dick Webster. He turned down Emerson's offer of a ride and trudged off down the hill. Emerson drove us home to Loomis, banking the car like a Gypsy Moth on the corners. He dropped Willis at his gate and me at the cottage. Felicity was going with him and flying home to Wellington later in the day. I kissed them goodbye and went into the cottage.

Well, I thought, I'm alone here now. I'll have to make the best of it.

But I have not been alone, in my *furor scribendi*. I have had more company than I have known what to do with. They are leaving me. I wonder if it's true I am acquainted with myself. In

249

a curious way I am both empty and full. The figure I see is an hour-glass. With Robert's burial the last of the sand trickled through. By an act of will (but an irresistible act) I up-ended myself. I let it all trickle back. The story ends.

I want very much to be quit of that metaphor. So—I'll put down one more thing. Rebecca and her husband drove up yesterday from Napier. He has applied for a job in Auckland. While he was being interviewed she came out to visit me. We talked about her brothers. She is not, it seems, satisfied with them. They've both "fluffed about" and wasted their chances. We talked about Fred Meggett's appeal against his sentence. But as far as she's concerned four years is not enough. I smiled at her and tried to make it seem that I agreed. This loud stranger was my daughter. That was more than I could understand.

We walked up to look at Peacehaven. She is not sentimental about the place. "It's a good job you got out. It was a bloody millstone round your neck. That was a good price you got from old Tinkerbell."

We stood on the verandah looking over the little piece of new Loomis at Merle's house. I said, "How do you know how much I got?"

"Well . . ." Some of her confidence slipped away. She got on to the business that had really brought her out. "I went to see Dad last night. He told me."

"How is your father?"

"He's getting by. . . . I won't beat about the bush. He wants to see you."

"Did he tell you that?"

"He's too proud. But I know."

"And what will Miss Neeley say?"

"Miss Neeley? Where have you been, Mum? Hasn't anyone told you?"

"Told me what?"

"For God's sake, that only lasted a week. She walked out on him."

"I see." And I did see. I saw it all.

250

"He's quite funny about it. Like, when she found out he had false teeth." But he had found out things about her too. "You know that letter you got, saying Dad and her were having it off? Well, she wrote it. Just to get things moving. She told him. Poor old Dad, he couldn't get over it."

"What's he doing?"

"Plumbing again. He's a plumbing repairman. He's got this little van. *F. Sole. Plumbing Repairs.* It's a bit of a come down."

I smiled. I smiled in praise of him. He had re-made himself a second time. It had taken longer than chopping down a tree.

Rebecca and I walked back to the cottage. She said, "I'm not your bloody keeper. All I know is that he'd like to see you." She grinned at me anxiously. She has always loved him more than she loves me. "Think about it, eh?" She drove away.

I have thought about it. She left me his address. I'll visit him tonight. There's room for him here if he wants to come. We'll have to get rid of the hospital bed. I am trying to be realistic. He can carry on with his plumbing repairs. I shall work in the garden. I'll paint the kitchen. For the rest of our days we'll treat each other kindly.

Well, that's what I've come to hope for in the last few hours. Not a large hope, surely; and one that has no undue sentiment in it.